Savage LOVE

Rocks & Stones Between A Rose

Series

Book Five

A

Smokey Moment

Novel

Become a Social Media Friend!

Follow me on:

Twitter: smokeymomentbo1

Instagram: smokey.moment

Facebook: smokeymomentbooks

Join our Book Family

Text SMOKEY to 66866 to stay notified on this series plus new releases, cover reveals and more exciting book stuff!

Acknowledgments

Dedicated to all the readers who love a good book that keeps you guessing, laughing, cursing, crying and all caught up in your emotions. To my readers a special thank you for letting me entertain you. If for a moment!

Table of Contents

Chapter One – Masked 19

Chapter Two – Sins of the Father 43

Chapter Three – Crumbling Walls 68

Chapter Four – More Money More Problems 78

Chapter Five – Indebted 103

Chapter Six – Wife on Paper 123

Chapter Seven – Officially Tired 143

Chapter Eight – Illusions 178

Chapter Nine – Slippery Slope 202

Chapter Ten – Sins of the Son 232

Chapter Eleven – Ride or Die 265

Chapter Twelve – Blindsided 318

Chapter Thirteen – Filtered Through 351

Chapter One – Masked

"Where's Tina!" Rose said in a frantic tone, as she shot past Jerry. Her eyes scanned the perimeter in search of her mother. She needed her right then. She felt she was losing her mind. Jerry could see Rose was frazzled. It was the same look he saw the day she went to the church looking for Tina. He wondered what was really going on with his usually laid-back stepdaughter. She didn't wear her heart on her sleeve yet his last encounters with her had shown a Rose coming apart at the seams.

"She's here. Probably asleep. I haven't heard a peep out of her in over an hour. Is everything okay?" he asked.

"Yes. Sorry Jerry. I'm just losing it. I need to talk to her. I have to wake her," Rose said, as she walked through the living room and down the hall. Jerry shook his head in disbelief. Mother and daughter both had issues and he would love them through it. Like Tina, Rose's issues ran deep. She was in his prayers. She didn't need Tina, she needed therapy. Some of the stories Tina had shared with him were eye-opening. It was a wonder she was functioning. The kind of abuse she suffered would take down the strongest of human beings. But then, she was Tina Walker's daughter.

"Tina!" Rose said, as she shook her woke. Her mother jolted up. "What! Oh... Rose... You scared the shit out of me," Tina said, holding her chest and taking controlled breaths.

"I went to see him. I couldn't do it. I am such a push over. He looked at me with those eyes. With that smile. And I let him have his way. I swear," Rose said, as she sat on the edge of her mother's bed.

Tina kicked the covers off and grabbed her robe. Rose wasn't prone to these types of breakdowns. Tina didn't understand blatant promiscuity. Sex for sex sake. Rose's problems all stemmed from her inability to keep her legs closed and Tina was having a hard time putting the pieces of her daughter's puzzle together. Her disturbing childhood had morphed her into a woman that her mother had struggled to understand.

Tina's promiscuity was fueled by a drug habit and a need to survive the streets. There was an exchange of money she used to survive on. But she wasn't so sure the reasoning behind Rose's affairs. She was rich the moment she married Boston. There was no need to use sex in order to eat. And there was no drug habit eating away at her and driving her to make foolish decisions that involved using her body Which meant her affairs were coming from a place of pain. Tina always thought she should get help. But until she did, Tina *was* the psychiatrist. She was also the shoulder. The pastor. The counselor. Her emotional rock and the ever-present and concerned mother she needed to be.

"That's called love Rose. You love him. What do you expect. Yes, he can get to you. Pull at your heart strings. That's your partner. His issues are yours and vice versa. Right?" Tina consoled, as she sat next to her daughter. She hadn't seen Rose in such an uncontrolled state in a while. Her and Boston were supposed to be on the mend. The affairs were a setback she wasn't sure Rose would be able to overcome.

Tina had something to say. She hadn't mentioned the conversation she'd had with Ashley that day. The day she went to *Truth Center* to make sure the women didn't get into an altercation. She pulled up as Ashley was pulling off. A quick decision to follow her, led to a conversation at the end of the block after Ashley pulled over and gave her an earful.

Tina was angry that day but glad that Ashley confided in her. The conversation got heated a few times. Tina was proud of her ability to handle it without lashing out physically at her daughter's former friend. It took all her willpower and strength to resist the urge to slap Ashley and reprimand her for the betrayal. She flashed back to the day. Ashley spoke her truth. And she had to rationalized the most obvious reasons not to avenge her daughter's pain. She remembered staring into Ashley's eyes and thinking; *What good would it do to hurt her! These girls are just damaged women. Toxicity breeds toxicity. They both need help!*

The truth was it wouldn't undo the fact that a child was conceived. Tina wasn't even sure the baby was Boston's. Ashley was never a one-man woman. It was why Max was dealt the blow he was given during his brief fling with her. And the discovery that the child had been fathered by her mother's abusive boyfriend. Ashley told her she never told

Boston for fear he would have tried to take her baby. Tina didn't think it was something that would have actually happened. Taking the baby would have meant he was ready to expose his affair to Rose and Tina didn't see that happening.

Tina sat as Rose expressed her feelings. All she could do was hear her daughter out. She had been advising Rose but the issues within her marriage were continuing to grow. Rose was worried about the wrong things. Boston's freedom was hanging in the balance. She hoped her daughter would vent then move on from it. A simple pay-off if the baby was his, would allow them to move on. It happened. He wasn't the first and he wouldn't be the last. Tina believed their biggest issue was an enemy unseen, who was determined to put Boston under the jail.

"Every time I want to confront him something happens and I fold. He asked me to step up and finish the sale of his invention. Me! Do a billion dollar deal! Right when the shit has hit the fan. He looks like the victim right now. If I pull away from him when he needs me the most, I won't ever live it down. I pretty much have to keep my mouth closed and help him however I can. But I want to know if he fucked her. When did it happen? And do they still contact each other. Like how deep is this. I'm was being good. We were in a different place. Having my babies did something. I can't have them be the children of a slut," Rose said, as she looked away. Tina's eyes widened from the shock of her words. "Rose! Don't ever call yourself that. Ever...you hear me," Tina said, putting her arms around Rose's shoulder.

"But I was. I was...His love helped save me because he never gave up. My babies saved me. But now I can't get past his affair with her. I have nerve. I know. I just want answers. How can we move on? How?" Rose cried, as she pulled away from her mother. "I'm such a child. Crying after all I did to him. I don't even need to know why. I know. It was because I slept with Denver. And Phoenix. And...um Bronx. This is my karma," Rose said, shaking her head as she tried to reason with herself. Tina touched the top of her hand.

"You will get yourself together and you will be there for your husband the same way he was there for you. Affairs... Babies... Yes, it's a lot. Enough to destroy even a strong marriage. But you had damage. He knew what he was getting into when he met you. He understood your past," Tina said. Rose wiped her nose then looked fiercely at her mother. "What do you mean by he knew," Rose said. Tina leaned away. Her eyes giving away a secret she held for years.

"Ma! What do you mean he knew what he was getting into? How would he know that? He doesn't know my past. He only knows what I told him which wasn't much," Rose said, looking deeply into her mother's guilty looking eyes.

"Oh Rose," Tina said, dropping her head.

"You told him that stuff?" Rose asked. Tina paused then grabbed her cigarettes and tapped the bottom. She pulled one from the package and lit it, then exhaled into the air.

"Yes. I did," she admitted. Rose jumped up from the bed.

"What! When?" Rose asked. Tina took another puff.

"He came to me way back after he first met you. After the affair with Denver. He wanted to know how it could happen. Wanted to understand why it happened. I had to tell him some of it Rose! How else would you have kept him. He needed to know that some of that was an illness. Not just the sex addiction, but where it stemmed from. The struggles. Your childhood. He had to be told. He was contemplating cutting his losses. I was trying to save your marriage. Don't be angry," Tina said, her eyes watering and filled with emotion.

"Wow mom! Wow! So he pities me? Thanks for that one. He thinks I'm sick. Like some kind of mental case. How could you. And you never said a word," Rose said. Tina looked off.

"He doesn't pity you. He is in love. He just wanted something that would guide him. That's all. I gave him what he needed to go on," Tina added. Rose shook her head slowly. She was in disbelief.

"You should have told me," Rose said. Tina looked up at her as she stood over her.

"I know baby. I just wanted you to be happy. I needed you to heal. I knew you would, with time. Especially with a man like him. He waited you out. He didn't think you were just blatantly going after his brothers. He needed a reason. Something! He thought they had something on you. Like they were forcing you. He wasn't sure what to think," Tina said as she paused then continued.

"They have betrayed each other before over women. It wasn't all that new to him. He waited for you to be the wife and mother he believed you would be. And you two are

27

better now. Don't mess it up over Ashley or anybody for that matter. Fuck them bitches. You and him will be the most powerful couple in Chicago. He will not rock the boat with you. Plus, no matter what he's done there's still the matter of Bronx. You did him wrong Rose! So whatever he did in the past, you must forgive him. You both have your crosses to bear," Tina said. Rose was angry but she couldn't pretend Tina wasn't speaking truth.

"I just wish I knew about that baby for sure. I still want to know. I don't want him to see her ever again. But if they have a baby, then what. I have to consider that," Rose stated, as she sat back down. Tina looked intensely at her.

"What?" Rose asked. It seemed there was more.

Tina feared her anger. She didn't want Rose to think she couldn't trust her but there was one more thing. Something she did out of anger. She had gone to see Ashley and the conversation almost caused her to attack her. It was time to tell. Tina was prepared for the outcome. This was her chance to come totally clean.

"I went to see her. And...um...She told me the baby was his," Tina acknowledged. Rose shot her a look and jumped up from the bed.

"What! She said that? When did you talk to her?" Rose said, as her wide eyes began to fill with fear. She had held out hope that it wasn't true. It seemed reasonable given that Ashley had not made financial demands and didn't look to be living off his wealth.

"That day you drove there and I told you I was on my way. You had pulled off but I still went anyway. She had left. One of her coworkers told me she'd just pulled off. I caught her about a block away. She was hesitant to talk. She fears something. She did eventually tell me that he came to her looking for information on you. Probably to corroborate what I had already told him. Ashley said he looked destroyed. He seemed desperate," Tina said. Rose listened intently. She could only imagine what he was going through. A newlywed man with a dishonorable wife. It was a lot. But his affair still stung. Tina continued.

"She said it was around the time when you had moved back to your old house. Right after the fight I had with Tacoma. When we left, he sought answers. That's when he came to me and then eventually to her. I don't think you and him had reconciled yet. But then you found out you were pregnant and he came to get his wife back. Can't you see Rose...This has no winners. No losers. You two hurt each other. Pick up the pieces and move on. But if you can't, leave. Just make sure you don't want him anymore. Don't leave because of your pride. Leave because the love is gone," Tina said. She looked at her daughter. Rose was hard to read. It was a lot to absorb.

Tina hoped her daughter wasn't stewing over the information she withheld. Tina didn't believe the conversation with Boston or Ashley was betrayal. She had hoped to help. But she also knew it was something Rose would cringe at. She wasn't ready to face her past. And she hadn't forgiven Ashley for Max let alone anything she would do with Boston. Tina usually fought Rose's battles, even violently. But not that day. She allowed Ashley to speak freely. Openly. No arguments. No threats. She couldn't do it anymore. She could see that Rose held some responsibility in what happened. Rose had dug her own grave with Boston.

No matter what he did, he would be justified. She started their affair plagued life. Tina could only imagine that deep down Boston toyed with the idea of leaving her. According to what Ashley told her, he expressed embarrassment at her behavior. Tina didn't doubt he was. She just wished he would have chosen someone else to fuck on the side besides Rose's former best friend.

Rose sat quietly. She rubbed her hands along her thighs and continually closed her eyes tight, looking like she would pop like a balloon. Tina worried. Rose was acting strange. She seemed defeated.

"Listen baby...You need to talk to someone. This can't be good on your mental health. I wasn't ready to tell you with all that was going on but I think this is a good time. And I can't have you thinking I keep stuff from you. I know you were trying to make it work. You've been trying to do what's right. But you two need counseling. This marriage can be saved. Fuck a baby. He'll pay his child support and you two will go on. You have a baby too. And you need to speak your truth, let him speak his, and see if ya'll can survive this," Tina urged. Rose took a deep breath.

"I'm not troubled. Don't say that. I'm fine," Rose said. Tina didn't agree. It appeared her daughter was in denial. "No! This isn't healthy. Healthy women don't have affairs so close to home," Tina replied.

"I knew what I was doing. I don't need to talk to anyone," Rose shot back in anger. "I thought I could talk to you. But not if you can't tell me everything. And not if you're going to share my life without my knowledge. I love him and I will try to stay until the next court date. But we can't continue on. Too much has happened ma. And it's not me who will leave him. He will leave me once he finds out about Bronx. This is just so messed up," she replied, as she stood and grabbed her purse. Tina scrambled to make amends and get her daughter to look inside herself. The answer was in where she came from. Her past. She had to face it. Talk about it. Heal from it.

Rose could hold a grudge longer than anyone she knew. Tina jumped from the edge of the bed and followed behind her distraught daughter hoping to make it right.

"Stay here honey. You need to calm down. I was doing what was best for you. He's in jail now. Don't do anything yet. He needs you. That bullshit can wait. Think about the girls. What's best for them. Think about what's best for you. Seek your truth Rose. He wants you still. He will stay if you tell him from your own mouth. He would have left already. Don't you see...He loves you," Tina shouted, as her heart broke in two. Rose never looked back. Never gave a hint at where they stood. She'd lost her before. This was too much to bear. Tina burst out her door running after her daughter. She couldn't lose her again.

Rose walked towards her car. Thoughts about conversations that she had no idea had happened, raced through her mind tormenting her soul. She couldn't speak on anything else. It was time to gather her feelings. It was time to take a look at what she wanted. Then make a move. It didn't seem probable that their broken marriage would remain intact. There was still the worst scandal of all. A baby that may not be his. And there was currently no way to find out without going to Bronx and telling him of her fears.

It was a closed door she had no plans of opening. An old chapter in her life. He was a man who had stolen her heart but for a brief time. His shunning of her opened her eyes. Her reality check that closed the door for good. She had let her feelings get away from her and Boston was her true love. It was never supposed to go that far. But Brooklyn could change things.

In the end, she would be the villain. Boston had everyone's support. Even her own mother. Tina sounded like she was on Boston's side. It was the first time Rose thought maybe he had bought her too. It seemed her husband owned everyone around him. The way she saw it, there was one thing to do. Secure the deal and secure her future. The one she would be living alone.

"Hey girl," Kendra said, as she opened her door wide. Rose walked in slowly. Kendra smiled. Their schedules were not permitting for much socialization. But the visit was odd. Rose didn't do pop ups. Kendra immediately thought about what Rose was going through. Boston was locked up. Everyone was stressing. She was wondering how Rose was holding up.

"The girls are not here. And Memph is out of town. He and Austin went to DC. Austin may be moving there. I don't have to tell you how that has Cicely all in her feelings. She been at it for days, talking about her baby leaving. He a grown ass man," Kendra chuckled. Rose gave a quick smile. She hadn't realized Kendra was so immersed in what was going on within the family. It was news she didn't know. Rose was envious of Kendra's fast acceptance into the St. Rock family. She was new, yet she was privy to information as if she'd been there for years. It hurt, given that Rose was on the outs. She couldn't blame them. She had done things unforgiveable for the women of the St. Rock family and it was the women you had to get past.

Aurora, although laid back, pulled the strings on a lot of the family members. Tacoma could be convincing and was bold with her opinions. She was known to sway the wives of her brothers with ease and she hated Rose with a passion. And everyone tried to keep Raleigh happy. So her voice was strong as well. The St. Rock sisters along with Cicely was instrumental in how the family came together, what they shared and what they celebrated. It was better to be on their side. Rose was the wife and partner of the bread winner. The one whose wealth generated the wealthy of the others. Yet she was ridiculed and was now silently outcasted.

"Rose…What's wrong. You're not saying much. You alright?" Kendra asked.

"Yeah. Can we um… talk," Rose said.

"Sure! Come sit. I'll fix us a drink. I have white wine. And I have something stronger. I can make you a Martini. You know I got drink skills girl. You name it I can make it," Kendra said.

"Something strong," Rose replied. Kendra was surprised. Rose wasn't really a drinker. Something heavy was on her mind.

"Here you go," Kendra said, as she handed Rose the drink and sat next to her on the plush black suede couch. Rose took a sip then sat the drink on a coaster. Kendra took a sip as she waited for Rose to get comfortable. The tension was thick. They'd had conversations about Boston before. Kendra was concerned. She was there for her friend. Rose had two babies and a man in jail. It had to be hard on her.

"I don't know how to say this so I'm going to just come out and say it," Rose said, lifting her drink once more. "Okay," Kendra replied, an eyebrow raising slightly.

"I had an affair on Boston. And um…Brooklyn might not be his. I um…found out that he had an affair on me. At least two that I know of. He has children. And I don't know how to fix this," Rose said, her voice cracking under the weight of the words. She kept her eyes straight. Only Kendra's sound advice and non-judgmental attitude would help her come to some kind of resolve. She was disappointed with Tina and there was only one other person she trusted with information that was touchy, embarrassing and utterly destructive.

"Oh Rose! No! What? Who? I thought that was all behind you. I mean…You never talk about the details of Denver. Or Phoenix. And I never asked. I just supported your process afterwards. You were trying to put it all behind you. I know what you went through. This is shocking news. How did this happen?" Kendra asked. She was careful not to ask too much about the past affairs. Rose had only told her so much. Memphis had enlightened her on all the sordid details. It was shocking that after everything, she had found herself in the same boat once again. Kendra was perplexed as to why.

"I can't say. I want to but… I love you and I trust you. But it's best if I keep their name out of it. He doesn't know. It's crazy! I know. Oh Kendra…I feel so ashamed. I was working so hard on being a good wife. And now that I have the girls, I wanted to be the best mom," Rose said, as she nodded at her words. It was a blow. A fear she had throughout her pregnancy. It was Noor all over again. Rose feared losing Boston for good.

"The only thing I know is I have never seen a man love a woman so much. You have to talk to him. And if you can't talk about it, write a letter. Not now. It was kill him to get that kind of news in jail. But when he comes home, and he will, you tell him then. Be prepared for his response. His emotions. Maybe even his anger," Kendra said, touching Rose on the shoulder and hoping she found the courage to be honest with him.

"Yes. You're right. It's something I just have to deal with. Talk to him. Thanks Kendra. Keep this between us. No one knows. Not a soul. Please don't talk to Memphis about it. I know you don't like to lie to him. Please don't say anything," she said.

Kendra agreed. She was open with her husband, but not at the expense of her friend's marriage. But Kendra was worried. It meant that it was one of the brother's again. Or perhaps Max. Otherwise she wouldn't keep the identity hidden.

"I won't say anything. But I have to assume it's one of them, or you would say," she said looking intensely at Rose. Her curiosity was getting the best of her. Rose looked down and shrugged her shoulders. Kendra sighed loudly. It was definitely a St. Rock.

*T*he night's warm and comfy breeze blew on Rose's wet skin as she lay underneath a single white sheet. She had managed to put her troubles behind her while she decided what was best for her family. In the meantime, Boston was calling her nightly and making love to her over the phone. Rose was struggling with her sexual needs and was fantasizing about him non-stop. Affair or not, he was still the man who made her feel like no other. Even over the phone.

The faint sound of her vibrator buzzing under the pillow between her legs had Boston ready to paint his ceiling with warm fluid. "Uhh," Rose moaned, as Boston rubbed the tip of his manhood gripping himself firmly and gliding up and down as he pictured his wife's mouth.

"You picturing me deep inside you baby," Boston said in the low deep tone usually reserved for her ear. But they were separated by space wide as the sea. He may as well had been on the moon. He couldn't touch her. He couldn't lick her. He couldn't make warm circles with his tongue on her wet and waiting vagina. And she wouldn't feel his kiss or the massive penetration of his weighty penis inside her.

Boston missed her head. He missed her pink crinkled mouth. The lips that caused many men to think sinful thoughts. It was his favorite part of her body. Second to her tight muscle filled vagina that gripped like a virgin on her first night. He was at war with men in his own family who also desired the woman that lurked beneath that perfect frame. Her head game was scandalous. She could suck a pit from an apple with one forceful take and he was sprung still.

"What you doing to my pussy? I wish I could suck it right now" he said. Rose moaned again. Boston's voice was deep and engaging. She was doing a lot of things to her wet and ready vagina. The vibrator was doing a good job, but it wasn't him. And despite the present state of their relationship, she still wanted his powerful thrusts.

"I'm...about to cum," Rose said, in a low voice. Boston closed his eyes.

"You feelin me baby," he asked. Images of his wife riding him then jumping down and giving him head had weakened him. Going to bed with a hard on was making a tough situation tougher. And it seemed they wouldn't get a chance for another tryst in the bathroom. Someone had snitched and guards had told him there would be no second round. So, this was it. Phone sex he hoped would satisfy his sexually addicted wife and himself.

Rose dropped the phone from her ear and arched her back. The powerful waves had taken over. Boston could hear her vibrator at work. The distant moans confirming she was cumming. Boston increased the pressure.

Soon he could feel his nuts tighten. The precum and jail lotion worked wonders as he slid along his shaft bursting into his own hand, as the side wall caught what he couldn't. Boston's body jerked. He chuckled at the power of his own nut. He hadn't cum that hard since he was there. It was only the third time he'd jacked himself.

He refused to do it at first, until pride had him blue balled out. He still had his fond memory of the day she came there and they were allowed private time in the bathroom. It wasn't the most romantic of times, but it served a purpose. He got a chance to make love to his wife. And it was still magical. Rose was a trooper. Head in the car. At parks. Behind building just for kicks had helped make her voyeuristic and game for whatever. It was what he loved about her. And what he hoped not to despise. If one more person touched his bombshell of a wife, he wasn't sure what he might do.

"You there?" Boston asked. "Umhmm. Now go to bed! I'll talk to you tomorrow," Rose assured.

"You gonna be ready. You not nervous, are you? Thomas is doing all the legal filing and drafting the papers. I'll find out when everything is set to be signed," he said, as he held his penis in his hand playing around with it. He wished he was home. He would go for round two. But it was time to talk business. The deal that would make him rich beyond his dreams was coming up. He hoped Rose wasn't still nervous about closing his deal.

"Okay. I'm as ready as I can get," she said. Boston could hear the tension in her reply.

"You got this. You're better than me at business. You're further than I was after owning your business for only two years. It took me longer. You are built for this. Don't ever forget that," he said. Rose looked off. She had never heard such words. She *had* accomplished a lot in two years. She could envision it all. Rose was overwhelmed. It was a good feeling to be viewed as a powerful, business-savvy woman.

Boston could hear footsteps. It was time to turn in the phone. "I love you. I miss you babe. Wear something sexy next time you come," he said. Rose giggled like a school girl. Boston was incorrigible. He was all in on her sexiness. If she wanted to tone it down, he was forever encouraging more.

Rose hung up the phone and tossed her vibrator on the night stand. She sighed as she stared into the blackness. A hint of dimmed lights peered through the edge of her blinds. The shadowy images on the wall looked like a man hanging from a tree. It was a chilling visual given the fact that her husband was in jail facing a hanging of sorts. If found guilty, he would be hung out to dry. Life for him would end. Boston wasn't equipped to be anything else but a man who took care of things. He was a powerhouse. A provider. She couldn't deny it. And even as she lay there thinking of all his positive traits there was still the negatives. There was still Ashley and Jodi.

Chapter Two – Sins of the Father

The St. Rock house of parents Orlando and Cicely was filled with laughter, music and the smell of cinnamon buttery goodness. Cicely had rolls in the oven for her grandkids and was trying to relax amid the troubles of her son Boston. She had spoken to him that morning. His voice sounded different. Gone was the strong, deep resounding soundboard that reminded her of Orlando. She could tell he was just pretending to be ok.

But she knew better. No one understood him the way she did. Even his father, who adored him above all others, did not see what she saw. He did not read him with such profound accuracy. Cicely could feel a breakdown coming. And it hinged on Rose. The only woman he ever gave his heart to. The woman who held their family in the palm of her hand unknowingly.

If he fell apart, so would his father. And it wouldn't be long before the others started to lose some of their shine. She didn't have time. But time was not in her control. The courts went at a snail's pace. Unless a miracle freed him, he would have to be processed like everyone else.

Cicely peeked inside the oven. "Just a few more minutes," she said, her mind racing. She wondered where Orlando was. She had something to say. The plight of their family was weighing heavily on her. It was time to talk.

"Can we talk," Cicely asked, as she entered her husband's study. The office that doubled as a library was Orlando's favorite room in the house. The mahogany shelves held a treasure trove of books. Some signed by the authors themselves.

"Sure dear. I was just reading the paper. Is it more bad news. Not sure I could take any more," Orlando said, as he raised up from his desk and sat down on his leather sectional. Cicely sat next to him. Close enough to feel his breaths. They still did it for each other after all the years and children they'd had. They considered themselves the luckiest parents in the world until recently. What was happening to the St. Rocks was difficult to comprehend. Cicely didn't know where to begin.

She was sure her husband was just as stressed about their boys as she was. And she worried about him. Orlando didn't like his family to worry. He did things to keep them from worry like make appointments to doctors and never tell anyone how they went. He would go for test and then never talked about the results. Cicely assumed he was fine. He was still very sexually active. It was surprising how much so. He was youthful in his appearance. A greyed version of Phoenix and Boston with a body very similar to theirs. Orlando didn't have an ounce of fat on him. He was impressive by older men standards.

"You okay?" Orlando asked, as his hand moved slowly on top of hers. "No! I'm not. I haven't been in weeks. Why is this stuff happening to us all of a sudden? We lose our grandbabies in a horrific way and Bronx is not the same. Boston is in jail. All of these horrible things within such a short time. Now Austin wants to move to Washington DC. We won't be seeing him and his kids that much. I can't take all of this. Why can't he pursue politics here? He could do a lot of good right here at home. Why does he have to go five hundred miles away to pursue his dreams," Cicely voiced, as she closed her eyes, appearing to be in prayer. Orlando sighed loudly then squeezed her hand.

"I'm doing everything in my power to help Boston. And Bronx just needs time to heal. We all do. It's going to take some time sweetheart. I mean...He suffered the unimaginable. He seems to be doing better. He cried when I walked into his room the other day. He's in shock still. I promise you he is my number one priority. Even more so than Boston. I will make sure he is healing," he said, as he paused before continuing.

"And Boston is just stubborn. Won't take any counsel sent to him. Feels everyone is an enemy. That they are happy to bring him down. I have to get him to relax and trust. And Austin...He is ready to be independent. He said he needs to get away. He said it feels toxic. He's just ready for a different atmosphere. Plus, he wants to expand on that political science degree he's been sitting on. He has a calling. He wants to be at the forefront of laws and decision making. I think it's a good thing. You're not losing him Ceecee. He feels this is his calling," he said. Cicely turned her head quickly towards him and scoffed.

"He needs to stop. All the trouble he put us through when he was young, and now we're the ones who are toxic. He is the most selfish out of all our kids. I swear. But if he feels this is something he must do, then so be it," Cicely assured. Orlando agreed.

It seemed the death of Bronx's boys had affected him deeply as well. And it seemed his way to deal with it was to embark on a journey he'd had interest in for some time. Austin was always interested in laws. Politics. Right versus wrong. Back in the movement days, when the Black Panthers were thriving, Austin would have fit right in. Their symbol of strength and unity would have surely been something he would have jumped into without a second thought. He was always the people's fighter. Always looking for ways to improve the outcome for the forgotten and disenfranchised.

Cicely and Orlando usually agreed on things as it related to their children. She didn't think Bronx was the one who needed so much of Orlando's time. He was mourning but he was coming along. Cicely could see it in his eyes the last time she visited him. Her concerns were more for

Boston. The judge denied bond for the murder charge and she was sure he was slowly coming unhinged.

"Have they said who the witness is?" Cicely asked. She had vague details from that night.

Orlando told her of the night he went to *Sam's Liquor & Convenience Store* on Freemont and Russel Street and walked behind the building, his gun in his hand. He was going to save his son from a group of hoodlums. When he got there, Memphis was leaning against a building with two men standing three feet from him. Orlando kept his gun in his pocket, but his hand on the handle. He was ready to shoot. The men had the wrong young man cornered. That was his son. And he was willing to die for him.

The darkness hindered him from seeing the situation clearly. Memphis stood quiet. He was young. Inexperienced. And he was terrified. Orlando was sure the men had a gun. They snickered at his request to leave. The young thugs were part of a gang and Memphis had disrespected one of their main runners. The two men that stood ready to make Memphis pay for not knowing better, were also prepared to call Orlando's bluff.

The facts of who shot who were made unclear, possibly on purpose. Cicely understood her husbands need to keep her out of it. But she wanted to know. It would help her prepare for how much trouble her son was really in. She wanted to know who shot the young man. It was why she was sitting next to him.

"Hun…Tell me what happened that night? Please! Is it possible that he could be found guilty and spend the rest of his life in prison? Did he do it?" she asked. Orlando leaned over and pulled her to him. Cicely laid her head on his shoulder. He didn't like secrets, especially with his wife but she didn't need to hear the answer. She would have sleepless nights. And he just didn't have the heart to confirm who did what that fateful night.

"He is innocent. He was there to protect me. They don't have hard evidence. I'm trying to get Max Stone to represent him. He will beat this," Orlando said.

"Max! They don't care for each other. Him and Phoenix are friends but that doesn't mean he'll help Boston. Can we trust him?" Cicely asked. She was concerned because of the men's past. It didn't seem like a good idea.

"Boston seems to think he can. So does Denver and Chicago. We'll see!"

"Max!" a distinguished voice yelled in the distance. Max had a firm grip on his briefcase and was headed across the street when the voice stopped him dead in his tracks. Max turned around. The face of a goddess in an all-white Carolina Herrera pants suit and black YSL heels stared back. Rose gave an infectious smile to her ex as he approached her slowly.

"Rose," Max said, looking around as if he was being punked. Rose waited with her hands intertwined in front of her, as she stood with her head slightly cocked to the side. He was more handsome then she'd ever seen him. His confidence wore on him like an armored suit. Rose was sure Brooke was the reason. Max was only truly happiest when he was in love. His bad boy ways would have cooled soon enough had she stuck around. Word had it he was faithful to Brooke. Rose didn't doubt it. He would not have been able to survive a second heartbreak. Changing his ways would have been the best choice for him. It was admirable that he actually took control of his life.

"Rose. What are you doing here?" Max asked. Rose leaned in and planted a tender kiss on his cheek. She had a favor to ask. There was nothing between them but pain. A break up and the disappointment at finding out Noor was not his. She was sure he wanted her to be. It could have resulted in her swift exit from Boston back to him.

"I need your help," Rose said, her seductive and piercing eyes ripping through his delicate soul easily. He still felt something after all the time that had passed. But it wasn't enough to make him turn from Brooke. He had responsibilities. He looked at life through a different set of eyes. Rose still did something to him. She could still arouse him with just a look. He still had her naked pictures. Throwing them away was not in the cards for him. Not yet. He still liked to look at her. Admire her. But that's where it ended. He wondered what she could possibly want. His mind raced for just a second. Then the answer hit him swiftly.

"I will not represent him. I can't! You know this Rose. Why come to me? Huh? Asking me is insane. This is insane," he said, running his fingers through his thick hair and turning from her. He looked out at the busy street. Rose stood still looking down. She was embarrassed, but her love for Boston had her facing his scrutiny with unguarded determination. Max got close to her. He looked her over. He had never seen her so serious. So sure. Her smile and unraveled confidence were commendable.

"Did you think I would help the man you left me for? If it was a parking ticket and he was offering a million dollars I still wouldn't take the case. You made a mistake coming here. I am angry that you have so little regard for me that you thought this was okay. I am still not over it. Is it true?" he asked. Rose looked intensely at him.

"Is what true?" she asked, fearing the question. Max stared intently as if he was trying to reach her soul. He glanced down at her mouth. His once favorite place to be. He remembered their tender kisses. Her wet orifice that he would plunge deep inside of. She was a tease. She was his first love. And she was someone who could still affect him. But he had one question. Something Phoenix told him one drunken afternoon at Club Mint. He wondered about it ever since.

"Did he fuck you in our condo?" he asked. Rose took a step back.

"Max! What? What! Are you serious? Where did you get that from? Don't ask me that. Don't...," she said, as she looked away. The question mortified her. That was information she never talked about. And Boston was not one to spread all his business around. But he had told someone and they had ran their mouth. Rose suspected it was Phoenix or Memphis.

"Save it. I already know. And I can't represent him. Now go home," Max said, as he turned and walked towards the parking lot. He glanced back once. Rose stood in the same spot. He was humiliated. It was an admission of sorts. He never believed it. It was pain resurfacing again. Max entered the parking structure his heart racing from the stress. He bit his lip as he hit the unlock button on his car remote. Max got in and slammed the door. He looked out at the sky then hit his hands on the steering wheel. He wished he could take it back. It was better not to know.

*R*ose pulled up to Aurora's massive estate. She was there to check on her girls before she went home. They were spending the night so she could rest sound before the meeting with Thomas. Rose sat for a moment with the car idling then shut it off. She always felt less than when in the presence of Aurora. It wasn't Aurora's fault. It was just the way it was. Aurora's seemingly perfect life made her feel inadequate.

Aurora lived as lavishly as Boston, and all on her own dime. She and her successful husband made their money without the help of their well-off families. Rose got out and walked the graveled walkway that was brightly lit by dozens of in-ground lights. Aurora's electric bill had to be worth a fortune. A huge, elegant water fountain with a large stone statue sat in front, lit with blue lights that changed periodically to a pale-yellow color. Rose was impressed. She had told Boston to get one for their home. Seeing Aurora's was a reminder that she still wanted one. It was breathtaking.

"Hey," Rose said in a low voice, as she entered the estate. Aurora smiled and shut the door behind her, then walked towards the back of her home. Rose had been there just a few times. Aurora had an enviable life. There was never any gossip or talks of behavior that would shame the family. She walked, talked and behaved with style and grace and Rose loved her simplicity and the ease at which she lived her life. Even when tempers flared, Aurora would be the calm voice of reason.

"The babies are resting. Brooklyn needs more milk by morning. I have just two bottles left. She cried herself asleep. I think she missed you. Breast fed babies are so attached. Noor was good. She's a busy body. They're both just a dream. So adorable. I can keep them anytime. All you have to do is call," Aurora said.

"Yes. And thank you. This is such a big help. I have to meet with the lawyers in the morning to sign some paperwork. I have to get some kind of sleep or I won't be able to focus," she said. Aurora furled her brows.

"What meeting? Is this about that eye thing he invented? He's still selling?" Aurora asked, trying to get what information she could about her brother. Rose nodded.

"Yes. Boston wants me to do the deal for him. That's a lot of money. Its why I'm so nervous," she said, as she walked quietly in Aurora's daughter's room and looked into the crib. Brooklyn slept peacefully. Rose touched her curly brown hair then bent over and kissed her head. She took a moment to smell her scent. The hint of baby powder and milk blended warmly. Rose loved her children. She held her nose to Brooklyn for a few seconds longer then made her way to the bed where Noor slept. "My sweet baby," she whispered, as she kissed her hand. Aurora smiled. She didn't care for some of Rose's choices in life, but she did love the mother she was. It counted for something.

"Call me when you settle in and I will drop them off. I have to go over my mother's. I'll be out. I will take them to see her. We'll be there until you call," Aurora stated as Rose left out the door. "That's fine. I shouldn't be all day."

Rose walked into her empty nest and slung her shoes nearly across the room. Her children were at Aurora's house. She needed to drop off breast milk for Brooklyn in the morning, if she wanted to avoid being the brunt of the family's latest gossip. She liked Aurora, but her sister in law spared no time talking about things she deemed inappropriate. For the moment she could rest knowing that the whispers were on Boston and Bronx. Boston in jail topped the list. But the family worried tirelessly about Bronx's state of mind. He was too quiet and no one was buying Orlando's narrative that he was okay. Even still, life went on for the St. Rocks. It seemed they were in denial with both St. Rocks men's fates. They believed Boston would fight his way out like he always did. And they believed Bronx would be pull through fine.

Rose walked through the darkness until she reached her foyer table. She clicked on the lamp and sat her purse down. She had a long day planned the following morning. All she needed to do was drop off the pre-pumped milk and get to her meeting. Part of her wanted to go back and get her babies. But there was no one around to help her. Mary had an emergency in the family. She had to fly back to her hometown to be with her daughter Menara, who had been in a car accident. Rose was glad everything was okay. Menara would be fine and Mary would be returning soon. Her 7:00 a.m. meeting was too early to try to care for the girls alone. It was better to just leave them.

Rose made her way to the kitchen. A warm cup of tea with chamomile would be a great way to relax and wind down. Her phone pinged with a message. Rose looked at it as she filled her tea pot. "Missed call," she said, checking her phone's ringer. Rose immediately recognized the number. It was the throw away phone Boston was using from the prison to make outside calls.

"Damn," she blurted. The caller i.d showed he called three times. Rose made the decision to leave her phone in the car while she ran in Aurora's home. The meeting with Thomas was crucial and she was sure her husband had some last-minute request and thoughts. She was still fighting the temptation to spoil it all with a verbal lashing about his affairs that were now permanent scars on their marriage. Talks of babies made by outside women. An embarrassment and a blow that had shook her even if she *was* managing to play doting wife.

Bzzz...Bzzz, the phone rang. Rose snatched it up quickly an answered. "Hello," she said. "Hey. Where were you? I've called a million times. You know I can't keep this phone. I get it for a few hours at a time," he griped. Rose sighed.

"I know. I was over Aurora's house. She got Noor and Brooke," she replied. "Oh! Well, I know its late. I'm not going to keep you. I have something important. Thomas came to see me today. He believes Mr. Fritch wants the company. I am giving you permission to sell it. No one can run it but me. Denver wants his own company. He's already reestablishing Twist Media. I don't blame him. He has been ready to do his own thing for a while. And with me not there…," he said.

Rose closed her eyes. He was taking her fast. She was flooded by emotions that did not go together. The mixture of happiness at their success, mixed with sadness that he was locked up plus the anger from the discovery of children by mistresses, was a lot. She had not weighed-in on one single thing. She was going with the motions. Doing what Boston wanted done. She wanted to sleep through the confusing feelings and emerge the next day with a game plan. She wanted him safe. Home with his family. But she also wanted to part from him until she could decide if she could go on. Rose knew she was being ridiculous. She had her own dirt. The reason she needed time away. She was questioning whether they would survive it all. First things first. She needed to do what he wanted as far as his business. Then she needed to help him get out of jail.

"Why you change your mind? You said you'd entertain offers later. Now you're saying sell it?" Rose asked. He didn't sound like himself. His voice lacked the vibrancy and assuredness that it usually had. Rose held the phone. She wondered what he was hiding. What he knew. His life was crashing around him including his relationship with her.

"They're saying a weapon has been found. I had a newspaper delivered to me. And the story states they had part of a building removed so they could dig underneath. They found a gun. I swear...someone in my family is talking," he said. Rose put her hand over her mouth. This was not what he originally told her. The narrative was changing. Why would he worry about a gun if he had nothing to do with what they were charging him with. Something wasn't right.

"I'll do whatever you need. I told you that. I'm here," Rose said. Boston paused. Rose held the phone. Soon he would tip the scale her way.

"Is there something you want to ask me?" he said. Rose's eyes bucked. She had a lot to say. But what exactly did he mean. If he was speaking on the fact that she pulled up on Ashley then it proved they were in contact. Rose decided not to ask him what he meant. She hoped he would reveal his hand.

"No! I don't. Nothing matters right now," she said.

"You had something to say when you came to see me. You said you were mad at me about something. What was it?" he asked.

Rose walked into the grand room and sat back on the couch and crossed her legs. She sat in the darkness as she tried to outthink him. He was figuring things out. Which meant he probably had an angle. Rose refused to play her hand. She was too angry to indulge him. But if he knew she had been to see Ashley and was ready to talk about it, so was she.

"I'm mad about everything! We were doing good. Starting over. We had forgiven each other for the past. But you haven't told me everything. You are locked away, and I feel selfish for thinking about anything other than your freedom. This is just messed up. I don't want to harp on it. I just want things to work out. I want you home. Okay! And when you get home, we have things to talk about. Right!" Rose replied.

Boston held the phone. The silence was deafening. She was sure he had something else to say. She waited, nervously rubbing the pendant on her delicate necklace. She wanted to get it off her chest. Air out all that was left in the balance. She wondered what all she would say if he confessed to what he had done. Would she tell him about Bronx. The one last secret. The bombshell that would annihilate an already devastated man. Boston continued to hold the phone. And with that, Rose decided he was not mentally prepared for that much pain.

Rose said her goodbyes to her complicated husband. She jumped up from the couch and made a beeline to her bathroom. The pressure was producing mild aches behind her temples. It would be a full-blown headache, if she ignored the signs. She held the phone. It was apparent he didn't want to hang up.

"Boston...I have a headache. I need to get off the phone now. The meeting is in the morning. This is overwhelming. I need rest," she said in frustration. His lack of a response was telling. Rose could see he wasn't quite ready to part ways. And if he wasn't ready to come clean, they needed to hang up.

"I miss you," he finally said, his voice low. Rose closed her eyes. That was code for; *I'm not getting off the phone yet.* Rose popped the top on the bottle and swallowed two pills. He wanted phone sex. She sighed then shook her head in frustration. This was the love of her life. The man who *got* her. The only one who made her feel like a queen even after she had done things that weren't majestic. Rose surrendered to his will. She would need to get him off so he could get *off* the phone.

An hour crept by. Rose stared at the ceiling. She engaged her husband until the sounds of his sexual release tempted her own desires. It was the first time he'd cum alone. She was much too distracted to fondle with her privates. For the first time, sex took a backseat. Rose was amazed at her ability to control the need to cum.

Her phone sat on her chest with the speaker on. Boston was snoring on the other end and she was in shambles. She couldn't sleep despite her best efforts. Her headache was gone, but freedom from the pain did nothing to improve her odds at getting some type of rest. Tears rolled down the side of her face soaking her pillow just enough to cause irritation. Rose flipped the pillow then tried to get comfortable again. She raised the phone and put it closer to her ear. The guards had forgotten to take it from him. It was the first time he'd had it that long. And he used the opportunity to fall asleep as if he were lying beside her. A comfort for him that didn't sit well. How could he sleep, like he was at home, while things crumbled all around them. It didn't seem fair.

Rose pictured him with Ashley. She hated that her friend knew him intimately. He was addictive. The best a woman could get. He did everything, and for as long as a woman could stand. His head game was flawless and he had a huge cock. He had all the things that would ensure a woman would likely want a repeat performance. She understood the reason for a baby. Between his money and the sex, what more could a girl ask for. He was good enough to play side chick for. Rose was livid that Ashley experienced even a small portion of what was hers. First Max. Now him. And she had been clever. There was a St. Rock heir to seal the deal. It wasn't easy plotting an exit from a man like him. It would kill her if somehow, he and Ashley became an item. The baby made it a possibility. She pictured Ashley in her house. Wearing her clothes. Fucking her man. Living her life. Assuming the role that was hers. Rose sat up. It was too much to take.

"Boston!" she shouted. She could hear his breaths. It angered her that he'd fallen asleep now that she was ready to scold him. Now that she was ready to tell him she was hurting. She listened to his rhythmic bellows. She was all too familiar with a *sleeping* Boston. If he was in a deep sleep, he would be hard to wake unless she was next to him and able to dip below the covers and place him completely inside her mouth. Otherwise, he was oblivious to any words spoken. But that didn't stop her from ranting.

"Boston…I want to know why you fucked her. Just tell me why? Was it all to get back at me? I hate you. I do. I hate you right now. I…I can't do this with you. I won't be there. This is the last thing I'm doing for you. Do you hear me," she cried. Rose placed her hand on her forehead. The headache was returning. Rose sniffled then wiped her nose. Her pain was deep.

"We are so toxic. So fucking… toxic…," she sniffled, as her voice quivered. If he was listening but choosing not to respond, it didn't matter. She said her *peace*. It was a release that needed to happen. She died a slow death since the day she pulled off and looked in her rear view mirror at the woman she once called a friend. The woman she never wanted to lay eyes on again. He needed to wake and hear her out. There was still something else. One last set of words.

She hoped some part of him was listening. If so, then what she would say next might jolt him awake.

"I'm leaving you!"

Rose waited. Divorce was their best option. He had a baby and so did she. He was facing murder which meant he was probably capable of it. Boston was capable of a lot of things including killing her if Brooklyn wasn't his.

"Boston," Rose said in a now worn voice. The emotion of the last few minutes stripped her soul down to the bones. The snoring ceased but Boston said nothing.

"Did you hear me?" she asked. She could hear talking in the background. The words of the guard were crystal clear. "I need that back," he said. Soon the sound of movement.

"Good luck tomorrow. I love you," Boston said. Rose's eyes popped. He had no response to her rant. She wondered if he caught any of what she said.

"Yep!" she replied. Soon the call ended. Rose plopped backward onto the pillow and wept. It wasn't over. He was being Boston. His normal self who tried to control the outcome. She wondered what his plans were. He was no longer in the driver's seat.

Chapter Three – Crumbling Walls

The smell of bacon had Aurora's husband ready to feast on his wife great cooking. Ralph Simmons walked into the kitchen to check out what was on the breakfast menu. Gone was the usual liveliness of his children's rambunctious nature. Aurora had allowed them outside to play in the early morning sun. The only children in the house were Boston and Rose's babies. And they were still sound asleep.

His beautiful wife, whom he adored, was up early doing what she thrived at. Being a mother. A loving aunt. A caring wife. She was his best accomplishment. It bothered him that his wife didn't respond to his entry into the kitchen. Not even a glance. Her mind was somewhere else. It had been for weeks. The loss of her nephews and Boston's current situation were weighing heavily on her. Ralph tried to be a comfort. But Aurora was brought to tears with any mention of either, and so he had stopped asking. She needed to mourn. She needed to keep abreast of the latest news on Boston. He understood. He worried as well. Boston was his favorite brother in law. He understood his drive. His vision. And he admired his success.

Ralph remembered when he first met Aurora. She walked onto the elevator at a company his father owned and he was immediately smitten. He remembered the nervous way she made him feel. She was beautiful. Poised. And his arrogance almost destroyed his chance at meeting her. She was there for an appointment, never to return. He remembered biting the bullet and doing something he had never done. Chase after a woman.

It was a decision that would spark a conversation and ultimately end with them going to lunch. He could kick himself for nearly losing her. His father threatened him if he didn't abandon the relationship. Ralph contemplated not marrying her. He was under pressure from his parents to marry another young lady. He had been groomed for greatness and that meant keeping his options open or marrying someone with status and wealth. But he continued to see Aurora, whose family was not wealthy at the time.

He was twenty four and she was twenty, when they first met. Later he would find out that she was from a large family, with scores of protective brothers and an overbearing father. Despite the pressure, they fell in love. But because Aurora's family was not quite the powerhouse they are now, his father was against it. She was from a family shrouded in mystery. In particular, her brothers who had reputations as hoodlums.

Ralph had heard the stories. It seemed Bronx, Denver and Boston were one step ahead of their tough father. Their ability to keep secrets and blend into their surroundings made for a dangerous cocktail. When Orlando made the move to the Englewood after losing his high paying job, it was a move he soon regretted. The charismatic brothers made their way through the rough neighborhood. Soon they connected with an older man anxious to take advantage of the well-known and impressionable young teenagers. It didn't take long before Orlando found out. It was an intervention that came just in time. Boston and Bronx had started delivering drugs to several designated places. Soon they had a crew. Orlando moved swiftly, approaching the man known only as

Vado and telling him to stay away from his boys. It was a threat that would ultimately put his sons in danger. Vado made threats of his own which caused Memphis to pull a gun on him. And life changed for the St. Rocks.

It was a move that put the St. Rocks in the limelight. No one threatened Vado. Many residents secretly praised Orlando for standing up to the ruthless low-level drug dealer. Memphis was fifteen at the time.

Orlando understood how the streets worked. He had fought the urge and lure of easy money from those same streets. He was much like his sons, well-known and well-connected, when he was young. He knew everyone. It would have been easy for him to dominate. He was naturally aggressive. Mean when he needed to be. Quick witted and sharp. And he was known to carry pistols. He had all the calling cards of a Street Don. But he knew the risks. He vowed to be different. He used his smarts to keep out of trouble.

Instead of selling drugs he sold homemade candy to the neighborhood kids. His grandmother's taffy and chocolate covered wafers were a hit. And when he had sons, he knew the pressure they would be under. He vowed his sons would never be swept in the power of the streets. By the time Aurora's husband Ralph came along, the St. Rocks were on their way. Orlando had secured a college degree and was working on furthering his education. All which then took a back seat to his child prodigy. Boston.

"You good? I'll be back soon," Ralph said, as he walked up to her from behind and planted a kiss on her shoulder. Aurora stood at the kitchen counter stirring pancake mix to create her bunny and bear shaped pancakes for her large family.

"I'm fine hun. I would like one favor," she said, as she flirted with him. Ralph was a corporate *big wig*. His role as the Chief Financial Officer for a parts manufacturing company, made for a comfortable living without his wife's several million dollars plus inheritance. Aurora never needed Boston and had never asked for his financial assistance but money was still provided and it was sitting in an account earning interest. She didn't have to ask. A check was cut and given to a sister he loved with all his heart. She would never want for anything.

"What do you need," Ralph said, as he hit his wife's derriere.

"A bottle of my favorite wine. Rose is coming to get the little munchkins and I'll be able to relax," she said.

"Sure thing," Ralph said, as he smiled then turned and left the kitchen. Aurora waited to hear the door shut. Ralph was her well-intentioned and easygoing husband who loved all his brother-in-laws to a fault. She wanted to call her parents but it was a conversation she didn't want to have in front of him. They were close. She told her husband everything. But not this. She didn't like to say things that might upset him. Her ears perked up. She heard the door slam closed. Aurora wiped her hands on her dishtowel and grabbed her phone to dial Orlando.

"Sweetheart…How are you? You're a hard person to catch up to," Orlando said. "Hey dad. I called you last night. But then I looked at the time. I'm sure you were sleep. You getting old now. Gotta get those naps in," Aurora joked.

"Hey now! Don't you count your pop out. Cicely said I'm like a young man," he chuckled. Aurora bursts into laughter.

"Oh really," she replied, as she listened to the voice of her mother in the background. Cicely was fully engaged in whatever had her attention on the television. Aurora waited to get her father's full attention.

"Everything ok?" Orlando finally asked, pausing as he tried giving Cicely feedback on her favorite soap opera. Aurora paused and waited for him to finish. She hated not knowing about what was going on in her family. Rose's revelation of having something to do and mentioning paperwork had her nervous. Boston was in jail. He didn't involve her in his business. Aurora wondered if involving her now meant he didn't see himself coming home and was making moves to secure things.

"Sorry baby. You know how your mother is. She acts like these are real people in real situations," he said.

"It is real. Its real enough. Now Connor will have to tell Amy he lost his job. And that damn Emily is walking into an ambush. Don't go in there!" Cicely shouted at the tv. Orlando laughed then focused back on his call.

"What going on sweetheart?" he asked.

"Well, just a concern. Nothing really. Rose was here last night to check on the kids and to bring me things to get them through the night. She mentioned having to do something for Boston. It involved his new technology. He wants her to do the deal. Why? Is he not coming home ever? Why are the circumstances surrounding Boston's arrest so quiet? He's still in there and now *she's* going to do the deal," she said.

Orlando's brow furled. Boston kept him well-informed of his business but this information was new. Rose wasn't tied to the business. She had her business and he had his. He didn't want to speak on Boston's troubles with Aurora. She would only worry more. He had faith. Once Max was on it, it seemed a waiting game. He was sure Boston would be exonerated. The information they DA had was all fluff. There was one so-called witness. And the DA still had not named who it was because the man or woman had not come forward yet. The information provided led to a gun that was discovered. Fifteen years in a moist environment probably destroyed the evidence even though it was in a plastic bag that was buried in dirt, under a newly constructed building.

"Listen baby. Boston is getting his defense together. He's innocent. Someone is doing this. He has enemies. Men who want to see him fall. Men from his past. We will beat this! Don't you worry. And as far as Rose is concerned...I will go see him. Find out what's going on. That *is* his wife. He wants to make his life with her work. I know this family has had its share of drama, but Boston is methodical in his moves. And if he is using her to finish the deal, it is for a reason. He always has a reason. Stop worrying. And kiss my grandbabies for me," Orlando said.

"I will. They miss you. And I'll stop worrying. I'll keep Boston in my prayers. That's not right. Murder is a serious charge. How can someone pin a murder on someone? I mean...they have to have something. What do they have?" she said. Orlando sighed. Aurora wasn't ready to let the conversation go. She was no fool.

Orlando listened to her clear her mind, then glanced over at Cicely. She gave him a stern look. One he knew well. *Don't tell her anything to make her worry*, was the understanding between them. All the strife and hard work was done behind the scenes. All in an effort to make their family solid. Orlando sipped his coffee. Aurora continued. Soon she rested. He could tell her mind was trying to wrap itself around the facts. Orlando jumped in. She needed to calm down and wait for his latest update whenever he had one to give.

"Ro…I will find out. He will get Max or Rupert King. The best lawyers in Chicago. Between those two brilliant minds, he will beat this. I promise!"

Chapter Four – More Money More Problems

*R*ose walked confidently into the towering structure on Michigan Avenue tired but confident. Her four-inch heels added to her confidence. She felt like power. She looked like money. She was there to do business. A simple deed for her significant other. The job was simple. Sign off on papers that would give her the power she needed. She was ready. She dressed in her finest, complete with a Piaget watch and Cartier necklace with a small, white and yellow gold heart charm. Dressing the part was half the battle. She would be the shark he told her she could be, and that would take care of the other half.

She had to admit her husband's word the previous night caused an adrenaline rush of new felt power. He would make a great motivational speaker, not that she would benefit from it. In her current state, she could do nothing but wish him well afterwards. She would do this deal, then tell him what was still tormenting her in case he missed her long rant as he slept.

"I'm here to see Mr. Thomas Ford," Rose said, as she entered his law firm.

"You must be Mrs. St. Rock. He is expecting you. Have a seat and I'll let him know you're here," the secretary said. Rose looked around then sat down in the bold looking black and white striped chair while the secretary alerted him.

"This way," the woman said. Rose stood and followed the secretary down the wide hall towards an opened office door at the end. She looked inside several of the offices. Eyes met hers with smiles. It was a different feel. There was an assumed prestige and power automatically granted to her. She could see why Boston relished in the deals. The ability to command such money with the stroke of a pen was powerful. Owning clothing boutiques, no matter how much money they were generating, never felt so good. The looks from Thomas' team fed her self-esteem in a way that had never been done before. For the first time, Rose was completely aware of what being Boston's wife meant. Who he was. Who she was. It was intoxicating.

"Mrs. St. Rock. Nice to meet you. I'm Thomas. And this is the notary, Ms. Callaway," Thomas greeted, as he stood and shook her hand. Rose smiled and looked at the woman sitting across from him. She stood and introduced herself.

"Hi. My name is Kelsey Callaway. I will be the notary for your signature on the legal documents," she said.

"Hi. Nice to meet you," Rose said, then sat next to Kelsey in a stately looking red leather chair. She crossed her legs, ready to get right to it. Thomas requested coffee and tea be brought in for his client then sat at his desk and flipped through a small pile of papers.

Rose glanced around. It was obvious Mr. Ford was good at what he did. His surroundings were opulent. He fit the bill of a high-end attorney. His refined look topped off by a smooth navy blue suit and distinct cuff links looked like a badge that showcased his accomplishments. Thomas Ford,

Esq. looked like royalty. His salt and pepper hair and beard, made him look like an aging prince. Max was the only sophisticated lawyer she knew. Rose thought most lawyers looked like dressed up waiters. But not Mr. Ford. His look was first-class high fashion. And he was quite handsome for an older gentleman close to retirement age.

Mr. Ford looked her over closely. She was gorgeous. Much prettier than he'd imagined. He expected the handsome and dashing Boston would be married to a woman who would command attention herself but Rose was much more. The soft pink low cut, button down blouse and black pencil skirt were classy and sophisticated.

Her ability to glide like a stallion in the five inch heels she wore, only added to her attractiveness. Thomas loved well put-together women. If she wasn't Mrs. St. Rock, he would find himself offering his services for free just to get in her good graces. She was stunning. He'd known Boston a year and hadn't had the pleasure. He understood why. He would keep her locked up in a dungeon if she were his.

Thomas cleared his throat. He would need to get a grip on the sexual attraction he felt towards her. This was business. And from the look of things, Boston wasn't above killing someone. He was being held without bond for murder. He wouldn't be testing the theory.

"I spoke with Boston. He told me that you've been briefed on the deal. I have drafted the papers transferring the remaining portion of the company into your name. I noticed you didn't bring a lawyer with you so I assume you are trusting me to act on your behalf as well since he *is* your husband. I can represent you. That's no problem. But if you want to return with your own attorney, we can reschedule," he said. Rose was perplexed. Her name was already on the business. There was no need to transfer anything.

"Wait! I *am* named as an owner on my husband's company. What do you mean transfer his business to me?" she asked. Thomas looked puzzled. "Didn't he explain. Just this morning he asked that I transfer the company to you. His portion. It's easier to sell it outright if it's under one name. That way two people don't have to be present for meetings and you don't need two signatures on all the paperwork. There is a lot to sign off on. It's just better if it's under one name."

Rose sat stunned. This was not part of the deal. She remembered him saying that he would entertain selling it one day. The only deal on the table was the medical device he talked about. Rose looked off.

"That's not what we discussed. He wanted to wait. Is he sure? I need to speak to him again," Rose said. Thomas looked at her. He was sure. Boston had made it quite clear.

"I went to see him. That was his words to me this morning. He said you would be shocked. He literally made the decision this morning. But he wants to move on this now! He has several interested parties. Fritch Packard will likely be the most viable option. They have the money. Mr. Fritch will probably make a solid offer. Boston wants 2 billion. The purchase will include the rights to the eye scanner as well as a few other copyrighted items that have not been released yet. He was very clear in what he wanted," Thomas replied.

Thomas was an astute and crafty lawyer. He had made the deal with a man who had no interest in the groundbreaking technology he was prepared to spend handsomely for. Fritch was in it for the recognition. Once Thomas found out he was dealing with a man who liked to bask in his accomplishments, it was easy to propose that the deal move forward. He was right. Even though Fritch was skeptical about Boston and his background, the blemish of being arrested didn't erase the fact that his technology was innovative. And it didn't overshadow Rockwater's presence as a powerful force in the technology world.

"It's fine. What's his is mine. So I guess that means you too," Rose said. Thomas narrowed his gaze.

"Yes…um…So let's go over the deal," he said, as he pushed the papers in front of her.

Rose pulled her chair forward and glanced over the legal documents. She guessed that was the purpose of his call to her that morning. A call she missed and tried to return but got no answer. If he would have answered she might be sitting in on a different meeting. She wanted out of her marriage. It was the last thing she said before the call ended that night. But now her mind raced. The more money he had the better. It would be easy for him to give her something in the divorce, for herself and their girls. They could rebuild their lives splendidly with that much money. Rose was ready.

"Is this legal and binding?" she asked. Thomas stared at her. It was an odd question.

"What do you mean?" he asked. Rose sat back and crossed her legs.

"I'm asking will this hold up in court. Is it a real transfer? Will I *own* Rockwater?" she asked in a matter of fact tone. Thomas sat back.

"Yes. And the only way he would get it back is if you signed off on it or sold it back to him. This is a binding legal transfer of ownership," Thomas replied.

Rose leaned forward and glanced over the wording. Thomas' stomach tightened. He wondered why she asked the question. Her demeanor was hard to read. She seemed on board. But the question was puzzling. It sounded like she had a plan. Thomas thought for a minute. They appeared to be happily married with two kids. Or at least that's what Boston had eluded to one night at Emilio's.

Thomas was sure Rose meant nothing by it. He relaxed as he watched her eyes scan the documents. He believed her inquiry was specifically to make sure the deal was full proof and that he had done the paperwork properly. But just to be certain, he would need to ask Boston if he truly trusted his wife. If he didn't, it would be too late. She was there to sign and accept ownership. And if Boston was wrong about her, it would be the biggest mistake of his life.

Rose signed the extensive papers. The tall pile that required a signature on almost every page was daunting. Rose could see that Boston had already signed them as she placed her *John Hancock* under his, sealing both his fate and hers. Rose stood up and extended her hand. "Thank you. I would like a copy of this faxed to my attorney," Rose said. Thomas furled his brow. "Oh! So you do have an attorney. Was he unable to come here with you today?" Thomas asked. "Yes. He had court this morning. He'll review everything. Here is his business card. Please fax him a copy of everything," Rose said.

Thomas looked down at the name. He recognized it. Jeremy London was one of the most expensive and successful business attorneys' in Chicago. The young, eccentric son of a millionaire Investment Banker, he had a reputation that preceded him. Thomas looked quickly into her eyes. Jeremy was known for playing hardball and sometimes working on deals that were unscrupulous and dishonest. And he had a reputation with the ladies.

"Are you familiar with Mr. London?" he asked. Rose smiled.

"He came highly recommended. I'm sure he'll suit my needs. I just need him to review these documents," she replied. Thomas would need to see Boston soon. The fact that she was working with a known shark and ladies' man was not good. But it was too late.

"I'll get these to him right away," Thomas said.

"Today please. And I'll take copies for my own records now" Rose said.

"Yes, Mrs. St. Rock. The meeting with Fritch is in a few days. We won't get a second chance. He leaves the country after that. I will definitely have everything sent to your lawyer today!"

*B*oston passed on breakfast once he heard what was on the menu. He requested turkey bacon and bagels and the night shift guard was doing his best to get it delivered. He was the main benefactor of Boston's generosity and he was on call for the jail's most popular and generous inmate.

"Here you go," the guard said, passing the food through the bars to an awaiting Boston.

"Thanks man," he said.

The bag of basic yet deliciously edible food was a nice distraction. His stomach was still in knots after receiving a blow to his case. Another inmate told him he read somewhere that the prosecution mentioned the discovery of some damaging items, including a weapon. It would surely be brought up at his next court date. What should have been hearsay was now much more, given the details of the story.

It was now confirmed that the snitch was someone close. Probably family. A guard had brought Boston the daily paper. He read the article that glorified him as a wealthy troubled man. Boston was upset at that label. He was the most stable person he knew. But he understood the drive to sell papers, and sensationalized stories did sell papers.

"Let's go. You have a visitor," a guard said, as he stood waiting. Boston furled his brow, as he gulped down the last of his fresh squeezed orange juice.

"I'm not expecting anyone. Is it my wife?" Boston asked.

"I don't know. I'm not your slave. Come find out. Or deny the visit. I don't give a fuck! Are you coming," he said.

Boston walked towards the cell bars. He didn't like this particular guard. A smart mouthed young newbie who tried him on several occasions. Boston wondered what his problem was. If it was envy. Jealousy. Or plain old anger at the fact that he wasn't in on the payout. It wasn't Boston's fault. He didn't pick whose palms got greased and whose didn't. He left that up to the guards he was already acquainted with. It was their unanimous decision to leave the troublemaker on the outside.

"Pop," Boston said, as he approached the table and sat down.

"Son," Orlando replied. Boston got right to the point. He was curious as to his loving father's visit. Orlando was a doting father. Always was. But two visits within days of each other was alarming. The family was healing and now trying to handle him being locked up. He hoped it wasn't bad news. He couldn't take much more. But he was glad to see him. There was something bothering him. There was an enemy close by. A rat.

"I have enemies all around me. Even within my own family," Boston said, as he looked deeply into his father's eyes.

"What do you mean son?" Orlando asked, as a feeling of intense anxiety came over him. It wasn't the time to talk about his wife's indiscretions with his brothers. It was old news. They were past it. Even the family had brushed the incidences under the rug. There were no other issues. Orlando wondered what his son meant.

"Enemies?" Orlando asked.

"Yes! And right now, I don't know who to trust. Dayton ain't been here and he won't answer my calls.

Neither had Bronx. Bronx been acting funny. Even before I got arrested, he did some shit after the boys died that fucked me up. He was mad at me. Lashed out at me. For no fucking reason. Then Austin went ghost. Ain't checked to see if a nigga okay. Phoenix still got his drawls in a fucking knot over my fucking wife. I mean…Where the fuck is everybody," Boston replied. Orlando shook his head side to side.

"No, son. You're assuming wrong. They think this will be over soon. They think you'll be home. No one is turning their back. This is a family built on love. We support you. Anything that has happened in the past is past. You have to let that go," Orlando said.

"How can I when it is still going on. Someone has betrayed me. Someone fucked my wife! Again! She told me she wants a divorce. She wants to leave! Why would she want to leave. I'll tell you why, cause one of them has betrayed me again. . What I can't figure out is how deep that betrayal goes. Someone wants me in jail! And if I find out that Phoenix or Denver has touched my wife again, they might as well keep me locked away in here because you will be going to another funeral," Boston warned. Orlando leaned back. Those were strong words coming from his son.

"Why do you say that? I spoke to Phoenix. I continue to talk to him. He is seeing someone. A woman named Reina. That chapter of his life is over. And Denver is in over his head with Natalie. He told me he thinks she's pregnant. He is furious. He has no time to do anything but keep a constant watch over his own life."

Boston looked down. His mind raced. Someone was working for the other side.

"Look pop. I don't expect you to see what I see. I know for a fact that my problems are coming from within my own family. Who else knows details about Freemont. Someone is feeding information to the cops. And to add on more bullshit, someone told Rose about Ashley," he said, as his eyes pierced through his father's. He hoped his father would stop playing devil's advocate and see things for what they were. He needed his help. Time was running out. They needed to id who the betrayer was.

"What? Is this why you are dumping your company. Giving your wife control. I don't think that's a smart move. The cops have nothing. What information are they feeding you in here? They are putting pressure on you so you will get scared and cop to a plea. That is the game they play. No one from our family is working with them. I promise you," he said, his eyes darting between his sons.

"Pop. Take the blinders off. They are. I wondered at first. I thought all this was just lucky breaks for the cops. But naw...I don't think so. I need you to find out who told Rose about Ashley. Whoever did that is probably the one," he said.

"And then what? You're giving up. Selling everything. Aren't you going to fight?" Orlando asked.

"I'm selling Rockwater Technologies. That part of my life is over. I want the money. I'll make history with this deal. My plan is to cash out, then open a new firm called *Rockland Enterprises*. Totally new! I will concentrate on expanding my reach. Still developing high-tech products but also buying the copyrights to others. I want to have money like Fritch Packard. I want to be the one *buying* companies, not the one selling them. I'm talking about making billions of dollars. Not just one or two billion. This move will put me in the ring. I get to go up against the big boys. But first I must do this deal. He won't wait. He'll just go invest in something else. And this could take a year or longer. I have to strike now. I know you don't trust her. She would never cross me like that. She knows me. She knows better. Plus...I love her.

We love each other. She can do this. She is not the problem. One of my brothers is," he said.

"You need to wait. Deal with the charges first. You'll beat it because they have nothing. Then when you come home, sell if that is what you wish. You don't have to do this now," Orlando pleaded. Boston became nervous. Orlando could see the shift in his son.

"What is it? What are you not telling me," Orlando asked.

"It's complicated," he said, as he hesitated. Orlando waited, as his heart rate went up. He could see his son was pacing his words in order to drop a bombshell in his lap. Boston looked deeply into his father's eyes.

"I...Um... I may... have to take the plea," Boston said. Orlando was confused for a brief moment. He didn't hear him right. But then, the words took form. The sentences came into focus. Orlando slammed his hands on the table.

"Plea my ass! What has gotten into you. What are you thinking? You have no will power? No fight. You've been in here nine weeks and already you're giving up. I have never seen you throw in the towel on anything," Orlando said, his voice carrying with it the passion of a father ready to give his all for his son.

Boston paused. Orlando stopped his rant and stared. There was a seriousness in his son. A serious look coupled with fear. Boston looked intensely at his father. Then rocked his world with an admission.

"They found the gun," Boston said in a whisper low voice. Orlando trembled slightly. It was a blow that hit straight in the gut.

"What!" he said.

Boston stared. It was a game changer. The gun was wrapped in plastic. He was young when he disposed of it. He didn't remember wiping it of any fingerprints. He didn't remember what else was in the bag. He remembered being handed a tee shirt, a gun and other small items.

His job was to take it and dump it in the river. But fear and his lack of experience had him bury it instead. A hole he dug with a small gardening tool, never to be seen again. He remembered the day he came home and told his father he had tossed it in the Chicago River. He lied. This revelation would hurt his father. Orlando was clear with his instruction that day. Boston felt bad. He thought he'd done a great thing back then. It had come back to haunt them.

"How is that possible? The gun you were supposed to…" Orlando asked, as reality set in.

His memories from that fateful day had him handing the bag to Boston to ride his bike to the river and discard of its contents. He chose the bike over driving in a car in case police pulled the car over. It was a clever way to travel with the damaging evidence. A methodical plan that had been diverted by his careless son. He couldn't speak. Fear had Orlando paralyzed. If Boston had just stuck with the plan this wouldn't be happening. Boston stared at him. He couldn't answer him. He had fucked up. The pain cut deep.

"I see! Well… that changes things," Orlando said, as he stood to leave. He was too upset to sit. Soon there would be tears and a look of fear that would make his sons predicament worse.

"I better get going. I will find out if there is any truth to what you are saying. But I must tell you, there is no way I'm going to let you take a plea for something I did," he continued. Boston looked around. He couldn't believe what Orlando had just said. There could be ears listening in. The guards had already told him the tables weren't bugged because it would be inadmissible in court, but he didn't trust that.

"Don't pop! Don't! Please! Let me handle things. You want something to do, get me Max. Talk to Phoenix and get him to come here. I know he hates me, but I need to speak to him. Between you and I, he will relent. I know you want to take my place. You can't. I won't let you! You would never survive in jail," Boston said.

"Neither would you," Orlando replied.

He was angry for the first time in years at his son. The one who made no mistakes. The one who was always two steps ahead. Orlando had a bad feeling. There was more than the cops to worry about. There was also the boy's family. They never believed the St. Rocks had anything to do with their son's death. This would cast a shadow.

Boston rubbed his hands together as he now had a new worry. Orlando was a man who followed his own mind. And if his mind was telling him to confess and save his son, he would. Boston needed to keep hope alive. Neither one of them needed to be locked up. The St. Rock men did in fact have enemies. One in particular was doing 15-to-life, for second degree murder. He was the brother of the man they called Vado and the cousin of the man gunned down on Freemont Street. He was the last person they needed to see. A huge powerhouse of a man named Chains. And Chains hated the St. Rocks with a passion.

Orlando gave a fake smile. He hoped his son was right. The charges could be fought and still won. Orlando needed to get Max on board. Many rich men got slaps on the wrist. Money bought everything including freedom. A lawyer would just need to cast enough doubt. But there was still Rose. She could break him. Jail was nothing compared to the power of a woman. Men toughened up in jail. The strong survived. And Boston was physically strong. It was the heart that would do him in. He was weak for her.

He could see Boston loved her the way he loved Cicely. Orlando couldn't imagine Cicely doing anything that would make him ever leave her. He would forgive the worst of what she was capable of. And he had raised his sons the same way.

It was why Bronx loved Heather through all her faults and drug use. It was why Chicago still loved Jan after finding out she'd had an affair with not a man but with another woman. It was why Dayton was hopelessly attached to April.

And it was why Denver, although divorced from Nina, was still there for her. There for all his baby's momma's. They had seen nothing but a great love story unfold before their own eyes. Cicely and Orlando were the greatest real-life love story. And Orlando could not pretend to not understand. He just hoped he wasn't right about her.

"I am here for you. Whatever you want...Whatever you need...You just ask. We will be here. I will talk to Phoenix. I will try to see if anyone is upset enough to want to hurt you. This kills me to say. I can't see your brother's being that type of enemy but I will enquire. Okay," Orlando said. Boston shook his head. The father and son hugged. They were on the same page. Boston was relieved. He admired Orlando, and even as he continued to build the life he wanted, he couldn't help but continue to mold himself in his image. His father was the greatest man he knew.

*B*oston sat in his cell in eye blinding darkness staring at the wall. He was waiting to see if one of the night guards would bestow another gracious favor, and get him a phone to use. The guard he spoke to mentioned the fact that six months prior, there was a mass firing because of guards granting favors to inmates. Another wealthy man, locked up for attempted murder on his wife, was given a phone to use. He then misused the special privilege and began stalking his wife from his cell. His harassment of her resulted in three guards being fired. Boston assured the guards he had no issues at home or with anyone. It was now a waiting game. Boston paid ten thousand for the honor with the promise to make his calls and return the phone. The guard agreed but couldn't make any promises. If he did get a phone, he would not be allowed to keep it past an hour or two. It was too risky.

"Hey!" the guard said, as he reached in through the hole in the door. Boston walked up and took the small untraceable phone from him.

"Thanks man," he said.

"I'll be back for it in a few hours. No threats! No calls to the prosecutor about your case. No calls to restaurants trying to order food. And no calls to anyone tied to your case. Understood," the guard said. Boston nodded in agreeance and walked back to his bed.

He smiled as he dialed Rose's number. He hoped she was awake. He needed to hear her voice. Hear Noor and Brooklyn breathing. The sounds would remind him of home. Relax him. No talks of affairs or divorce. She couldn't have one. She was being silly. Once he was home, they would get back to doing them. For now, it was him and her on the phone expressing themselves through the only means available. He wanted to hear her moan. Hear her cum. It would make his night. He had no other calls. No business to tend to. This night belonged to her.

Boston waited anxiously as the phone rang. He hung up and called again. Each minute was tense as he hoped against all odds that she would pick up. Rose was the mother of a newborn and a toddler. Her body yearned for a different kind of sleep these days. There was a time she awoke easily. Boston missed those times. Her life was different. Everything was different. And if she didn't answer, it was because she was as exhausted as a woman could be.

"Damn!" Boston mumbled under his breath as he looked off. His dreams of fun times with his sexy wife were dashed. Boston sucked his teeth, laid back across the bed and put his hands behind his head. His dick had already plumped up to a massive size and would not be released as he had hoped. He would need to rub it out on his own. Again.

Chapter Five – Indebted

Northwestern hospital staff were working diligently to keep Max and Brooke comfortable. Max lay next to Brooke on the small hospital bed playing a game on his phone as Brooke ate strawberries. Max had stopped at the market and got her the fruit she requested. He was camping out at the hospital daily until Brooke was cleared to go home. She was weak but otherwise seemed fine. They were waiting for the doctor to come in and tell them whether or not Brooke was healthy enough to go home.

She had gone for several tests that morning and the results hadn't been disclosed. Max was nervous but tried keeping his mind positive. Brooke was keenly aware of his moods and he didn't want her to read the terror he felt. An anguishing hopelessness resided in him. Brooke had expressed not wanting to abort the baby. Which meant she wanted the baby to live even if it meant she would die trying to bring her unborn child into the world. She was avoiding treatment and Max was terrified. The drugs alone had harmful side-affects that could have devastating affects on their child. What the doctor said this afternoon would matter. And Max didn't look forward to it, although he was anxious to know if she was at least okay to leave.

Max moved quickly from the bed and walked over to greet Dr. Nunez and Dr. Freidkin. "Mr. Stone," Doctor Freidkin greeted. Dr. Nunez walked over to Brooke.

"How are you feeling Mrs. Stone?" he asked. Brooke made an attempt at smiling to hide her fear. It was her best effort but a failed one. The doctors' faces said it all. Brooke looked between the two of them, hoping to see something encouraging in just one of their eyes. But soon the words they said only confirmed what she had suspected. Max walked back to the other side of the bed and held her hand. Doctor Freidkin delivered the grim news.

"You heart is losing the fight to pump sufficiently for you and your baby. We must do the surgery now. The risk is very high. We have the best surgeon among our staff here at Northwestern. But even with his skill, there is no guarantee of success. Your ejection fraction has reduced since you've been here by a few percent. That is significant. It means we don't have much time," he said. Max looked at Brooke. She leaned back on her pillow then placed her hands over her eyes and began to weep. Max sighed.

"Me and my wife researched the best surgeons in Chicago. A doctor by the name of Samuel Lim came up as the top surgeon. A renowned heart surgeon who travels all over the world. Are you familiar with him? We would like to consult with him. Possibly get him to do the surgery," Max said.

Dr. Freidkin glanced at Dr. Nunez. He hoped Dr. Nunez would address what he was sure was an impossibility. Dr. Lim was booked through the next two years. He was certain he would not be able to take the case. They had consulted with his office before about another surgery for a wealthy family seeking to hire him and the family was a lot wealthier. He was sure Dr. Lim would find it impossible to do, even if Max offered five million.

"Dr. Lim is phasing out of surgeries and concentrating more on education. He flies around the world teaching his skills to surgeons in third world countries. He is driven by something other than finance. I can get you his office number. But I can't make promises," Doctor Nunez said. Max looked down at his wife. She was optimistic still. Her husband had negotiated deals that would surprise the most skeptic of critics.

"We will reach out to them. My husband and I will call their office every day until we are heard. Why do good all over the world when you can do good right here at home," Brooke avowed.

Max reached down and kissed Brooke's forehead in a show of solidarity. No matter what the doctors that stood before them said, they would be undeterred in their quest to get Dr. Lim to do the surgery. Dr. Nunez and Dr. Freidkin walked out. Brooke broke down after they were out of view. Her situation seemed hopeless.

"Baby don't cry. I have his office number. I will call him every day. I will show up at his office every day until I get him. Don't you worry," Max said, as he held his mouth to her head and kissed her gently.

"Uhmm," Brooke voiced, as she closed her eyes. She couldn't imagine life without the baby whose face she hadn't seen. It was cruel to take the baby she wanted so badly. The last of their offspring. Brooke had no plans of conceiving again. She would have her three children and that would complete their family. It was a selfish thought to hope the baby survived instead of her if it came down to it. She had Ciara and Nevaeh to consider. They deserved to have a mother. If she died, it would rob them of the most important woman in their lives. Brooke agonized over her own wishes. Words she couldn't say to Max even though she was sure he already knew. She had been nesting heavy. Talking nonstop about the baby they would name Heaven, if it was a girl. Or Max III, if it was a boy. Even though Brooke came from a large family that consisted of three sisters, there was no replacement for a mother. And as great a father that Max was, he still wasn't a mom.

*B*oston walked into the visitor's room prepared to meet with Phoenix and Orlando. They would be allowed to visit with him, one at a time. He smiled when he saw Orlando's face. The man with wise eyes and a strong presence. The father whose words and actions had carried him through the toughest of times.

"Pop," Boston greeted, as he hugged him. He would be allowed. The guard was one of his favorites. He allowed a lot as long as one didn't go overboard. The men sat down. Boston intertwined his fingers and prepared for an update on everything and everyone. Orlando was his connection to all that made him who he was.

"Phoenix is here as you requested. I won't take long. Just needed to see my son. See how you're holding up in here," Orlando said, his face becoming filled with emotion. He looked in Boston's eyes for weakness or any sign of breakdown. Orlando felt good. Boston had not been broken. He couldn't say what he really wanted to say. Boston had already sent word to him that he was not to interfere with the case or speak to the DA regarding the events surrounding Freemont. Orlando always said he would never let any of them take the fall. He wanted his sons out of it. Memphis' beef with several neighborhood boys was Orlando's problem. It hurt to see Boston caged. He would not be able to back down and let it play out. But he was prepared to see what happened when Max took on the case.

"I love you pop. I'm good. But I do need your help. Rose won't pick up my calls. Probably because she doesn't recognize the new number. Tell her that's me calling from a 514 number. Tell her to pick up or hit me back tonight after twelve. And I need you to wire Thomas some money. Send him forty thousand," Boston said. Orlando nodded then took a seat.

"Sure son. But what about your representation? You won't take a meeting with anyone. You have to select someone. You can't keep representing yourself at these hearings. And you have to be prepared in case Max refuses," Orlando said. Boston chuckled.

"Yes I can represent myself. At least until I get someone I know can beat it. I want Max," he said. Orlando sat back.

"Son...He already declined. Have you forgotten your history with him? We should go with Rupert King. He is phenomenal," Orlando said. Boston was aware. He was still hopeful of getting Max.

"I'm hoping Max reconsiders. If Phoenix can't get him to do it, I'll think about hiring Rupert," Boston said. Orlando was glad to hear it. They were running out of time. A court date was approaching. And the prosecutor claimed to have a witness. Orlando didn't see anyone else in that dark alley that night. It didn't mean there wasn't someone there.

Phoenix walked in solemn and not feeling good about being inside prison walls. He was only there by urging from his persistent father. He could see Boston sitting, waiting at a table. A feeling of dread moved through him like a wave. This was the bomb he saw coming years prior. The murder on Freemont that involved his brothers and was the dark secret of the St. Rock household. His heart pounded a more vigorous beat. It was better to keep a distance from the brother he quoted as "Ruining his life." Yet still he was there. Still ready to listen. Possibly ready to help. It was more than he believed he would do for him.

Phoenix walked confidently. A woman waiting for her husband caught his eye. She stared at him. He stared back. It looked as though the woman had the weight of the world on her shoulders. The look was fitting. They were in a place that housed the troubled. The dangerous. The unstable. The destructive. His brother was the latter. All was fine as long as you played by his rules. The reason he stopped playing long ago. This wasn't his battle. And frankly, he didn't care what happened. He liked to think of it as karma. He knew his inner circle would say he was jealous. Envious. The celebrated success, and marriage to a woman a man once loved, would make any man spiteful.

"Hey," Phoenix said, as he sat.

"You don't look too happy to be here," Boston said. They had their differences, but this wasn't the time to showcase them or lean into what ailed them. They were still brothers. This was a time to come together. To fight for the greater good. Boston was only one year older. They had a lot more in common than who they dated or slept with. They were both headstrong and accomplished men with similar tastes and drive. If they could only stop fighting and respected what each could bring to the table, they might enjoy the fact that their differences complimented one another.

"Did you ask to see me?" Phoenix said.

"Yes! Is that so surprising. I need your help getting Max to get on board. Otherwise, I'll have to go with a stranger. My fear is it could be a lawyer who is friends with an enemy. A lot of this city's finest lawyers have tried to get to me. But I don't trust it. The murder charge was brought on by an anonymous caller," Boston revealed. Phoenix raised a brow.

"What? You're kidding right?" he asked. It was shocking news. Boston glared intensely into Phoenix's eyes hoping to see something that would exonerate him. It was possible Boston was looking at the snitch. Phoenix still harbored resentment. It wouldn't be above him, since he'd threatened to squeal once before. But his eyes showed nothing. If he was the one working with the prosecutor, he was doing a good job of covering it up.

"Max won't! Remember! I'll ask him again but I doubt it. Especially now," he replied.

"What do you mean by that," Boston asked. Phoenix looked seriously at him.

"Brooke has a bad heart. The meds they need to put her on are harsh. The baby could be born prematurely. They have an option for surgery, but that is just as risky. Max is upset because she won't make a choice. He's afraid he'll lose them both. They tried to get some popular heart doctor but he won't get involved," Phoenix informed.

"What's the doctor's name?" Boston asked. Phoenix looked perplexed. He was sure Boston wouldn't know the man. From what Max told him the man was constantly out of the country on do-gooder missions. A Japanese doctor with homes in other countries.

"Um...Lynn. Or Lim," Phoenix replied. Boston sat straighter.

"If I get this doctor on board, will he take my case then?" Boston said confidently. Phoenix hesitated. He was surprised. Boston didn't bluff, but he couldn't help but wonder how he planned to pull it off behind bars.

"I'm sure he will. He'll do anything for his family," Phoenix replied.

"Good! Then have him come here so he can be briefed. He'll be getting a call from Dr. Lim. I know who he is. And I will make him an offer he can't refuse. You just make sure Max is here within the next couple of days," Boston said. Phoenix stood up and gave a single nod before turning and exiting. He had been there longer than he cared to be. The smell. The stale air. The sounds. The depressing color. He couldn't wait to get home and wash the dirtiness off. He didn't hold out hope for Boston. He was doing this for Max. The doctor would be the answer to his prayers.

Max walked into his house as quietly as he could. He had taken his children to his parent's home so he and Brooke could have some quiet time and relax. He was sure she was asleep. She had been depressed all week since Dr. Lim called them back and turned down their generous offer for his services. Max felt like a failure for the first time. All his connections, money and influence did little to deter the decision of the only doctor he and Brooke had faith in. Now, he had the momentous task of finding another skilled and highly reputable doctor to do the surgery. It was an uphill battle. He was running across the same names he'd already listed. Their credentials were somewhat impressive, but failed in comparison to Dr. Lim.

Max placed his briefcase on the foyer table and flipped through the pieces of mail. He could feel his phone buzzing. He wasn't taking any calls because he was done for the day. It was three in the afternoon and the rest of the days hours belonged to his wife.

Bzzz… Bzzzz.

His phone sounded off once more. Max decided to check. It could be his mother Linda calling with something important about the girls. He looked at the caller i.d. It was Phoenix again. He had been avoiding calls from him after Phoenix asked him to represent Boston. He had no interest. He didn't wish anything bad, he just didn't want to take the case. The wounds delivered by Rose and Boston's affair right inside his own home felt just as fresh as the day it happened. He was getting to a point of salvation. He just wasn't there yet.

Bzzz. Bzzzz.

The phone vibrated as Max slept. Brooke lay with her leg over his, snoring the night away. Max twisted to his other side as the phone continued to buzz, eventually awakening him from a good slumber. It was rare in the Stone household. Nevaeh was still waking many times throughout the night and requiring bottles before she would go back to sleep. Max grabbed the phone and looked at Brooke. He was instantly angered at the caller. It was twelve at night. Unless something bad had happened, they would get an earful of the worst words he could think of.

Max looked at the caller i.d. The number was an unlisted number with no name on his display. "Who the fuck," he protested, as he looked at the clock. He eased out of bed. He was curious. Whoever it was, they were persistent and he wanted to know why.

"Hello," he answered quickly when the phone began to ring again.

"Hello," the deep voice said. Max sighed loudly. It sounded like Phoenix. He had already told him, in no uncertain terms, that he was not taking Boston's case.

"Max it's me, Boston," the voice said.

Max took the phone from his ear and looked at it. He wanted to chuck it against the wall. He paused then placed the phone back to his ear. The men were stuck in a perpetual silence. Max could hear him breathing. It was awkward. Boston was on his phone to beg for his services. He was now one of the richest men in Chicago. He could afford everyone. He could have ten of the top lawyers sitting side by side. Seeking him out was insane when he clearly had options. There were only a handful of billionaires' in the city and he was one of them. Anyone would take the case for the notoriety alone. It was the type of case that made careers.

"Boston…Look…I'm going to tell you what I already told your brother. I can't take the case. I am up to my fucking neck in cases and I have personal issues that I can't just brush off. I can refer you to…," he said before Boston interrupted him.

"I made a call. I took a phone meeting with Samuel Lim. He has agreed to do the surgery. He said he'll call you first thing," Boston said.

The men held the phone. Max wasn't sure he heard him right. He took a moment to absorb the words. But then, he needed clarity. It wasn't possible. He had offered everything he had. Millions. But money wasn't the driving force for the world best surgeon. And Max wasn't sure what had just happened.

"Wait! What? What do you mean? He can't. I know this because I called his office over a hundred times. I stalked the man like a maniac. What are you saying?" Max asked.

"I called him. It wasn't the offer of money. It was a promise I have to make good on. To build him a prototype of a mechanical heart. One similar to the one I made that was featured in Forbes and The American Journal of Medicine. He's all about ingenuity. Advancement. I told him its far from being complete. But he wants in on it now. He heard about the eye scanner deal. And he wants to work with me on a few things. He wants to change the world. Help the poor. I told him about my work on mechanical heart valves and a fully functional heart. More innovative technology to move us into the future. It was right up his alley," Boston said.

Max closed his eyes as a tear fell. He couldn't believe his luck. It felt strange coming from his sworn enemy. He was proud of Boston. His work had taken a new direction. It was something Brooke could possibly benefit from. Or perhaps people in similar situations could benefit from.

"You there," Boston called out.

"Yeah. Um…," Max replied, unsure of what to say. Boston held the phone nervously. He could only hope his gesture would cause Max to take the chance and represent him. It was a large step he wasn't prepared to do. He waited quietly. It was now or never. There was a chance he and Brooke had picked a replacement surgeon. Max took a deep breath and let it out.

"Thanks man! I owe you for that. Brooke was heartbroken. She really wanted him. She will be so happy when I tell her he'll be doing the surgery," he said. Boston smiled. A part of him felt good about it. He'd met Brooke before. She was a sweet and loving woman. Even if Max still refused, the promise he made to Dr. Lim would still proceed.

Boston sat up. He could hear footsteps coming. It was time to turn in the phone. "I have to go. They won't let me keep the phone," Boston said. Max paused. Then spoke a final response before hanging up.

"I'll be there on Friday. You'll have to bring me up to speed," he said. Boston said a quick prayer. He was thankful. It was a miracle. He was not Max's favorite person. But Max was still gracious.

"Thanks man! See you then!"

Max walked back into his bedroom and tried to be quiet, as he crawled back in bed. "Hey baby. How was your day," Brooke said, startling him. Max looked at her and gave a gracious and loving smile.

"Hey baby. I thought you were sleep," he said, as he scooted closer to her then held her tight. "Mhm," he moaned as he kissed her neck. He kissed her repeatedly on her cheek then smelled her hair as he held his mouth on her face. Brooke smiled. It felt good to be loved so powerfully. "I have good news," Max said. Brooke pulled back.

"What?" she said, excited as it was obvious the news would bring her joy.

"Dr. Lim is going to take you as a patient. We got him baby," Max said, as his emotions took over. He wiped his eyes before anything could surface. Brooke put her hand over her mouth. She couldn't believe her good fortune.

"For real. He has time. Now! See me like now," she asked, in disbelief.

"Yes! Now," Max gushed. Brooke hugged him. She wished she wasn't so sick. She wanted to make love but the energy exerted made her exhausted. But there was something she could do.

Brooke pulled Max's arm. He grinned. It was what she did when she wanted to *lazy suck* him. Their endearing term for a quick head job in the middle of the night when they were both too tired to do much of anything else.

"Mmmm," Max moaned. Brooke was still the best lover when it came to using her mouth. Max held her head trying not to go to town. He wanted to. He missed her. The power sucks and hand job she was so skilled at, would render him finished within a few minutes.

"Mhmm. Shit baby," Max said. Brooke chuckled then increased her pressure on his massive hard manhood. Max turned over on his back and Brooke mounted him quickly.

"No baby! What are you doing. We can't fuck," he said.

"Shut up and fuck me. Go slowly," Brooke said in his ear. Max held her face then dove his tongue inside her mouth. He planned to slow fuck her until she said stop. This was his queen. Thoughts of Rose faded long before she put him in her mouth this night. And the pictures he still had would need to be deleted. It was not his battle any longer. Brooke's heart was.

Chapter Six – Wife on Paper

*R*ose walked down Clark Street headed to Bushwick Buildings 10th floor. She walked alongside her lawyer Jeremy London, keeping a fast pace and trying her best to calm the flips of her churning stomach. She was there to move forward with the sale of Boston's invention and his company if the price was right. It was an area of business reserved for the wolves of wall street and the titans of the financial district.

She had a plan that not even Jeremy knew about. Her plans changed that morning. It didn't matter what Ashley wanted to reveal. And it no longer mattered that Jodi was

MIA. The private eye she paid so handsomely to find something that could corroborate Dayton's claims had called to update her on his findings. And what he had to tell her was shocking and heartbreaking.

Jodi did have a baby. A girl. The private eye also found proof that Ashley had listed Boston as her child's father. She had his name added to the birth certificate with a fake signature. The private eye compared Boston's known signature with the one on the document and was able to tell it was not the same handwriting. Rose was hurt. Naming him was not proof. But it still dug deep.

Then there was Carmen. Her thirteen year old child had another man's name down as the father. Carmen's husband. The private eye discovered a witness. Carmen's old roommate. A woman who gave details of the hot steamy affair between Boston and Carmen. The dates match with the age of the girl. Carmen's husband didn't come on the scene until at least a year later. It was damming evidence. It seemed Dayton was right. Rose was inconsolable despite looking fresh faced and calm.

"Once the meeting starts, do you want me to do most of the talking or am I here just to back you?" Jeremy asked, as they approached the cross section. He wore a grey pinstriped Armani suit with a crisp white shirt and a blue Louis Vuitton tie. His matching Louis Vuitton "LV" cuff links and tie pin were sophisticated and eye catching. He walked like the powerhouse he was. Rose glanced at him and smiled. She too was self-assured. Clothing was her business. She dressed stars and their children. Evident by her Alice and Olivia black wool blend dress and black red bottom Louboutin's. She wore a one-of-a-kind Chopard watch with a blue face and diamond bezel and her fourth finger carried the weight of a solitaire five karat ring on it.

Rose looked self-assured. Jeremy wasn't sure what his role was and she had dodge many of his calls that would have helped him prepare. The research he did on Lawrence Oliver Fritch had him both impressed but worried. He couldn't dig up dirt on him which meant he was either a saint, or very good at covering his tracks. He couldn't help but wish the meeting was uncomplicated. He was a shark, but he felt like a goldfish. It took a shark to deal with someone as savvy as Fritch and Jeremy was outmanned and unprepared. He was sure Mr. Fritch had lawyers. A billion dollar agreement was a huge deal. It would be in the papers the next day.

"I will take the lead. I needed you here for moral support. I started to bring my mother but she doesn't do well under pressure. Sorry I haven't briefed you on my plans. But feel free to interject if you hear something that sounds off or anything that you feel could have legal ramifications down the line," she replied.

Jeremy looked at her. Rose kept her gaze straight ahead. The light turned red and they crossed and walked up to the door. Jeremy had never seen Rose so fierce. She walked different. She was talking different. It seemed she was armed with something he had no knowledge of. Gone was the demure kitten who looked like she didn't so much as purr loudly. Her laid back demeanor had been replaced with a woman who seemed certain of herself. Powerful in her own right. The billion dollars had turned her into someone else overnight. And Jeremy hoped she had wisdom to back up the self-assuredness he was witnessing.

"Mrs. St. Rock," Fritch said, as he bent over slightly and kissed her hand.

"Call me Rose. And thank you for your decision to move ahead with this deal," she said. Fritch was taken aback. He looked at Jeremy and then at his own lawyers.

"Is Thomas coming?" he asked.

"No! I told him I was bringing Mr. London. And unless he is acting on your behalf, his presence is not needed," Rose replied.

Lawrence Fritch liked the fiery woman in front of him. Her sharp direct eye contact and winning smile was admirable. She was as fiery as she was beautiful. His kind of woman. Someone he could work with. Build something with. He could use her on the board of one of his companies.

"No. Mr. Thomas does not represent me. He is your husband's lawyer. And as far as I am concerned, his presence is not needed unless you are requiring it," Mr. Fritch replied.

"No! I was briefed by him. Jeremy has looked over everything and has given his own stamp of approval. I see no reason why we can't proceed," Rose said.

The small group sat down at a large mahogany colored conference table as two secretaries entered to take notes and dictation. Rose smiled at the women then looked at Jeremy as she waited for Mr. Fritch to lay out the deal and the agreed upon price. He glanced over the paperwork pulling his eyeglasses down on his nose as he read the fine print. He noticed a spot Rose didn't initial and proceeded to read the paragraph.

"I noticed you didn't initial section g," he said. Jeremy flipped over two pages until he got to section g. He scanned the words as Rose did the same.

"Yes. I also didn't initial sections k, l, m and B1. Those were the areas that would make Rockwater still liable. Section g mention time to allow for feedback from a third party. Sections k, l and m open the door to the possibility of suing the creator for false or exaggerated claims and section b1 is worded in a way that ties the inventor to the product after the deal has closed. It would make Rockwater liable in the event of serious bodily injury or harm and any and all side effects associated with the ESD810. Once we close this deal, you assume all responsibility." Rose said.

Jeremy was shocked by her knowledge and recollection of the paragraphs and what they meant. There was a part of him that wished she would have leaned on him. He excelled at such tasks. This was his ring. And he was a heavy weight.

Mr. Fritch sat back. His lawyer whispered in his ear. Rose's foot tapped under the table out of view. She was nervous. She hoped she hadn't offended him. Men like Mr. Fritch thought of women as delicate and more valuable inside of the home. She read an article on him dated eight years prior. In it a simple sentence told her everything she needed to know about him He was quoted as saying;

There has always been great men doing great things. And if you follow them home a great woman will answer the door.

Rose waited as he continued to side bar with his lawyers. Whispers followed by wide eyed glares began to make her nervous. Rose tapped the top of Jeremy's hand. He had been practicing law since he was twenty four. And he was on top of the world by age thirty. Rose knew he felt some kind of way. She also knew he had a thing for her. His lust filled stares and constant touches meant to look innocent were not. She was past that part of her life. Sex for sex sake would not happen with the flashy and handsome young attorney. He touched the top of her hand. He had an attraction to her that bordered on obsession.

The calls to hit the gym. The unannounced pop ups at Little Rascals. He was now a member of a growing club. The list of men who sought a chance to get a little closer. Rose was in a different space. She was looking for her calling. For a shot at real power. Pussy power was fleeting. It caused confusion. It would destroy her. It would destroy her children's future. In another space and time, Jeremy's touch may have led to an open door that he would have been able to walk through. But not this day. She needed him. But in a different way. Anything more would have to build over time. She was still Boston's wife. And he would never let her be anything else but his. But she sought to change all that. And this was her time.

"Do we have a deal minus those sections?" Rose asked. Fritch leaned in.

"Yes we do. And I am prepared to buy Rockwater outright. That is, if you're interested," he said.

Rose looked at Jeremy. It was his cue to read the room of players. A billion dollars was on the table for just one invention. It was Boston's greatest work. One of three medical devices, and it would change the world of medicine, travel and even law enforcement. She was prepped by Boston. He predicted that Fritch would want the whole company. This was her shot.

"Mrs. St. Rock is not prepared to sell the company. She is here to close the deal as stated. You will own the unit outright with confirmation that there will be no other more advanced unit produced by Mr. St. Rock. Anything related to the EDS810 and any upgrades on the current technology will be at your discretion. Meaning, you can hire Rockwater to create a second prototype if you so please. But right now, the deal is for the copyright and all rights and monies generated from the EDS810. That's the deal," Jeremy stressed.

Fritch looked at Rose. "Then we have a deal. I am interested in the purchase of ESD810. But what if I was interested in the company. What if I made an offer that would compensate your family handsomely? Would you be willing to sell?" he asked. Rose tried not to break a sweat. She was the deciding factor in a deal that would make the news. Every magazine in the country would want an interview. She could expand on her boutiques just off of the closing of her deal on Rockwater. But she was out of her element. Her boutiques netted her a six figure income yearly and that was a big deal. This was the big league with players whose decisions ran countries.

"My offer is to buy the company Mrs. St. Rock. You can stay on as acting COO under my direction, of course. A board will be appointed and I will act as chairman," he said. Rose almost peed her pants.

Did he say I get to stay on as COO, she thought, as her leg shook. Rose had been armed with a piece of information about Mr. Fritch that weighed heavily on her mind. Thomas told her that he had a reputation of buying whole companies and dismantling them or selling them outright. Rose looked intensely at him.

She paced her breathing as she tried to consider what Boston wanted. She was still angry at him but she also wanted to be fair. Which was more than she could say for him. His indiscretions where prominent at this meeting. Fritch had no idea the thoughts that were running through her mind. But Rose knew a little something about money. If Boston had already agreed to sell and his price was met, anything over what he wanted would be hers. The company was hers.

If she secured extra, to pocket money for her and her children, no court in the world would make a judgement against her. Her and Boston were on borrowed time. Eventually the secret between her and Bronx would be out. Rose was prepared to secure her future and part ways with her cheating husband who had whole families that he hid. Their dirt was equally yoked. They were even.

She had been faithful to him since the affair with Bronx. She was done hurting him. She had recommitted herself and had stayed from affairs. It was why she kept from Phoenix and Denver. Even Dayton, who she was sure had a thing for her. And her love for Bronx was tucked neatly in her heart. They'd had their heated moment and it was over. And now, so were her and Boston.

"Can we speak alone. One on one," Rose asked. The request sent everyone into a panic.

"Wait! This is a multi billion dollar deal now. I don't advise…," Fritch's lawyer interjected before being asked to leave.

"It's fine. The best deals in the world were made with two people at a coffee shop. I think her and I can handle a billion dollar deal," Fritch said, as he kept his eyes on Rose. Jeremy shook his head *no* as he locked into a stare with Rose.

"Jeremy please! It's fine," Rose said.

The *five men and one woman team* left out. Jeremy stood up. "I'll stay close just in case," Jeremy said, as he walked to the door. Rose uncrossed her legs and pulled her chair closer to the table. She wasted no time making her demands.

"I won't waste your time Mr. Fritch. Rockwater is not for sale. The thought about selling outright, if you showed interest, was discussed between my husband and I. But one billion is for the unit and only the unit. It will make you ten times that. It is the next best thing since the invention of the computer. Every hospital and clinic will want one. There are capabilities that would make it easy to replicate for home use. Every family would want one. My husband told me the details. And I think that this is an investment that would ensure the forward growth of Fritch Packard. But buying Rockwater is another matter altogether. Surely, the company is worth more than you are probably willing to pay. You have the best of his work. The eye scanner is his best invention. That is the deal. And a mighty one at that," Rose spoke confidently. Boston had prepped her. She was surprised with what she could recall. Her stomach still turned but she handled it with pride.

Mr. Fritch was a force to be reckoned with. He looked at Rose without blinking. His peering gaze made her question what she had said. She wondered if she somehow had turned him off. *Did I say too much*, she thought, as she waited for him to say something.

"I am one of the richest men in the world young lady. I made my first million before you were born. I am interested. Your husband has a viable company. He positioned it for profit and you should strike while the iron is hot. My offer is 2 billion. Which is to include the eye scanner. I think selling a company that is only nine years in business for a billion dollars is an awesome achievement. Most companies never see that kind of money. The world listens when you have the title of billionaire behind your name. No matter how profitable a company appears, no one wants to take the risk that the company will continue to grow. Your husband is a genius. There is a chance that the company won't be as profitable under new leadership without him. There is a risk! Let's face it…Rockwater is the brainchild of Boston St. Rock. You married a tech god. Do you have any idea of his capabilities? I do. But I also know that the company will struggle without him. I am willing to take that risk," he said.

Rose leaned forward and put on her charms. She could see he wanted the company. And now she understood why he wanted her to stay on as COO.

"Mr. Fritch. Rockwater will sell for no less than 2.5 billion dollars. I can confidently say that, because the company is a combination of my husband and his brother's hard work. Equally brilliant minds. My husband will part ways but Denver will probably stay on. Especially if you make it worth his time. Pay him what he wants, and he will stay. But the price is 2.5. Non-negotiable," Rose stated with clarity.

Fritch was a man of many hats. The sly grin on his face was in stark contrast to who Rose thought he was. In an article she read, he bragged about life as an astute and fair minded business man. A description that wasn't befitting of the man looking at her that moment. He looked like he held a card.

"I'm a businessman. I do my homework. I am aware that your husband and his brothers Denver, Austin and Bronx were listed as the executives of this company. I am also aware that your husband is the real master mind. I don't expect him to stay on. Why would he! I have some brilliant minds working for me. I want the Rockwater name. Doesn't matter to me if they stay on or not. It's not imperative. But it would make for an easier transition," he said. Rose gave a serious glare.

"Besides… what makes you think his brother won't resign?" Fritch asked.

"Because he's interested in making his own mark. He has wanted to part ways from my husband for a long time. There are other scientists. There is another brother. He is the youngest. He too, knows technology. He was groomed for it. I can't make promises. I can only tell you that I have influence with the St. Rocks," Rose replied.

Fritch tapped his finger on the table. "Tell me something. If I'm being too nosy then I'll back off but there is something I'm curious about. When you first married, he put half of his company in your name. Why did he do that," he asked. Rose narrowed her gaze.

"Well…He wanted to make a promise to me. He said we would never part. He wanted us to be partners for life. I guess it was a way to show his commitment," Rose replied.

"Not because of these charges he now faces. Maybe he foresaw this day. Maybe this was to protect his money from lawsuits. If you own half, they can only sue him for the portion that belongs to him. Was this to protect the money," he asked. Rose was surprised at his line of questioning.

"I don't think so Mr. Fritch," Rose said, as her mind raced. Fritch wasn't really concerned. He only really wanted Rockwater. She believed she could have gotten another billion. Rockwater was the Microsoft of the future. It was worth much more.

"You have yourself a deal. The money will be wired within thirty days after all the papers are drafted and signed. That gives enough time for the lawyers to look them over. Congratulations Mrs. St. Rock. You're pretty savvy yourself. I usually have a price in my head that I stick to. I definitely want you on my team," Fritch said.

Rose smiled to hide her anxiety. She would have 2.5 billion in her account. More money than she ever dreamed of. She was already wealthy. She was the wife of a multi millionaire. Now a billionaire. And it couldn't have happened at a worse time. He had betrayed her. She had betrayed him. And as she sat signing documents and passing them to Fritch, she couldn't help but think about Boston. He would be enraged with her staying on as an executive of his company. That wasn't part of the deal. Neither was a divorce. It was only a matter of time before he would seek answers and find out about Bronx, signaling the end of their union. Rose hated to sign on the dotted line. This was going to hurt him. It was like stealing from him. But it was a half billion in her pocket. She'd secured the extra with a promise to help keep the company going in the right direction.

"And you have yourself a new company Mr. Fritch. My lawyers will be in contact with you. If you can send over a proposal that matches what we talked about that would be great. I accept your offer, but I must be allowed to name at least one person as a member of the board. I know that's not the traditional way it's done, but it is the only way the deal will go through. Think about it," Rose said. Fritch didn't have to. He was sure about the deal. Rockwater was a heavy hitter. He had plans to grow the company. Fritch gave a hearty handshake. He had faith in her. And he had faith in Rockwater Technologies.

Rose walked with a quiet and pissed off Jeremy to their cars parked in a parking structure a block away. "You're mad?" Rose said, as she beamed. She had secured the biggest deal of her life and couldn't see why he was so upset.

"That was not cool. I have no idea what's in those papers. A whole new deal? What were you thinking? Deals that huge must be reviewed. And just when you think you've read it over thoroughly, you read it again. He's nothing to fuck around with. That good boy image he polishes every day is a mask. He's not dirty but he knows his shit. He knows how to protect himself. He'll find a way to fuck you. Literally," Jeremy said.

Rose stopped walking. Jeremy looked back at her then stopped. He was angered beyond anything he usually felt. He liked Rose. And he refused to see her get tricked. She was playing with a man who took no prisoners. So the fact he wanted her to stay on meant he had other plans. Jeremy believed Fritch wanted her to stay, so he could make a move. He was fresh on the market after a bitter and lengthy divorce, he was probably ready for a fresh start. And Jeremy was fired up with jealousy.

"Don't talk like that. It was a business deal. Without me he'll never get the company to be what it truly is. Innovative and forward thinking. Boston and Denver are geniuses. I have a drawer full of sketches and drafts Boston created in the middle of the night when he couldn't sleep. If he had men capable, he wouldn't ask me to stay on. He hopes that with me as COO, Denver will stay and Boston will come around eventually. It's not sexual for him. I can tell. Trust me. I know when a man wants me," she said, as she resumed walking and walked right past him. Rose stopped at the elevator. Their cars were parked on the third floor. She pushed the button the turned to him. Jeremy got in her face.

"No you don't know! Cause if you did, you would have realized that I wanted you," he said, as he pushed her against the elevator door and kissed her before she could thwart his advances. Rose pushed him away and wiped her mouth. He was new in her life. He had no right to invade her space with an aggressive display of his affection. If he only knew the depths of her past, he wouldn't move so quickly. She had two children at home with her husband and because of her disloyalty, she was facing another issue with paternity. A fact that would probably paint her in an unpleasing light with him. She could tell he liked perfection. And she was anything but.

It was tempting. He was attractive. The pencil-legged pants and jacket with a white shirt and blue tie gave him a modern appeal and an undeniable sexiness. His caramel skin and neatly cut facial hair showed that he took himself serious enough to pamper himself from head to toe. He looked like a roaring flame ready to engulf her and she was reluctant to start an affair. She could see he was fearless. It would be an affair she would have trouble ending.

"I do know. And we can't. I have a history of poor decisions when it comes to men. I can't," she said. The elevator door opened and they stepped on. Jeremy pushed the button and rode up in silence. He had gone too far. He hoped she would forget the quick decision to make a move on her. He still wanted to be her lawyer if nothing else.

"I'm sorry. I went overboard," he said. Rose touched his shoulder.

"It's fine. You are handsome. In another life I swear I would. But you don't know me. My past is horrible. Trust me...I'm not that girl. I have skeletons. I do! I am still trying to make right of my past wrongs. And I wouldn't want to hurt you. This deal I just did is not exactly what my husband would have wanted. But because of something I did, I have to cut my losses. He did me wrong. I did him wrong. And it is what it is. But don't hold me to any high regard. I am not her."

Chapter Seven – Officially Tired

"Orlando," Rose greeted, as she opened the door. Orlando stepped in and looked around. He got right to the point of his visit. His family was in chaos. An article in the local paper had a front-line story that no one believed. Boston was beside himself. And Orlando had many fires to put out.

"Did you see the Chicago Tribune and Black Enterprise Magazine's stories on Rockwater?" he asked. Rose folded her arms.

"Yes," she replied. She could see he wasn't there on friendly terms and was agitated at his and Cicely desire to probe into their adult children's matters. She knew the family would be unhappy with Boston's decision. And she had secured what he asked for. But she was also blindsided by the ultimate betrayal and she could care less what Orlando, Boston, Cicely or anyone else thought of her. She was leaving. She'd done her deed. It was over.

Orlando walked towards the living room. The walk would help in easing his anger. And his stress. His next question was a simple one and the answer would either settle the St. Rocks or blow the lid off of an already tense family. Many extended family members panicked after Boston's arrest. And if the article was true, this was another thorn.

"You sold my sons company and stayed on as CEO. He will not take that lying down. You were supposed to sell it. He told me the deal was for 2 billion," Orlando said. Rose trembled slightly. Orlando could be intimidating. It was all in his stance. The direct and unwavering way he looked one in the eye. Or the purposeful tone of his voice. It was hard to keep it together. But Rose was ready. She understood what she did. Facing Orlando was the least of her worries. And she was ready to own up to it.

"He wanted 2 billion dollars. I got him what he asked for. It will be waiting on him when he gets out of that hell hole," she replied.

"Hmm… The article states that you sold it for 2.5 billion," he said. Rose looked confidently in his eyes. She was done playing word salad.

"Yes! I was able to negotiate more. There's nothing illegal in that. He signed Rockwater over to me. And I did exactly as he asked. I am his wife. I did not break any laws. We are looked at as one in the eyes of the law in case you didn't know that. I'm keeping the half billion for myself. I'm the one who negotiated the deal. I should get my share of the profits. They'll give me that much in the divorce. He has children. A whole damn other family. So, I don't care who doesn't like it. I am doing this for my kids. For my future. He has more than enough money to create a new technology company. I don't support him. It's over. He'll get his money. But if he tries to take my children or cause me any pain, I will become his worst nightmare. I know about Freemont. I overheard him talking about it. I've always known. But I won't say anything. I just want him out of my life. No more controlling me. No more hurting me with his lies and this fake ass life," Rose said, as she burst into tears. She wiped them quickly as she gazed upon a shocked and disgusted man.

"You listen to me good. I know you are my grandchildren's mother. I have to respect that. But I don't have to guard my words since you have disregarded my son's heart. You step on him like an ant. You sell his company for more and you pocket the rest. That *is* a betrayal. And it will kill him. Do you have an ounce of decency? He met you. Fell in love with you. And married you. Tried to make a decent woman out of you. And what did you do... Fucked nearly half of his brothers. You single handedly tore my sons apart. And now, when he needs you the most, you bring up women he doesn't give a damn about. You started this thing between you two. It's because of what you've done that he struck back in such a vicious way. Because no matter how much he showed you he loved you, you refused to stop fucking his brothers," Orlando fumed.

Rose was in shock at his choice of words and tone. She had never seen her father-in-law so livid. She took a step back. A thought crossed her mind that made her think he wanted to slap her.

"Don't worry. I'm not the one you should fear. He's got many family members who hate you a lot more than I ever could. I don't hate you. I think you're just damaged and I wish my son had never met you," Orlando said, as he made his way to the front door. "You really need to be careful. You're playing a dangerous game," Orlando advised.

He left without uttering another word or asking to see his beloved granddaughters. He needed to leave her with something to consider. It wasn't a friendly visit. And if Boston was home, he would be in jail again. Only it would be for whatever he unleashed on Rose. Orlando had many stops to make. First, he needed to go to the county jail. Boston would need to see his face. Be comforted by his words. And given hope for what was the ultimate betrayal. He was rich beyond his dreams but it was at a heavy cost. The company he worked so hard to build from nothing had just been sold. He would have never sold Rockwater. It was his baby. His first born.

Rose crossed her arm as she tried to refrain from a response. She hated they had words. She was doing his son a favor. Taking her money upfront and exiting before the storm. This was the best way.

*B*ronx sat in darkness with a ball point pen in his hand. He had flicked it over a hundred times as his mind raced with images of his boys. The clicking sound of the pen seemed to fuel his incessant need to picture their faces. He had already cried most the day away, ignoring calls and several knocks on the door. His family had become steadfast in their attempts at keeping him close. Cicely was dropping by unannounced and he was not responding. His days were a mixture of good and bad ones. This was one of the worst.

He watched a father with his three sons at the park not too far from his home. Bronx pulled over to catch a glimpse of his interaction with them. He laughed at times, then cried during the most lovable displays of affection from the man who he'd seen before. Eventually the man noticed Bronx and stared piercingly back at him. The awkward exchange ended with Bronx driving off. The man was a neighbor. A family that had recently moved into the neighborhood. His sons looked like good kids. And it hurt Bronx that his boys would never be able to play with them. They would never be able to make ice cream runs or take trips to the local fair.

Bronx threw the pen then put his head in his hand. His problems were compounded by the fact that Rose's infant could possibly be his. He was determined to find out. Boston being locked up had its advantages. He could go freely to their home, walk right up to the door and ask her without worry. Rose could be honest with him without the pressure of hoping Boston didn't come home. Bronx sniffled as he tried to clear his nose. He was too distraught to go at that moment. A rejection from Rose could send him over the edge and his sanity was fragile.

Bronx was always good at thinking logically. He was the master of time well managed. Words well said. And movements that were deliberate and direct. He had to think on it. Weigh the options. She had taken her children to stay with Cicely for a day. So there was the option of waiting for them to go back to his parents. Then there was Eboni. He knew her well and could easily get inside Boston and Rose's home when she was out. Bronx calmed himself. He mourned for his boys and he yearned for the baby girl he believed was his. There was one way to find out. A DNA test.

Bronx awoke, his hand on his penis as he turned and looked out at his property. He stretched then adjusted himself and grabbed for the remote control. He missed sex. Waking up with his balls tight and his manhood hard was becoming irritating. Thoughts of the only person he would enjoy making love to was pushed to the background. He hated he loved Rose and lusted for her. The worst thing he'd ever done was to be intimate with her. She was in his head still.

More than anyone, Bronx understood risks and chances. He needed time to get over her. It was inevitable that one day he would. Things would be better. But Brooklyn was an issue. He had a feeling he was her daddy. He wanted to see her tiny face. See if her eyes were grey. If her baby hair was sandy brown. Cicely had described him with those features that eventually went away. His sons had grey eyes that turned brown. It was also a trait that his mother said he shared with siblings Chicago, Dallas, Austin and Raleigh. Their children all had those features until they got older. No one mentioned Brooklyn having grey eyes. He feared asking. It could cause the family to take notice and curiosity could open the doors to something he wasn't ready to talk about.

Bronx flipped channels. Suddenly a thought came to him. He could ask Chicago what color the baby's eyes were. Bronx picked up the phone. He dialed Chicago's number. He waited for the phone to start ringing.

"Shit! I can't. He'll get mad all over again. Fuck!" Bronx said, as he placed the phone next to him. His mind raced. Soon another idea. *I'll see for myself,* he thought. He knew Rose took her kids to Memphis' house and to Aurora's house on occasion. Even Cicely took care of them. He had options. Both his son's eye's didn't change color until they were almost a year old. He had time.

"Pop," Boston said, as he approached. His father's face was a pleasant sight among the other's in the prisons visiting room. The serious look on Orlando's face caused him to pause. Boston approached the table and sat down. He had good news but it looked like Orlando did not.

"What's wrong pop. This is a good day. We should be celebrating. The money will be transferred in a few weeks. . Your son will officially be a billionaire. We can do a lot more for the family. I'll make sure you have extra in case anyone needs help," he said. Orlando smiled warmly at his generous son. His happiness would be short lived. Orlando braced himself for the fallout and prepared to tell what he knew. But Boston wasn't done delivering good news and he paused to let him finish.

"I spoke to Max finally. He has agreed to take on the case. I did him a favor. I got a doctor to take on his wife's case. He was grateful. You and mom can rest easy. I know this look on your face is worry about me not having a lawyer.

I got one," Boston said proudly. Orlando was elated. It was good news. But he had something that would overshadow everything.

"Son…I have some bad news. It's…um…it's about your company," Orlando said. Boston's stiffened. He sat back and straightened his posture as he waited for Orlando to elaborate. He had sold it. A detail he wasn't prepared to explain. No one would understand the heartache of such a decision and no one would have agreed. Especially his father. The one who helped pave his career.

Orlando hesitated, choosing to give his son a moment to prepare himself. "What?" Boston asked. Orlando locked his hands and leaned on the table. It was as close as he could get to his son who played tough, but was much more vulnerable inside. Orlando knew his kids. He studied them. Paid attention. The ones that seemed the toughest weren't. Especially when it came to things like loyalty and love.

Boston was a fighter. Physically strong. He snapped if someone hurt anyone in his family and would go at them with everything he had. He was a warrior in all aspects of his life except his love life. His grandmother told him one day he would soften just enough to fall in love. That he would know her when he saw her and would be forever in love. Orlando wished it weren't true. Rose was not good for him.

"Did you see the Chicago Tribune yet?" Orlando asked. Boston released a nervous laugh. "No! I figured the sale of the company would get people talking. I was going to tell you. I didn't think you would approve and I had made my decision. Doesn't matter. I'll be free soon and I'll start another one. I have more than enough money to feed everyone for the rest of their lives. And I'll still earn more. Don't worry," Boston said. Orlando was prepared to tell him the rest. The part he was sure was never Boston's intention.

"You sold your company. And you allowed her to walk away with half a billion dollars," Orlando said. Boston's smile disappeared. "What! No! I sold it for two billion," Boston assured.

"No! She sold it for 2.5 billion and pocketed the .5 billion in installments that she will receive so long as she stays on as CEO," Orlando said, as he pushed the magazine across the table.

"Rose wouldn't...," Boston said, as he picked up the magazine and read the story that was highlighted. The headline was bold. A picture of Mr. Fritch standing prominently in his old office. The title of the story jumped off the pages.

Rockwater Technologies Poised to Make an Impact on the Future.

Boston looked off then looked intensely at his father. "Where is Rose? I want to see her now!" he shouted, throwing the magazine clean across the room.

"Hey! Chill! Do that again and you will have to return to your cell" the guard warned. Boston gave a stern glare and was met with opposition. He turned from the guard who seemed ready to make good on his threat. Boston's emotions were running high. Rose had been crafty and made a power move. It meant only one thing. She was positioning herself to live life without him. It wasn't the money. He had what he wanted. It was her leaving and it couldn't have come at a worse time.

"I want her here now! Tell her I said to come see me or she'll be sorry. I will go straight to prison. No trial. Get her here pop. You better warn her. Why would she do this. Why," he said, as he held his head. Boston was numb. He couldn't wrap his head around her betrayal. He leaned on the table. Orlando was angered. His son didn't deserve all that was happening to him. It seemed he couldn't catch a break.

"Listen...I will talk to her. Maybe the story is exaggerated. I know she is angry at you. Kendra told Memphis Rose is heartbroken. Something about you having another family. Is that true?" Orlando asked. Boston stared at him. Orlando knew his silence meant there was truth to it. There was nothing he could do. A war was waged and Boston was not in position to fight. Orlando looked deeply into Boston's eyes. The words seem to break something in him. He was a solid man. Able to withstand the most trying of things. But not this. Not jail and a wife on the outs. Her move pointed to a woman done. And that would be his son's undoing.

"Boston...Answer me. Why are you just looking at me. How can I help if I don't know. Is it true? Is there another family?" he asked. Boston looked at his hands then sighed.

"I don't know. I shut everybody out. We were starting over. I wanted to push anything back that could destroy that until Rose and I were good. I planned on telling her. But not now. The timing couldn't be more fucked up. Rose knows about Jodi. I didn't have the heart to tell her Jodi had a baby.

I haven't even seen the kid. But If it's true, it will hurt her. I would lose her," he said. Orlando moved his head slowly side to side.

"What?" Boston asked, his worried filled face wondering what Orlando was silently objecting to.

"The name Ashley was mentioned. Who is Ashley?" Orlando said. Boston sat straight. It was a hit to the gut that dismantled his core.

"What! Ashley? No! I don't have a baby with her. I fucked that girl once. With a condom. Fuck no! Is that what's being said?" Boston said, as he became nervous and visually agitated.

"Kendra said the name Ashley. That's all Memphis mentioned. I will find out," Orlando said.

"No! What? No! What the fuck is happening around me. I swear... everybody is out to fuck me. Who told her that bullshit! As soon as I go ballistic on they ass, they gonna be crying talking about how cruel I am. And Rose better do an about face. She better come here and explain," Boston fumed.

"You are too smart and you have come to far to turn back or resort to brutal street tactics. I raised you to rise above things. I did all that so you wouldn't have to. I won't let anyone get you caught up. You hear me! Now use your mind. The same way you always have. You are brilliant. A thinker. Methodical. Don't you let no bitch...and yes I said bitch because at this point she is dead to me. Don't you let her fuck your life up. She has slept with your brother's. Disregarded you. And now crossed you. Take back your company or take the money and start another one. That company is nothing, without you and Denver coming up with new ideas," Orlando said.

Orlando understood his rage. He had already looked into the legal ramifications of her move. It seemed it was legal to sell something someone gave you for more, as long as you gave them the dollar amount they were expecting to receive. Orlando decided to hold off on telling Boston that part. He was still looking into loopholes in the law. Something his son could use. But there was nothing to do until he divorced her. So long as she was his wife, there was nothing he could do.

"I'll look into it. But I do know that she has power being your wife. You can't sue your wife. She has to be your ex wife. I'm sure of it. Probably would be a good idea to divorce her at this point. That shouldn't be too hard. It's obvious she has other plans. And they don't include you," Orlando stated. Boston looked ready to cry. Emotions rose up from the pits deep within and Orlando felt bad.

He could see Boston getting more emotional by the minute. It was hard to say if he was bothered by his words or bothered by Rose. Boston rubbed his hands across his face and laid his head on his arms. It crushed Orlando to see him break. It was something he'd never witnessed.

"You listen to me and you listen to me good," Orlando said, looking around to see if anyone was within ear shy of him.

Boston kept his head down. Orlando touched his hand and Boston glanced up then sat up straight. "We have to tackle this one thing at a time. First, we get you out of here. We handle this case. You will not do one day, you hear me. Not one day! I meant what I said. Your concern is coming home," Orlando said. Boston furrowed his brow.

"You stay out of this. I told you this is my battle. Don't you do anything to shift blame from me to you. It'll kill me," Boston said as he wiped his face. Orlando quickly reached across the table and took his hands. He looked at the guard who pretended not to see.

"Let's not worry about that. You're going to beat this fake case. They just need a headline. Anything to bring a powerful black man down," Orlando said with a smile, hoping to add some warmth to the coldness of their surroundings. Boston was slowly coming apart. He needed to redirect his thoughts. But he was serious in what he said. He wasn't going to let Boston do time. It was him who pulled the trigger that shot the young man after Boston's shot missed.

*T*he sound of a determined visitor awoke Rose from a peaceful slumber. "Who is this," she said, as she slipped out of bed and grabbed her robe. Whoever it was, continued hitting the door with an aggressive force. "Coming," Rose said, as she sped up. She peeked out the peep hole then took a deep breath.

"Have you lost your mind! You took money from him. Is there no fucking end to your bullshit," Tacoma shouted, staring her down and slowly shaking her head in disbelief. Rose felt like she was standing in the middle of a nightmare. This was another family member in her foyer talking shit about her marriage. The St. Rocks were intrusive. And she was done with their interference.

"You don't know what you're talking about. Don't come here threatening me. You're not part of this marriage Tacoma! I did what I had to do. Like I told Orlando, I got Boston exactly what he wanted," Rose stated, emphasizing her words and taking a stance against her *always in the middle* sister in law who she believed hated her most.

Tacoma was incensed. Rose was always doing something she had no business. She was fed up with her family's tolerance of it. The gloves were coming off.

"You are a real piece of work. And why are you not answering his calls. Answer his gotdamn call! It's the least your slimy ass can do. Why are you such a bitch? My mother is in tears. My father is upset. You have upset my whole gotdamn family. And I'm really trying to control myself right now. I want to know why you did that? Why?" she shouted.

Rose felt no need to explain. Tacoma seemed to be teetering on something drastic. She was passionate about her family. Even to the point of violence. But Rose was no longer afraid of her. If she wanted a fight, they would have one. Even if she lost. It was principle. This was her life.

"He has an outside family. He has children. Go yell at him for how I have been treated. Anybody standing up for me! I took what the courts would have given me anyway. This way he can go on. Love who he wants to love. Make babies all over the gotdamn city for all I care. I'm done," Rose said, as she crumbled under the weight of her own words. A tear fell. Then another. She stared intensely at her unforgiving sister in law. She could see a light go off in Tacoma's eyes.

"You leaving him? Wow! Taking the money and just leaving," Tacoma said.

"Yes! So you can go throw your party. I'm sick of everyone hating me. Rooting for my demise," Rose said. Tacoma calmed herself. She was still angry but Rose said the magic words. She was leaving. And as far as she was concerned, she couldn't leave fast enough.

"Well...I guess I don't blame you. Gotta get something out the deal. And no one is rooting for your demise Rose. But you have to see that this relationship is toxic. It's probably for the best. He would never accept what happened with Bronx. And there's no way I would allow that to remain hidden. That's my brother. If you stay, then I will be forced to tell him. Bronx will just have to face it. He shouldn't have fucked you. Boston is innocent in all this. I *will* protect him," Tacoma said. Rose tried to hide her shock and disdain. This was a threat. If she wanted to consider divorce, she was now being told to do it or else. Tacoma knew about Bronx which meant Boston would find out sooner than later. Rose could do nothing but deny it. She needed to slow down the gossip until she found a way to tell her husband herself. She owed him that. It was more than an affair. A child was also in the middle.

"You don't know what you're talking about?" Rose assured. Tacoma had nerve. Rose wanted her out.

She was beginning to lose her ladylike grace and poise. Policing her words in this family had become less important. Tacoma needed to leave. They had said enough. She was sure Tacoma was there speaking for her mother and sisters. The men in their family didn't hold such a grudge.

"I do know. It's no secret. We're close. You know that. Everything comes to light. And you had to know this shit would have killed him. He will be alright. Boston is strong. Plus, he has other kids. His life will go on. You should go. Take the kids and leave. Come back after everything cools down," Tacoma said. Rose walked slowly to her door and looked out. She didn't want her sister in law to see her tears.

"Wow! Ya'll hate me so much that you don't mind me taking my kids away. What a horrible mother you must think I am. To do so much damage, that my children's family don't want them either," Rose said, as she wiped her face.

"I didn't say that," Tacoma said. The words hit her hard. She was beginning to regret storming over to the house. She didn't expect to feel anything. But Rose's emotional reaction and words of children forsaken had struck at her heart. And she had said more than she should.

"Listen... I didn't mean it like that. We love them," Tacoma said, hoping to remove the sting. Rose turned from her door and walked slowly towards her staircase.

"It doesn't matter. Now please leave. Tell your family they don't have to worry about me. About us. Please go!" she said, refusing to shed another tear, as she ascended the stairs to the second level of her home. The slow drag revealed a woman taken down by a conversation. Tacoma looked off. She wanted to do damage control. Her emotions had her saying things just to cut at Rose's weakened spirit. Rose was leaving.

The one thing she knew about Boston was his rage ran second to his love. Of all her brother's he had proven to be the most adept at smoothing things over. Forgiving. There were no depths he wouldn't go in order to right a wrong. And no matter how angry he got, he would still be there. He wasn't into cancelling people out. He was deeper than that. And Rose was the only woman to ever possess his heart. It was a love that would sustain the worst of battles. Because at its forefront, was a man who loved a person to the moon and back. Not the money, company nor the fact that she had betrayed him would sway his heart. He would find the reason in her faults. And he would forgive.

She couldn't really be mad that Rose cut a deal for herself. She was entitled to something. He had the money he was promised. Tacoma understood where he stood with money. He controlled money. The money didn't control him. He was generous. The plan would have never been to leave her high and dry. He cared about what money could do. It provided for him and his family. They were now set for life. All of them. But even still, it wasn't what he lived for. He lived for love. Which meant he needed his family. He needed Rose.

"Rose! Don't just leave. Talk to him," Tacoma pleaded. Rose reached the top of the stairs and disappeared around the corner. Tacoma walked out slowly, taking care to pull the door completely. She shook her head in disbelief as she approached her running car.

Marti waited anxiously. Her lover was bold and unpredictable. She behaved more civilized when she was there. Marti feared for Rose. Tacoma flew off the handle after getting off the phone with Orlando. Talks of Rose pocketing money shocked everyone.

"Damn!" Tacoma said, as she got inside her SUV and closed the door.

"What happened baby?" Marti asked, as she touched Tacoma's hand. Tacoma sat wide legged in her Nike jogging suit, royal blue puffer vest and beige Timberlands.

"Man! I fucked up. I told her shit I shouldn't have. This was not how things were supposed to go down. Boston gonna lose it," Tacoma said. Marti looked stone faced.

"Tae. You didn't. That's his wife. They have kids. He doesn't want you to run her off. He knows how to get rid of her if he doesn't want her any more. What did you say?" Marti asked. Tacoma shook her head slowly.

"I said enough. I can't control myself with her. I just be wanting to slap the shit out of her. The shit she has done. Come on…It's fucked up," Tacoma confessed.

It was a lot to take. Their lives were seamless before he met her. Tacoma was hard to win over even without the mistakes and betrayal. It was her personality. Her lover could attest to that. When she first saw Tacoma she was immediately taken with the stud whose stunning good looks was hard to resist. Her feminine face and rugged persona were sexy. Her vibrant personality and rock star attitude made her noticeable. She exuded confidence and had a flare for drama. It was what Marti loved about her.

"Let's go. We shouldn't even be here. His life is his. He chose her. He refuses to leave. If you ask me it's admirable," Marti said.

"What is?" Tacoma asked.

"The way he stays. His resilience," Marti replied.

Tacoma looked intensely at her. Her brother seemed happy before the arrest. All did seem well. But this was a new dagger in his back. This time it was money and another brother.

"I wish he would let her go. She's no good for him," Tacoma said, as she looked back at the house.

"He's no angel either Tae. Ever wonder why he stays. Maybe it's because he's like her. Who else would put up with that shit. They're meant for each other," Marti said.

Tacoma glanced over at her. There was some truth to the statement. Boston was a handful. As were all the St. Rock men. Even her. Marti was her first monogamous commitment. She couldn't throw rocks at their house when her own was constructed of glass. And her brothers had more staying power.

Tacoma parted ways much faster than they ever could have. She wondered if it were her feminine intuition that guarded her vulnerable heart. Their strengths lie in different areas of their lives. Whatever the reason, she could agree on one thing. All St. Rocks had a weakness for the downtrodden with no regard for what may come. Rose was the epitome of hurt people hurting people. She had done damage.

*R*ose held her phone as it continually buzzed. Her girl's were sound asleep. The last week had been trying. Between the visits from Orlando and Tacoma, she had no more energy for it. It would be another hour before Brooklyn would be ready for another feeding. Rose looked at the phone number. She was sure it was Boston. Only he would call like a madman, and he had good reason. She was a rich woman off of the sale of his company. Then there was the matter of Bronx. It was hard to say what had him gunning for a conversation. The twenty missed calls was indicative of his desperation. Rose was panicked. It was possibly time to face the piper.

I could just talk to him. It's over anyway and he's locked away. He can't hurt me. I'll just tell him I'm sorry. I'll tell him the money was to help me move on, Rose mumbled to herself, as she watched another call go to voice mail. It was late and she needed to talk to him so she could rest up for her meeting with Fritch in the morning. She would soon be the Chief Operating Officer of Rockwater. A position she had to take in order to get to the money. Fritch paid out the two billion. The rest was hers with ten percent given up front and the rest to be earned over the next five years. She was set.

It was risky to ignore his calls. He had his ways. And she feared him getting out on bond. He would charge toward her like a raging bull. It was better to speak and let him voice his anger. Rose looked at the phone then at the clock. It was eleven p.m. He had about another hour then he would have to give the phone back. Rose answered, placing the phone slowly over her ear.

"Have you lost your fucking mind. Have you! What happened in the sale Rose? It was supposed to be a cut and dry deal. What the fuck! You sell it for more, then you pocket the change. What sort of dirty ass bullshit was that? Answer me!" he shouted.

Rose closed her eyes. It was a relief he wasn't talking about Bronx but now they were at war over something else. It didn't matter. Battles with him were difficult. He was angry about money. She was upset about Ashley. There was also Jodi and Carmen. Kids. Lies. Betrayals. They were fractured in an unfixable way. At least it appeared that way. But of all the shocking secrets, none would do more damage than her and Bronx's affair. He would die a slow death. This was her way to save him. He just didn't see it yet.

"Tell me about Ashley?" she said. Boston got quiet. He held the phone and released a long sigh.

"Tell me about Carmen's daughter. Or we can start with Jodi and her newborn baby girl. Where exactly would you like to start Boston?" she said, catching her breath and closing her eyes to filter through the feelings.

"The money is so I can leave and take care of our kids with or without you. We are so flawed. So damaged... You have been living a lie. I felt so worthless. So guilty. When all along you went to see my people. You went to my mother. You went and talked to my mother! Seriously! She told you about my past... About my issues... And you never said anything to me. I told you about her and I. That we had a terrible relationship and you used your money to buy her loyalty. Got her to tell you things I wanted to share with you on my own. She doesn't know the half of it. Did she tell you when I was ten I was the mistress of a grown ass man and his sons. Did she tell you that? Did she tell you she prostituted me out to her crackhead friends for drugs? Huh! Or what about the times I sat in the back seat while she fucked countless men in the front seat of her Volkswagen," Rose shouted as the tears flowed like a river. She was not deterred. They were having the conversation.

"I can't make excuses but I was coming from a dark place. It's still dark! I still struggle. And you were the only person I trusted. The only man I thought was good in this world. And you fuck my friend! You keep important information like children born by other women from me. That should have been a conversation, Boston! You know what…Take the money. I will wait for you to give me what I need. You want to control everything. Fine! But that will change the deal I made with Mr. Fritch. You call him and explain what happened. You set a meeting and re-negotiate the deal. I secured another five hundred million for you," she said, pausing and giving herself time to catch her breath. Boston held the phone. Tina had not mentioned prostitution or exposing Rose to sex in such a brutal fashion. She had made it seem like Rose was older when the sexual abuse started. Boston was floored.

"I'm so tired. I won't be here when you get out. I won't. I don't trust you anymore. You need to file for divorce. But you can't have my children. I will fight you this time and I will win. So don't come after me. Don't try to torture me. Okay! Just leave me alone. We're even. I fucked up. You fucked up. This whole relationship is fucked up. And I…I can't," Rose cried. Boston held the phone. Rose became angered at his silence.

"Say something dammit!" she yelled. Soon the phone went dead. Rose looked at the phone. She tried to call him back in a panic. Boston was never at a loss of words. She had said a lot. She wanted to take it all back. He was rotting in a jail and she had promised herself she wouldn't do this while he fought for his freedom.

"Oh No! Boston! No, no, no, no, no. I'm sorry. I didn't mean it. Answer this gotdamn phone," she said, as she called the number repeatedly. Soon the phone began going straight to voicemail. Rose threw the phone and cried into her hands. She had messed up. She still loved him. The reaction was not what she wanted. She wanted him to ask for a second chance. Beg for forgiveness and promise never again to betray her. And in the middle of him professing his undying love she could slide in the last betrayal. The night with Bronx. The one that could have produced Brooklyn. Rose cried uncontrollably. Her mind went straight to a reason for the silence. It seemed that maybe he was hoping to be rid of her. Glad it was her who initiated the break up. It was a debilitating blow to her heart.

Boston sat the phone on his chest and stared into the darkness at the ceiling. The jail was eerily quiet except for an occasional outburst from a mentally challenged prisoner who continually called out to the guards. His spirit was at an all-time low. He was locked away from Rose and unable to look into her eyes and explain himself. Carmen's daughter *was* possibly his. He never asked and she never said. Their on again, off again fling was never serious. Carmen wanted more and got angry when Boston wouldn't commit to her.

She started seeing a second guy and by then, Boston had started pulling away. They soon parted and Carmen kept her pregnancy a heavily guarded secret. By the time he found out she'd had a baby, she was already married to yet a third guy and he was named as her child's father. There was a chance the girl was his, but it was too late to question it. Carmen's husband knew nothing except that he and Carmen had three children. And Boston never wanted to stir the pot.

What happened between him and Ashley was nothing more than a hurt and devastated man looking to get answers for a broken heart. Rose was living back at her first home and they weren't together. Boston regretted going to Ashley's house to dig into Rose's past. But he couldn't go back in time and undo what had happened. The only thing he was sure of was that he used a condom. Her child couldn't possibly be his.

Jodi was the only relationship he could acknowledge. They messed around off and on, only after Rose continued her affairs. He didn't feel bad over his affair with Jodi. Her child could be his. It seemed likely that it was. He didn't use condoms with her. She was a side piece he trusted and cared for. But he and Rose were re-committed and he hoped the baby wasn't. Rose would be unforgiving and he still loved her.

"Hey," the guard blurted, as he stood outside Boston's cell. Boston walked over and handed him the phone. "You'll get it again tomorrow. Cheer up," he said. Boston turned and went back to his bed and laid down. He crossed his legs and put his hands behind his head. He was a tortured soul. Luck was not on his side. The timing of her finding out couldn't be worse. There was no way to smooth her over.

He couldn't call Jodi and put her on speaker phone and prove he had not seen her in months. Or apologize for not saying *no* to her sexually aggressive friend. It would have been easier to get Rose to forgive him if he apologized in her ear as he made passionate love to her. They had heated exchanges before that were always cured with great sex and the right words. Phone sex would not ease her pain. Boston was sick about it. Nothing made him happy the way his wife did. He wasn't sure what power she held over him nor did he care. Only one thing made him happy. Rose.

Chapter Eight – Illusions

*D*ayton pulled up at Bronx's home. He was doing a welfare check after pleas from his distraught mother to check on her emotionally unstable son. He was still ignoring calls from everyone and she wanted an update. Dayton knew what his brother's problem was. He wanted to clear his mind. He wanted to know if he had fathered Brooklyn.

Dayton hit his blunt once more then rolled his window up and turned off his car. Bronx stood in the doorway watching him. Dayton was surprised to see him. According to several of his siblings, Bronx would not answer the phone or the door. Cicely believed he would talk to Dayton since Dayton had recently stayed with him. Bronx had a soft spot for the youngest St. Rock. They all did. And Cicely hoped she was right.

Dayton hit the redial on his phone. His mother Cicely answered. "Hey ma. I'm here. He's actually at the door waiting for me to get out of the car," he said. Dayton could hear his mother begin to cry.

"It's ok ma. He looks good. I'm looking at his face as we speak," he assured.

"Oh thank god! Call me as soon as you leave there. I have to know what's going on," Cicely pleaded.

"Sure ma!" Dayton replied.

He hung up then sighed. He was sure Bronx was not ready to talk. He lost his entire family in a horrific accident. It wasn't the type of thing that just went away. And you couldn't rush someone's grief process. Dayton exited the car and threw up a quick wave as he approached slowly. If Bronx gave him the *what the fuck are you doing here* look he wanted to see it before it was too late.

"What's up?" Dayton said, as he approached. Bronx walked away from the door and straight to his kitchen counter. His huge spacious open floor plan was inviting. The sun lit the room up nicely and the home smelled of apple pie and cinnamon. Dayton looked around. It was obvious his cleaning lady had been there. "Smells good," Dayton said to break the ice.

"You hungry?" Bronx asked.

"Sure. What that smelling so fucking good?" he asked.

"Lucy made me a homemade apple pie. It's in the oven," Bronx replied.

Dayton walked over and pulled it out. He made the obvious first slice into it. Bronx hadn't touched it. He glanced at the casserole on the stove and it too was untouched. Bronx wasn't eating and it was concerning. His eyes had dark circles underneath. And his clothing was not his typical selection.

"Mom is worried. Everyone is," Dayton said, as he kept his back to him. If Bronx was going to go off, he didn't want to catch it head on. Bronx didn't respond. No response was better than a verbal assault. But he was there for it. If Bronx needed to go off to feel better, then so be it.

"Hey…talk to me. You good? I'm worried B," he said, as he walked closer to his older brother.

"I need something from you. A favor," Bronx said. Dayton took in a chunk of pie then moaned at the flavors.

"Okay. Anything," he said. Bronx side eyed him. Dayton regretted his quick acceptance hoping it wasn't anything too overboard.

"I need you to call me when Boston's kids are over mom's again," he said. Dayton's brow wrinkled from curiosity. He had recalled the conversation between Chicago and Bronx. The one he wasn't privy to. The night he hid around the corner of the hall listening as Bronx questioned the paternity of Rose's infant daughter.

"Sure. I'll find out where they are now. Hit you back in a sec," he said, as he grabbed his keys and headed to the door.

"Wait! Why aren't you asking me why?" Bronx said. Dayton looked to the floor. It was embarrassing to admit but he had to answer him. And Bronx was clever so there would be no lying or covering up.

"You think she's yours. I know. I heard you that night Chi came over," he replied. Bronx was in shock but could do nothing but nod. His baby brother had heard. He didn't care. It was no longer a secret but he was still not ready for too many to know. He would go from grieving son to the next brother to do his own flesh and blood wrong.

"Keep it between us. Alright?" he said.

"Sure B," Dayton replied, as he left.

*T*he sun warmed the ground comfortably. It was unusually warm for fall. Dayton sat outside April's sprawling residence. He was ordered to stay away from her. A command that did not come from the police or even his father. Boston was direct in his threat. If he went near her, he would be removed from the family's money tree. The money that seemed to be growing would not be made available to him. But Dayton was tired of Boston's meddling. April was his girlfriend. It was he who discovered her on the pole of a Miami nightclub and brought her with him to Chicago.

The silhouette of a woman in a long flowy gown caught his eye. He jumped out of his loud, bright-yellow Lamborghini and walked to her door. It was possible she had already seen him. Dayton walked with purpose. He'd heard Max was on the case and he was good at persuading things to go his way. He wanted to get to April before Boston got out. If Boston had brain washed her into keeping her distance, he wanted to speak his truth. She needed to know he loved her no matter what she believed she saw in his journal. Dayton wanted her back.

He did have a crush he believed was love. Sexual lust gone awry for a woman he knew he couldn't touch. He was like his brothers and she belonged to them which meant she was his as well. An illogical way of thinking about Boston's wife. He realized the insanity of it all. As much as he despised Boston he wanted to be like him. The truth was he wanted him put away. Because with him gone, he could flourish. He was smarter. He was destined for great things. But as long as Boston kept the family comfortable, he would remain king.

"Who is it," April shouted, as her hurried steps brought her closer to the door. Dayton didn't want to respond. He wanted the door opened or he would bust it open. She would be hearing him out this day. He was a bully like Boston. He pushed, in order to be heard. April opened the door and her smile quickly turned into a frown. A change that hurt Dayton.

"What's wrong? You were expecting it to be Boston. He still locked up," he said with a smirk. April became incensed.

"No, I wasn't expecting it to be him. I am well aware that he is locked up. I've spoken to him, if it's any of your business. It is over between us. Now please leave," April warned.

"The police have already been called Dayton. They have nothing better to do out here than respond to a call about a black man making a scene in this lily white neighborhood. You better go now!" April warned. Dayton sucked his teeth.

"You called the cops? Fucking whore. You did that cause you fucking my brother. I ought to go to jail. Maybe sit in a cell right next to his ass. You just like Rose. Loose pussy ass bitch. I should have known. Can't turn a hoe into shit but a paid hoe," he ranted. April shook her head slowly. He was being his same agitated self. When something didn't go his way, nasty words spewed out. The truth was she knew what it looked like.

She didn't blame him for the rage filled words that left him. If she thought he was fucking her sister, he would have been treated the same. Maybe worse. It was difficult playing hard ball. It seemed he'd said enough to part with. His slow walk back to his car was mellow dramatic. The sunken body posture wasn't him. April didn't want to dig deeper into the wound. It was why she kept from name calling herself. The family was dealing with enough. Bronx was in mourning and keeping his distance. Boston was locked away. And she was living under mysterious circumstances in a home purchased by his brother. He would need some of his sanity just to deal with it all.

Max walked into the Cook County State Attorney's Office ready to get going on his new case. He placed his briefcase on the conveyor belt and walked through the scanner. He nodded at the guard and grabbed his belongings and headed to the fifth floor. He had a meeting with one of the attorneys who would be providing him with a discovery package.

"Max Stone," he greeted the young looking gentleman. Max hoped to speak with the prosecutor directly. The young man he was greeting was certainly not briefed on all aspects of the case. He questioned why someone with more experience wasn't there to answer his questions. He had a right to fully understand what information they had and what charges would be filed against Boston.

"Is Mr. Hill or Mr. Cleary available?' Max asked.

"I'm sorry. Both are out of the office at this time. I was told you were just picking up the discovery," the man said. Max looked at the thick file.

"Yes. But since I'm here, I was hoping he could speak with me," he said. The young man was nervous and unsure of himself. Max figured he was new to law. Perhaps a student or an assistant.

"If they're not here, then perhaps you can answer my question," Max said, as he opened the file and scanned the pagers.

"Yes sir. Maybe. I have been briefed on some of the details," the young man said.

"Oh. Okay. Well I see here there are no witnesses named, yet the discovery mentions the case being opened from a phone call. How do you have a phone call that leads to a case being opened behind a caller that hasn't surfaced?" he asked. The young man stared like a deer in headlights.

"Um…Yes sir. The caller gave a verbal statement. That statement led to the discovery of a weapon and a possible suspect," he said. Max furrowed his brow.

"So the caller named my client! He was arrested based off of an anonymous call. Hmm. Okay," Max chuckled, as he scratched his forehead.

"Well yes sir. We recorded the...," he said before Max cut him off.

"Well...Thank you for your time," Max said, then turned and walked out. He'd been given enough. The young man stared at the back of the confident and straightforward man who had managed to ruffle his feathers with a look and two simple questions. The young man walked to the office of his boss and closed the door.

"Mr. Stone just left. He asked two questions," he said.

"I'm listening," the prosecutor said.

"Well sir. He asked how did we open the case from an anonymous call. And then he wanted to know how we arrested his clients from an anonymous call," he said.

"Yeah! I knew the questions before you asked me young man. That's why I am the prosecuting attorney. And I can tell you he's going to use that to get his client out on bond. That's why I need that witness. How close are we to finding out where that call originated from? I need a name! Otherwise, it looks like the caller is the killer trying to pin this on someone else. Or perhaps an enemy trying to get someone to take a fall. This caller obviously knows Mr. St. Rock. And I don't give a damn. This case will be epic. A rich murderer. Movies will be made about it. Books written. Careers made. Find that witness! I want you to look at that man's enemies. Someone among him is either the killer or the accomplice. Get me names of everyone in his circle. And everyone in their circle. And then everyone in their circle. Through a large net. I got a big fish to catch. I'll be governor after this one," he said. The young man looked off.

"Yes sir," he replied, as he turned to leave.

"Hey! You want to ride the wave? Then keep your mouth shut and do as I say. This will be an important career move for you. Now go," Allen Hill said to his young protégé. It was a news worthy case. Boston St. Rock was a well-respected businessman. He was rich. He was a powerhouse. And his conviction would lead to great things for Prosecuting Attorney Allen Hill.

*R*ose sat waiting for the bell to ring at the Truth Center. It was getting close to their afternoon break. She remembered the routine well. It was one o'clock. The normal hour the teachers and their aides took the kids outside for sun and fun. The window was cracked about two inches while she sat, her car idling and her radio down low.

Soon, the sound of the school bell rang loudly. Rose looked over the rim of her tinted Gucci sunglasses as the children burst through the door and made their way quickly towards the playscape. Ashley exited, looking casual in an old pair of jeans and a plain knit top. She looked nothing like the mistress of a billionaire, as she held the hand of a young girl. A child much younger than the group of kids she was supervising. Rose's mouth dropped slightly. She couldn't help but wonder if it were the child in question.

"Yay," a kid yelled, as she darted towards the see-saw. Ashley picked up the toddler and placed her on the opposite end of the see-saw. The time and attention she dedicated to the child made it obvious the child was some relation to her. Rose stared at the girl. She was brown skinned. Almost three times darker than Ashley. Rose's mind raced. The child was close to Boston's dark brown complexion. Ashley was light skinned. And so was Jay, the father of her first born. Rose hated to guess based off of skin color but it was a fact that she couldn't ignore.

Tormenting thoughts about mouths on places and exchanges of passion, was tearing at the very core of her. Ashley liked to suck dick and Boston was weak for a good head job. Boston ate pussy in the rawest and most disgustingly pleasurable way, and Rose was beside herself with jealousy. If it got good to him, he would go further. Maybe lick your ass just enough to drive a woman insane. She was sure Ashley was hooked on him and if she wasn't getting him, she would be nothing short of anguished. It wasn't beneath Ashley to beg. Plea. Throw herself onto whatever pleased her and he was pleasure time ten.

Rose teared up with thoughts of how deep things really went. But with her track record, deep down he was allowed such an indiscretion. "Dammit!" she said. She looked once again. She hoped Ashley wouldn't notice the car. It was Tina's work car. The only car she could get her hands on that wasn't new or flashy. An older model SUV with tinted windows. Perfect for such purposes.

Rose watched as the toddler tumbled to the ground. The thud causing her to burst into a roaring cry. Ashley picked her up and comforted her. She watched as Ashley looked at the other little girl and walked over to comfort her as well. It was a touching moment. Rose remembered that endearing trait about her old friend. Always there to protect and soothe.

She remembered the time she called Ashley after Tacoma's vicious attacked. How fast Ashley showed up with Tina in tow, ready to protect her even though she was very pregnant at the time. They had been through a lot. Ashley was always strong on all facets of life, except when it came to men. She seemed to be easily victimized by overpowering, overbearing men. She too had been assaulted in her youth. Molested by men who should have protected her. The result was a woman who ended up in one bad relationship after the other. It was the common thread between them. Their pasts mirrored one another.

As young teenagers, Ashley always wanted to be like her. It was first noticed by Elouise. Then Tina. Everything from the way she dressed, to the way she carried herself.

Rose watched as Ashley transformed herself into a mini version of herself. It was fine as young women. But they were adults now. This was her life. Max was her ex. Boston was her husband. It was not okay.

Rose looked down at her phone. She checked her texts and caller id as she began to question why she was there. It was a form of stalking and it was embarrassing to say the least.

"Either go over there and confront her or pull off," Rose mumbled to herself. Soon a shadow blocked the sun. Rose looked up and nearly jumped out her seat. Ashley stood. Her hands on her hip. And a look of total horror on her face.

"Are you serious? You're here! Again! What do you want Rose?" Ashley fumed. Rose held the steering wheel tight. She was broken down and suffering. Boston wasn't calling. He wasn't checking on her. He wasn't attempting to fuck her over the phone. All that they shared was now shattered. And she was there to find out if she was the reason. There were still a lot of unanswered questions. Her husband was a big mystery. And in order to solve the mystery, she needed to know a few things. One, were they still romantically involved. And two, was her child his.

Rose exhaled loudly as she tried to think of a nice way to ask. It was a yes or no question. She wanted the details but she was sure she wouldn't be getting them. Ashley was done with her. She was supposed to be done with Ashley. But here she was. Rose didn't want to admit that she was desperate.

She had a secret of her own. Ironically it also involved a child. Hers. She wasn't there to pick a fight. It was deeper than that. Her last baby was her undoing. She wanted a divorce. The divorce she figured would save her. It would free him. But if he had his own terrible secret, it would change things. She needed to know what she was up against.

"Is your baby Boston's?" Rose asked. Ashley peered into her eyes then turned and walked away. She got halfway across the street and turned back around, charging the car with the force of an unstoppable train.

"Do not come back here. If you do, I'll put a restraining order out on you. Do you understand me," she said. Rose looked straight ahead. Ashley was overreacting and hadn't given her a chance to explain herself. She *was* leaving him. In the lowness she felt over Bronx, she wanted a clear conscience. It would make them even in a sense. She had a right to know. He knew her dirt. All of it. Even the scandal of her youth, which she was too young to be responsible for. Rose believed, in some way, it would buffer the blow she was delivering. He was going to find out about Brooklyn. And he would hate her forever. She was a terrible mother and an even worse wife. He had slept with her friend. But she had slept with his brother's. Several. It was shameful.

Rose watched as Ashley stormed away. She pulled off looking in her rear-view mirror at the woman she once loved like family. "Dammit," she blurted out, anguished at the fast that she still had no answers. Something was wrong. Either Ashley was protecting him, or she was fearful of him. It made no sense not to say one way or the other, whether he had fathered her child. Which Rose took as a *yes*. She took a long breath in and release it, as she fought the urge to turn around. Her resting children in the back seat was enough of a reason to keep driving. Ashley could get violent when cornered and Rose wasn't sure how it would play out.

She could see Ashley get into her car. Rose looked in the backseat at her babies, as they slept in their car seats. The dark tinted windows on her car had obscured them from Ashley's view. She turned on the main street and headed back towards Kenilworth still reeling from Ashley's refusal to speak on anything. Boston was famous for controlling people. It was possible he was pulling the strings. Her outward appearance could be a clever rouse. Rose's mind raced. It was possible that the mother of Boston's child was still pulling up to a mansion, all while appearing to have less than. Rose had already been to Boston's other two properties. Ashley was not set up at either. It was back to square one.

If Ashley wasn't going to talk, then Rose would have to find a way to get the information. She hatched a plan to follow her home one day after time passed. Things were too heated to attempt it now. The answer would help put her mind at rest.

But first she needed to clear her mind. Find her power again. The strength she found after carving out a deal with Fritch Packard was no longer empowering her. The first installment of her portion was sitting pretty in an account. Twenty million dollars collecting interest and all at her disposal, yet she felt like a penniless bag lady. Down trotted and hopeless. She was dying to know if Boston was secretly involved with Ashley and spoiling her too. She would not stop until she had the answer. Until then, she needed to gear up for a new phase in her life.

Rose looked back at her sleeping babies. Tina was waiting on her. She had an earful of her life's drama and a huge check to hand her mother. The bond between them that was on the mend was back broken. It would take talks and more time to heal. For now, she needed her. A lot was going down and more drama was on the way. She could feel it. Boston's silence meant he was crafting his response. And she needed Tina's help while she decided what to do next.

*B*oston laid on his prison cell bed trying to keep his current environment from affecting him. The jail was finally calm after a chaotic afternoon. A young man with mental issues had to be carried out by five guards for attempting to hurt himself. He had been complaining of severe stomach aches and the situation escalated. He had been seen and basically dumped back in his cell. Boston felt sorry for him. This was just the sort of thing that got to him. The weak and vulnerable being mistreated.

Boston paid the guards off to get help for the man faster. But now he was in his cell without making so much as a moan. Boston yelled for the guards to come check on the man. His calls went unanswered. Other inmates that had blamed the guards and were yelling and throwing things, had finally calmed down. Boston hadn't moved. The smell of blood still filled his nose.

Boston had become acquainted with the eccentric son of a man who cut him off and hadn't seen him since he was ten. Boston didn't understand how a man had a child he didn't try to see. It was a cold fact of his life that he had come to terms with. If Jodi, Carmen or even Ashley had his child there would have to be an introduction one day.

The man's cell was right next to Boston's and he wasted no time plugging his own dreams and ideas to make money. Boston took the time to give him a few pointers and the man was beginning to believe in himself. His late-night talks of no family and no woman to love hit hard. Boston had a woman but they weren't doing well. He was ignoring her calls, which were now coming in every few hours. She had been consistent up until the last day. It was a solemn night. He hoped the man was alright. He was supposed to be on suicide watch, but the guard was on a smoke break and Boston was pissed that he would take the chance.

"Hey you okay? How you feel. You alright over there?" Boston asked, as he sat at the end of his bed closest to the door. The silence was painful. The impressionable twenty year old was in jail for vandalizing a government building. He was out of place among cook county's roughest residents. Boston called out to the young man again and another man chimed in.

"He doped up. I saw when they brought him in. He was spaced out like a muthafuckin zombie. That's what they do so they can mind control your mind. It's a government conspiracy. They did that shit as payback for writing on that wall. You know they experiment on prisoners the most. Easy pickings. Never get a shot in your arm. They put stuff in us. Take everything by mouth. Never nothin in tha blood. Neva," the man they called Professor said. He was always talking conspiracies and women. His stories were Boston's entertainment. But this evening, he was only interested in hearing from his next door neighbor.

Chapter Nine – Slippery Slope

Max sat at the table waiting on Boston to enter. He sifted through the paperwork in his briefcase. He was off to a good start. His day couldn't get any better since he and Brooke had an appointment with Dr. Lim the following week. The sound of a metal door opening caused him to glance up. Boston walked in. He looked unbothered in his tan pants and button-down shirt. His prison uniform was neat and new looking.

Boston looked well-manicured for a man in the county lock up. There weren't the same amenities as there were in larger prisons. But this was Boston. A man who always had an in. The man who always figured a way. Even from behind bars, he was able to pull off the impossible.

Even convince a world travelling, untouchable, semi-retired surgeon to take on a case when it was the last thing he wanted to do.

"What's up?" Max said, as he extended his hand. Boston shook it with a firmness that added to Max's ease. The men stared at one another for a brief moment. They had come full circle. Max was once again looking into the eyes of his client. Only this time the stakes were higher.

"So I've been to the prosecutor's office. I know Allen Hill. My father and his father knew each other from college. I also know the assistant prosecuting attorney John Cleary. I've gone through the discovery. They have some damaging information that will hurt you. But the information is coming from a witness. Not an informant. An actual caller. There's a difference. Sometimes informants give fake information and it's easy to discredit them. But not a cold call. This is someone who has facts. I'm not going to bullshit you. You have an enemy close to you," Max said. Boston nodded slowly.

He figured as much. He didn't sleep a wink the night before thinking of the situation and who he believed it was. His first mind told him to consider Phoenix. But then he couldn't make sense of it. Phoenix didn't play games. He would have never come to see him if it was a dirty deed by his hand. Denver also came to mind. With his past with Rose and the Twist Media fiasco, he wondered if there was some lingering deep resentment. Then there was Dayton. Their relationship had become strained. Boston had issues with several brothers. It hurt him to think any one of them would go that far. Max continued.

"They have information from that night and was able to match what the caller told them with what they already had. It was a cold case. There just wasn't enough to get a solid lead. So needless to say, now that they have something to work with, they're going to try and make a name for themselves. You are now the most well-known Chicagoan outside of Michael Jordan and Oprah Winfrey. This will be a game changer for them. But I noticed they have not leaked anything to the press," Max said. Boston listened intently. Max was a thorough and skilled lawyer. Boston kept quiet, as Max explained what he knew.

"The story the press has about the gun came from the shop owner whose building was partially destroyed in order for them to dig in the spot where the gun was supposedly buried. He was so angry, that he called the papers and complained about the city's handling of it. He was reimbursed for the damage but he's still not happy. I spoke to him. He was like an open book. He videotaped them without their knowledge. He planned to use it to sue them if he didn't get the payout he thought he deserved. I have the video," Max said with a smile. Boston sat back. Max's confidence put him at ease. It was a first since he had been arrested.

"So, can you get me out of here. Get me the fuck out of here man. Get me a bond hearing," Boston said.

"There's no bond for murder. Burying the gun shows some type of premeditation under the eyes of the law. I will request one, but I'm certain it will be denied. Let me review everything completely. I don't have my plan mapped out yet, but I need you to trust me. You have a lot working in your favor. You are an upstanding citizen. No criminal record. A wealthy tax paying CEO with tons of character witnesses. The prosecutor has his work cut out for him and he knows it. He wants you to get nervous. Take a plea. But we're playing hard ball," Max said. Boston felt good. He did trust Max. It was the reason he was determined to hire him.

"I trust you. I just know how it is when someone like myself is under investigation. Every enemy I ever had will root for my demise," Boston said, as he shook his head in disbelief. He didn't think he was such a terrible person. He wondered about the caller's motive. He tried to look brave in front of Max but he was riddled with fear. Max saw it anyway.

"Look…The citizens like it when old cases get solved. It helps get people re-elected. But the case is still weak because the caller has not stepped forward. I could argue that it was planted there a long time ago by the killer. And that jealousy and envy has an old enemy of yours wanting to see you fall. So for now, their only witness is someone they haven't even seen yet. I'll be able to get you out on bond on that bit alone?" Max said, as he shuffled through the discovery papers. His manner was harsh and direct but he needed Boston to see only facts. He wasn't there to blow smoke up his ass. He wanted Boston to know he was in for a fight. The only thing that could make it go away was if the caller never surfaced. They just didn't have enough for a strong case.

"They don't have finger prints. They have no weapon," Boston said, his voice laden with fear and confusion. Max stopped shuffling papers and stared at Boston.

"You don't know about the DNA?" Max asked. Boston leaned back.

"What DNA?" he asked. Max was surprised Boston didn't know.

"It's here somewhere in the discovery. I don't know the specifics. Did you look through the case file? You were representing yourself, so you would have been given what you needed, to do so effectively," Max said, as he tried to find the paragraph that talked about it.

"I was given a box full of shit. That's why I was so desperate to hire you. I can't sift through that shit," Boston replied.

"That was to throw you off. They probably gave you a bunch of papers explaining shit you can't even use. Legal jargon you wouldn't be able to understand in hopes that you would get overwhelmed and overlook it. It's in there! And they not gonna help you find it. Give me what they gave you. I need to compare it to what I have. I will go through everything with a fine tooth comb. Give me a couple of days," Max said.

"Ms. Rose, the baby is crying. She seems extra fussy," Eboni said, as she brought Brooklyn into the media room. Noor stood next to Rose eating cheerios. Rose rushed over to her baby.

"What's wrong pumpkin. Come here," she said, as she took the newborn from Eboni.

"She feels a little warm. I hope she didn't catch a cold from Aurora's kids. They all have colds over there. I didn't find out until after I picked them up. Can you find my thermometer?" Rose said, as she touched Brooklyn's head and then the inside of her armpit. Eboni went to the closest bathroom searching through the medicine cabinet.

"Go to the bathroom in my room. I have one in the drawer," Rose shouted. Brooklyn's small cries were hard to take. Rose rocked her as she spoke low into her ear.

"It's okay baby girl. Momma got you," Rose assured, as she anxiously waited on Eboni to return.

"Here it is," Eboni said, as she pushed the thermometer into Brooklyn's cheek. "She's too small for that. I have to do a rectal," Rose said, sitting down with Brooklyn and removing her diaper. Eboni looked at Rose. She had never seen Brooklyn so fussy.

"Should we take her to the doctor?" Eboni asked. "No! She'll be fine. Bring me some Tylenol. If the fever doesn't break, then I'll take her," she replied.

Rose had been down this road before with Noor. There was nothing to panic about yet. A slight fever and crying were to be expected since she was battling her first cold. There would be more.

Rose rocked her calm baby to sleep. A muffled low bell rang in the distance. The visitor couldn't have come at a more inconvenient time. Rose walked towards the front of the house patting her baby girl on the back and hoping that the visitor was her mother Tina or the delivery guy. Eboni had ordered take out and she was starved.

"One minute," she shouted. Brooklyn lay over her shoulder sucking a pacifier. She sounded congested and Rose's suspicion was confirmed when Brooklyn continually opened her mouth to breath around the pacifier. "Aww baby. You have a cold. Damn!" Rose griped.

Rose could see the silhouette of what appeared to be a woman through the new glass and wood doors Boston had installed. She opened the door and was pleasantly surprised.

"Cicely," she greeted, as her mother-in-law entered and looked around.

"I don't get to see my children's home life much. I thought I'd pay a visit. See how the babies are. How everyone is holding up," Cicely said. Rose rocked Brooklyn as she looked around for Noor who was now walking.

"Eboni! Is Noor with you?" Rose shouted.

"Yes Ms. Rose," she replied. Cicely walked to Rose and extended her hands.

"Let me see my grandbaby. And I will take some tea if you have some," Cicely said, as she made her way to the grand room.

"Sure. I'll get you a cup," Rose said, as she walked away. She could tell Cicely had something on her mind. And Rose was filled with anxiety. There was so much going on that it could be a number of things.

"Here you go," Rose said, as she placed a tea cup and saucer on the table in front of her. Cicely held Brooklyn then removed the pacifier from her mouth and watched lovingly as the baby then began to suck her thumb.

"Are you nursing still?" she asked. Rose paused.

"Well...I pump. I give her breast milk in a bottle now," Rose responded. Cicely kept her eyes on the baby but furrowed when Rose gave the reply. Rose saw the look and was not happy about the shade thrown. Cicely soon gave her rebuttal that Rose knew was coming.

"That's just extra work for nothing. Babies get much more from nursing than just nutrients. They bond. It is the ultimate love. I nursed thirteen babies. Each and every one of them, until they were well over one years old. No bottles," Cicely stated.

"I will breast feed more. I know. I just be tired," Rose replied.

Cicely looked over at an oil painting of Boston and Rose. It was regal looking. The painter was obviously very skilled. Missing from the oil painting were the children. And also missing was a smile on Boston's face. It seemed Rose struck gold giving Boston offspring. It was the light of his life. She was sure Boston and Rose's marriage would not have survived without the children.

Cicely couldn't help but wonder if he had regrets that he never told her about. Her son was open with her. But he was steadfast in his commitment to a woman who was slowly breaking his world and Cicely was no longer willing to watch on the sidelines. Her children, although adults, could count on her. She was there. And Boston was suffering in silence. So was Phoenix. So was Bronx. And now Dayton. Cicely wondered about the latter. April called her months prior and gave her an earful about him loving an older unavailable woman. Someone whose face he saw often. Cicely wondered if the woman in the journal that April had told her about was Rose. It wouldn't be too surprising.

"Have you spoken to April or Dayton? They are having issues and April is convinced he is in love with someone. I haven't spoken to her lately. I know that Dayton confides in you sometimes. He used to confide in me. I was the person whose shoulder he cried on. He's replaced me with you, I guess. And so, I must ask you how much you know about what's going on with him? Who this mystery woman is? Surely, he's hinted to you. April said he called you whenever they argued," Cicely asked, glancing down at her sleeping granddaughter. Rose was appalled. Her heart nearly jumped out her chest. It sounded like a sly way to ask if something inappropriate had transpired.

"I haven't talked to April lately. And Dayton is just trying to adjust to not being able to see her. I don't believe there is another woman. He loves her. I do know that they have broken up. I'm hoping they get back together," Rose said, hoping to erase any thought she had on there being a sexual relationship between them. Cicely nodded.

"Uhuh. Well...he won't because he is in love with someone else. He could get that girl back if he wanted her. He doesn't. And I just wonder what's going on. He's my baby. And if he is in over his head in something that will destroy him, I want to know," Cicely said, as she stood and handed Brooklyn back to Rose.

"She looks just like you. Both of your girls do," Cicely noted. Rose smiled to hide her humiliation. Cicely was pretty much stating that Rose was the woman in the journal. She didn't have to say it. It was in her eyes. It was in her sarcasm. And now, it would be spread amongst all her children whom she felt could exert control over the situation before it imploded.

"He's not like his brothers, you know. He's vulnerable. He loves hard. He's spoiled and easily misled. But he's also tough when he needs to be, and irrational if he feels mistreated. It's why April is having such a hard time with him. He is passionate. Sometimes overly. I worry about him. He hasn't had his heart broken. I'd hate to see when he does," Cicely cautioned.

The words felt like a threat. Her description of him was something Rose already noted. He broke things when he couldn't have his way. He had already broken her like a crystal vase. His tell-all, as he stood in the foyer that day, shattered her completely. She was still picking up the pieces.

Rose stood and followed Cicely to the door. She turned and gave a half smiled as she walked out. "Take care. And call me if you find out anything," Cicely said, as she left. Rose watched her get in the back seat of a black Escalade. She could handle conversations about Dayton. Nothing had happened between them. Her initial fear was that Cicely was there to talk about Bronx. That would be the news that would end everything as she knew it. Bronx was Boston's closest brother outside of Memphis. He looked up to him. Sought counsel through him. She would be disowned by the St. Rocks.

Cicely's driver gave a single nod then got in the car and pulled off. *Fuck! She's going to tell Boston. And I haven't done anything with Dayton!*

Cicely's car drove down the long driveway from Rose and Boston's sprawling estate. She was upset but kept her head up. Rose was beginning to disgust her. She couldn't figure her out and she could never get close. Rose always kept a wall between them. It was the same for her daughters. She was impenetrable.

But if you had a penis, it was cakewalk. She would let you in. Possibly open her heart. Her legs. Cicely didn't understand the woman she was. Or what had happened to make her such an enigma. She didn't understand how a woman could be so loosely bound. Cicely looked out the window. Her son's accomplishments shined bright. He was the reason for it all. And he deserved a wife who would support him, love him unconditionally and remain loyal

"Where to Mrs. St. Rock?" her driver asked. She hadn't thought about it. She didn't get out as much as she used to. She loved being home. Her children came to her. She was there to watch her grandchildren. She thought of food.

Deserts. Whether she had the things she wanted for the evening. A quick run through of the items in her refrigerator was all she needed to render her verdict. "Home. I'm tired," she said, as she settled in for the twenty minute ride back to her house.

Cicely felt a vibration. She felt the pockets of her trench coat and removed her cell phone. "Hello," she answered. "Hi. Is this Cicely?" the voice said. "Yes, it is. Whom am I speaking to?" she asked. The caller waited a second. Cicely was on edge. With the present state of her family, a call followed by silence was not the best feeling in the world.

"This is Heather's mother Marianne," the caller stated. Cicely was floored. She knew Marianne but hadn't spoken to her since the funeral. Marianne seemed upset at the family for reasons she never understood.

"Marianne. How nice to hear from you. How are you? I pray for you every day. Losing our grandbabies that way was just horrific. Bronx is still not right. He keeps disappearing. He won't answer the door when we go to check on him. How are you holding up?" she asked.

"I'm doing better. I couldn't talk about it before without crying. I still break down. But I'm healing. I pray. My pastor and his wife have been very helpful in dealing with all this. But I can't say I feel sorry for Bronx. I'm just so mad. This is all his fault," Marianne said, as she sniffled and then blew her nose. Cicely became angered but took a series of short breaths to calm her. Her heart raced the moment Marianne spoke of her son in a negative way. He was mourning. Probably more than she could imagine. It was his children. She had a lot of nerve.

"Marianne...Please don't point blame. Bronx has been devastated by this," Cicely rebutted. She wanted to shout. Marianne needed to be careful. She lost grandchildren too. Those were her boys. Miniature versions of the men she raised. She was enjoying the chance to do it right. The mistakes she made with her own sons were a learning lesson and she was robbed of the chance to love them though life. Talk to them about goals. About women. She was brokenhearted the same as Marianne. They both stood bedside for the children's births. Cicely wasn't having it.

"I have to go. This is upsetting. You blame my son! Heather had issues. They found a pipe in her car. I'm not saying she is to blame but I am saying that it could have been a factor. And how dare you look for someone else because secretly you blame yourself for Heather's troubles. I know the guilt Marianne," Cicely said.

"Now wait one gotdamn minute. Her drug screen was clean. No drugs. None! No alcohol. She was driving fast because she was upset. Bronx and Rose had an affair. And Heather was going to see that baby. See if Bronx was there. She wanted to find out if what Blake told her was true. You don't know what you're talking about," Marianne ranted.

Cicely closed her eyes as she relaxed her arm. The phone fell onto her lap. She lost her voice. Her breath. Her wind. She could hear Marianne still ranting then suddenly the call ended. Tears flowed like a river. Her driver glanced in the mirror at her.

"Mrs. St. Rock. What is it? Are you okay?" he asked. Cicely leaned her head back. She felt a massive headache coming on.

"I'm fine. Please just get me home," she said, her voice cracking. This was a bombshell. Bronx and Boston were close. Cicely was in disbelief. Bronx was not the type. He was not a woman chaser or oversexed like Denver, Dayton or even Austin. Bronx was rock solid. This would be the end of Boston. He wouldn't survive it. He would change. Cicely's tears flowed in a heavy uncontrolled downpour. She reached on the inside of her back door compartment and pulled a few loose tissues. She needed to think of what to do next. She wondered if there was any truth to it. Just because Heather thought it didn't make it so.

The driver pulled up to Orlando and Cicely's estate and opened her door. Orlando stood waiting in the doorway for his wife. He had been gone all day with Memphis and Dallas and had recently returned home. He smiled as he watched the love of his life walk up. His smile was met with a solemn and depressed look. Orlando opened the door and stepped out.

"Sweetheart. What is it?" he asked. Cicely took his hand.

"I need to sit. My head... I can't deal with all this," she said. Orlando waved Joe off and held his wife's arm as she entered the house.

"Talk to me baby. What happened?" Orlando asked. This was not his wife's normal mood. She was the rock. The strong but silent supporter of any and all things St. Rock. But something had her shaken. And he needed to give her space. They had no secrets. She would tell him once the wind got beneath her wings again.

Cicely walked to her sofa and sat down. She removed her coat and then looked down to the floor. Orlando would be floored the same as she had been. She didn't want to hurt him. Bronx was his heart. They were the three musketeers. Him Bronx and Boston. It was not the best situation when they had so many other children, but it was what it was. He just naturally gravitated to them. It was why their other boys were so jealous. So competitive. A tragic outcome that could not be erased. It could only be managed at this point. But the scars still showed.

"Bronx and um...Rose," she said, as she looked to him to finish the sentence. Orlando leaned back.

"Rose and Bronx what?" he asked. Cicely moved her head slowly up and down. Orlando's eyes popped.

"Don't say that. I know you joking," he said.

"No. I'm not. Marianne said they had an affair. And that Heather was speeding to the hospital to see the baby. How does this happen. He knows about Boston's history with her. Why would he do that. Why Orlando!" Cicely cried. She jumped up from the couch to walk away. Orlando jumped up and grabbed her by the arm.

"Wait! Are you upset with me?" he asked. Cicely looked intensely at him.

"Yes! Yes I am. Cause you share some of the blame. Our boys are not loyal to one another. They harbor resentment. They make bad choices. And money is used to cover it up. This family is falling apart. They are still doing things to one another with no regard or respect for each other. You had favorites. You did! And I tried to be there for the ones who weren't so lucky. You were their father. This larger than life character. The one they all tried so desperately to please. To be like. But you were only accessible to a few. And the others rebelled. Memphis ran the streets. Phoenix hated us. Austin left and never looked back. He barely comes to our functions. Chicago plasters a smile on his face to hide his true feelings. Columbus, Dallas and Dayton were just too young. Don't you see," she said.

Her eyes searched his for understanding. He had to see it clearly. Feel it with his heart. This was his doing. He needed to reach them. Each one. And see where they stood with him. See how much pain or anger they felt over his absence. And the ones who felt smothered by him needed to be talked, to see how they felt about his overbearing ways.

Orlando was frozen. He couldn't respond to her just yet. They were better than this. They had thirteen children, and it was hard for him to focus on each one equally plus provide a roof over their heads. Cicely had said the words before. This wasn't the first time she'd expressed her dissatisfaction at the way he fathered his boys. But it *was* the first time she blamed him for how they turned out. He agreed to a point. He wished he could go back in time. Undo a lot of it. Spend more time with them all. Do things together.

But Orlando also believed they wouldn't be wealthy if he hadn't focused on the ones with potential. The ones who excelled. It was because of Boston, Denver and Bronx that they were where they were in life. Those were the sons who paved the way for the others. Austin was sitting on two degrees from Harvard. Phoenix was a successful club owner. Chicago had a successful property management firm. Even Dayton, who was a coding and IT whiz, was gifted because of money provided for the best education through the most expensive schools. And the most successful of them all was now a billionaire. Orlando was hurt. He didn't know Cicely felt he had failed them.

"CeeCee...We can't fall apart now! We can't argue about the past and what we could have done differently. We had thirteen kids. It is impossible to spread attention evenly among such a large family when some of your children look like they may be headed for trouble. I had to stay on Boston, Bronx and Denver's necks. They were getting into things. Memphis too. But he rebelled and so I couldn't watch him as much. You can't hold it against me. I love them all. I love all my children. I love you," he said, as he touched her face. Cicely felt bad. She didn't mean to push the dagger in so far. But time was running out. If they didn't get in front of the train wrecks, more damage would be done. And they needed to get in front of the bomb that was Bronx and Rose's affair. It would level their family to a pile of rubble.

"Listen...Let me talk to Bronx. See what he says. He needs time. I can't do it yet. He is vulnerable. Its touchy. And if the affair resulted in Brooklyn, then it would only add to his sadness. She would be his only living child. Bronx is not the type of man to not have access to what is his. I will straighten all this out. If it is true, then I will have a hard talk with Boston. He has to leave her. She cannot be a part of this family any longer. If he refuses...Then he is on his own," he said. Cicely furrowed. She wasn't sure what her husband meant. She was sure he didn't mean that they would turn their backs on him.

"Just be careful. Boston is run by his heart. He plays tough, but that's just a mask he wears. This is his first true love. He will love her to the moon. You know that. He is like you. He loves hard. I think he should divorce her. But he won't listen to you on that. In the end, he will come to me. And I will tell him. He will do it for me. I know he will," she said. Orlando agreed. Out of all their children, Boston and Tacoma had the most loyalty for Cicely. If she pushed, they folded.

"When I went to visit him, I questioned his trust of her. He looked like he was weighing his options. I showed him that article. He didn't seem too pleased. I think he will," Orlando said, then kissed his wife on her head. Cicely smiled. They were on the same page. They always were. Her children were grown. Their actions would not tear her from her husband of forty years.

Orlando left out. Cicely hadn't thought of the position Bronx was now in. She wondered if part of his deep depression was because he had a living child he could not see. She didn't blame him for wanting to see. Another living offspring could help him get through his grieving process.

But his pursuit of it would come at another cost. Boston's sanity. It wasn't fair. Bronx would need to mourn and then get back to life. Fall in love. Have more children. It was possible. He was still young enough.

"Hey," Dayton said, as he entered Bronx's home. "What up," Bronx said, as he left the door opened but locked the screen. Dayton followed him into his massive kitchen complete with a large television hanging from the ceiling. Bronx poured himself a cup of Thai tea with milk then offered his brother some.

"Naw. I'm good. I bought you something," he said, handing Bronx a long thin envelope. Bronx lit up. The moment he'd waited for.

"When did you get it?" he asked, taking the small package from his brother.

"Rose took them to Memphis house. Now all you need to do is swab yourself and send it off. I wrote the address on the front. Send it in with a money order for one hundred and eighty dollars and you're good. I think the results take a few weeks though. Not sure," Dayton said. Bronx got emotional. Dayton looked intensely at his older brother. He hoped Bronx would be alright. It was the first time he'd seen him smile. It was a wonderful sight. He looked normal. Focused. He was on his way to being the Bronx everyone knew and loved.

"I better get going. I'm supposed to meet up with the fellas. We're racing in Harmony Park tonight," Dayton said cheerfully.

"Alright! Thanks man. I really appreciate this," Bronx said. Dayton smiled then hugged his brother. "Call you later," he said, as he walked out the door. Bronx watched him to the car. He looked at the package in his hand. Its contents would make or break a lot for him. Bronx exhaled. This was the first step. Now he would need to get the sample off and wait.

Alright boys and girls. Clap your hands and stomp your feet as we dance to the beat of the sing along gang, the fluffy bunny with the large pink nose and oversized feet said. Bronx moaned then shifted his body slightly. Soon a familiar tune played on his television. Bronx bolted awake. The cartoon had him dreaming of his boys. He grabbed the remote and turned the television off. It was Blake's favorite program.

Hare Fare was a daily favorite in his home. Bronx had seen every episode and knew every song. It hurt him to watch even a one second clip of it. The program was popular and it seemed he couldn't escape the images. Bronx sat up and held his eyes closed as he tried to undo the damage of the song. Tears formed that he refused to let loose. He had cried every day. He was not in the land of the living.

The sky glowed a reddish orange hue as the sun prepared to set for the evening. Bronx lay across his couch clutching his manhood through his pants as he stared at the ceiling. After several minutes, he looked at his watch then stretched his arms and stood up. He glanced out at what was left of an obvious beautiful day. Not that it mattered. His days were dark and gloomy no matter what the weather did.

Life for him was behind closed doors while people like his housekeeper or his brother's made special trip to bring him food and necessities. Bronx wanted to get back to normal. It was easier said than done. Everything reminded him of what he lost. He held the world responsible. Even Boston and Rose played a part.

Bronx was still finding the courage to mail the swabs. Finding out would change things for his family. It wasn't an option not to know. If Brooklyn was his, Boston would get a rude awakening. He was not Phoenix. Not even close. And Boston knew it. The envelope containing swabs from he and Brooklyn's mouth sat on his glass and stone table right near the door. It was now closer to getting in the mail box after sitting on his bedroom dresser for a week. Once he got over the shock that life had dealt him, he planned on getting to the bottom of his niece's questionable paternity. And time was running out.

It was best to do it while Boston was locked up. He could have a conversation freely with Rose without worry, if it turned out she was his. He hoped Rose would allow him to see her. Bond with her. And he would figure out what to say to his brother later. As much as he hated to admit it, Boston being in jail meant a chance to see Rose. The guilt he felt wishing his brother stayed in just a little longer, was ripping him from the inside out. He hated he still felt something for her. She would never be his. Boston would never let her go.

But if Brooklyn wasn't Boston's, he would probably leave her. He left once before. It would free Rose. She could then love him. He didn't doubt it would be rocky at first but smoke from fires always cleared. And he would be there to raise his child. Bronx thought about it. He didn't care what his family thought. He would take Rose *and* her girls and leave town. Maybe go to DC with Austin. Boston would have to do his time the best way he could. It was scandalous but what else was there to do. He couldn't undo the sex. Take back the semen.

But if Brooklyn wasn't his, then he would back down and suffer in silence. He could continue his battle to get back to normal even though his bleeding heart would continue to bleed. He would still desire Rose. Only time would cure that.

Bronx checked for missed calls then walked to the bathroom. He flicked the light on and walked to the toilet, catching a glimpse of himself in the large custom vanity mirror. He didn't like the eyes that looked back. He no longer recognized himself. He no longer understood his thoughts.

Bronx stood at the mailbox staring at the manila envelope. He flicked it a few times then clutched it in his hand. *What are you doing*, he thought, hitting his hand with the sealed contents of the possible life-changing event. Bronx was oblivious to the traffic around him. He stood on

Arlington, looking around feeling like he was in the twilight zone. A quick close of his eyes and tightening of his jaw propelled him forward to the metal container with red, white and blue graphics and the image of an eagle displayed. It was out of his hands.

Chapter Ten – Sins of the Son

Max walked up to the county jail. The doors buzzed loudly and he heard a click sound. "Hi. I'm counsel for Boston St. Rock," he said, as he placed his briefcase on the turnabout and emptied his pockets. He knew the drill. He was prepared for it. But not for the conversation he would need to have with Boston. The hearing was in another day. It would be determined at that point if Boston could get out on bail. Max was originally hopeful. But not in lieu of the new findings. And the new evidence meant his case just got harder to beat.

"He's on his way. Table three please," the guard stated.

"I'm his attorney. I need a private room," he said. The guard looked at the signature then looked on his paperwork.

"My bad. Wait here. I'll see if a room is available," he said.

Max waited a few minutes before being escorted to a small room for privacy. He sat down and pulled his notes and wrote down some things he forgot to look into. A warm thought entered his mind. Brooke was making progress under Dr. Lim's care. He had her on alternative medication that seemed to be helping and the baby was healthy. Brooke was improving although she would still need heart surgery one day. They pushed it off until after she gave birth. Dr. Lim planned to deliver the baby by c-section thereby reducing the stress on Brooke's heart. Brooke would have to go through a series of tests. The results would help narrow down what options best suited her. Max was relieved. He was comfortable with everything and could now focus on Boston's case.

Boston walked in and sat across from Max. He looked like a man with the weight of the world on his shoulders and Max felt for him. He didn't have good news but he was a brilliant lawyer. And he would work turning over every stone until he found a way to get Boston off. But there was the new discovery.

"I'm not here to bullshit you or sugar coat shit. So, I'm just going to come right out and say it. They have a spit swab that was collected and stored over ten years ago. A wad of spit near the crime scene that day. Right near the body. Do you remember spitting?" Max said with a look of worry.

"No. I didn't. Come on man! Someone is setting me up. Just like that they have everything they need. Spit. A gun. What next. My prints. If they had all that, then why wait until now. They could have got to me a long time ago. This is bullshit," Boston yelled, as he slammed his hands on the table. A guard opened the door and looked in. He gave Boston and Max a look. He had been paid well enough to allow Boston many freedoms inside the jail. But this was beyond anything he would ever allow. He couldn't. He still needed his job. Max nodded and he shut the door. Boston grimaced at the thought of such convenience.

"No one was there when we confronted him. And we did not shoot him. We left. I'm telling you it's a lie. It was just my brothers and my father. There was no one else around. It was late. Quiet. Chilly. No one was out," Boston stated. "Someone was! You missed it. How could you see all around you? 360 degrees in all directions! It's impossible! There is a witness and there is a murder weapon. So I need to ask. Did someone from your family shoot that man?" Max asked. Boston looked intensely at him.

"No! The gun they found was from my family. And the reason it was buried has nothing to do with this case. Nothing at all. It had nothing to do with that night we confronted that boy. Nothing! That gun was involved in something else. I hid it to protect someone. That's why it was there. Dammit! That's why," he shouted. Boston couldn't admit what was done. He had his father to protect. Max looked fiercely into the eyes of his former enemy. He didn't care for Boston, but Boston had possibly saved his wife and his baby's lives. He had to save him. And it didn't look good.

"Look man, I ain't gonna lie. Them having the same type of gun used at the crime scene is damming. Two shots were fired. Witnesses from nearby reported two shots! What the report showed was only one bullet entered the victim. They found another bullet in a wall nearby. Two different guns. Two different bullets. The gun found is the same type as the slug found in the cement of the building. It is damaging evidence. Give me something cause right now the evidence is hard to explain. Who is feeding them all this information? Give me someone. Who hates you?" he asked. Boston chuckled.

"You," he said. Max scoffed then laughed.

"Come on Boston. Who are you protecting? You're being vague as fuck man," Max said. Suddenly he looked off.

"Damn!" he said. Boston looked intensely at him. Max sat straight and folded his hands.

"I see. This is fucked up. Oh my god. This is so fucked up," he replied. Boston snickered.

"Tell me about it. If I don't divert their attention they'll go after him. No way can I let that happen. Would you let them arrest your father? The man who sacrificed everything for you. My family needs him. I need him. I'll do his time if I have to," Boston said. Max stared. There was nothing more to say. It was a battle he would fight. He understood the gravity of the situation. There was nothing else to say.

Max handed Boston a few papers to sign so he could be entered as his new legal counsel. Boston signed the papers. Max noted Boston was a lefty as he was. Boston finished and handed Max his high-end Mont Blanc pen. Max packed it along with the papers in his briefcase and closed it. He had final words for his new client.

"I'm confident I will be able to get you out on the next bail hearing. Its scheduled for the 15th. I know that's a few weeks away but the courts are backed up. Be patient. And don't worry. If you remember anything about that night, write it down so we can talk about it. I need to know what could possibly be happening behind the scenes. Why would someone decide to tell after all these years? You sure this ain't from within your family?" Max asked. Boston scowled at the question.

"I thought so at first. Now, I ain't so sure," he replied. Max nodded.

"Well…If the prosecutor does have information with regard to the witness that came forward, they can't keep their identity hidden until the last minute. That's against the due process and procedure they must follow. So, he'll eventually have to name them. It's a waiting game. In the meantime, I will fight to get you out on bail. They don't have enough to seek first degree. Not from what I see. They also stated you could be a flight risk. So if you were denied because you own a plane, that is prejudiced. It's unfair to deny you solely because you have the means. I will fight that," Max said, as he packed his briefcase.

Max glanced at him and gave a quick smile. It was becoming easier to represent the man he once hated. Rose was no longer on his radar. And Boston was being on his best behavior. Jail had tamed the big cat. He seemed humbled by the dagger in his back from an enemy unseen. Max felt bad for him. It was hard to fight a war when you had no idea who you were fighting. But the state was heavily relying on the mystery person to come forward as promised. Max had read the notes. It seemed the prosecutor was expecting to meet with the witness in the coming weeks. Max held out hope that the person stayed in the background. Even with the old evidence, it was still circumstantial. The gun had been tampered with over ten years prior and so ballistics testing was inconclusive. The barrel of the gun had eroded from acid and weather. And the spit on the ground could have been put there hours before the shooting. Max had his argument. It was solid. Unless someone was willing to testify that they actually saw the shooting, it would be a hard sell. The prosecutor would have to drop the charges and if they played hard ball, the judge could make the call and dismiss the case. Either way, Boston would be a free man.

"I have to go to my office. Prepare my argument. You go before the judge in a few weeks and I need to have my argument tight. We'll enter the plea of not guilty at that time. But I need you to be prepared. This could drag out. It could get ugly. And you still won't have a bond unless I can convince the courts that the case is weak and baseless. I am working on it. I want to ask the judge to dismiss the case but I can't unless I have a good argument of why. I'm on it. Call me if you need anything," Max said. Boston stood and extended his hand. Max shook it firmly. A shake that affirmed a bond had been established despite their past. Max never thought of himself as a forgiving man. This was the man who fucked his woman inside his condo. But it was also the act that broke one bond and forged another one even better.

Had Boston not taken Rose, he would have never been free to meet Brooke. She was the most amazing woman in the world to him and he couldn't see life without her. An ironic twist of fate. He knew he would never want Rose back. Proof by the erased pictures from his laptop. And the fact that he was willing to fight for her husband. Max turned and walked out. Boston was his only case and he was behind the carriage. It was pulling him instead of the other way around. He needed to get on top of it. Be clever and clear on all the notes gathered thus far. He had diverted all new cases to his staff lawyers. Boston was his priority. Something he was still getting used to.

"Son!" Orlando greeted Phoenix as he walked by him. Phoenix stood at the door in his Sunday lounge wear. A pair of cotton and linen Brunello pajama pants and a white tee. Soft music played in the background. It was 7:00 in the morning and he wondered what his father was doing at his house so early.

"What's going on pop?" Phoenix asked. He followed his father into the kitchen and offered a cup of coffee. "I was just getting ready to make some. You want a cup?" he asked.

"Sure. That'll be my third cup of the day. Been up since five. Couldn't sleep," Orlando said, as he walked over to the window and looked out at Phoenix's massive yard complete with a garden, gazebo and a pool. Phoenix poured water into his Keurig and selected the cup size. He was sure his father was there about Boston. His favorite son. It pained Phoenix to watch his father slowly die inside without him around. He didn't believe he would get the same energy if it were him. Nor the same fight. But he loved him anyway.

"What's on your mind pop? I hope Boston is not requesting my presence again. I did my part. Max is his lawyer. What else can I do?" he asked. Orlando turned around.

"You can answer a simple question. Is it you?" he asked without so much as the blink of an eye. Phoenix stopped mid stride. He sat the cup on the counter and stared into his father's serious eyes.

"Is what me? I know you're not asking if I am responsible for him being in jail," Phoenix replied. Orlando nodded slowly.

"Yes…That's what I am asking son. I spoke to Max. He went through the case. Someone with detailed knowledge has been feeding the cops every piece of information they need. Which means it has to be coming from either Memphis, Denver, Bronx or you," Orlando said without hesitation. Phoenix sighed. He narrowed his gaze at his father. He didn't know him at all if he was asking him that question. It was all he could take.

"What do you think. Hmm… Do you think I would do that to him? Or to anyone in the family for that matter. I've moved on from my past troubles with him. I've met someone and I am good with where my life is right now. Why are you in my house insulting me and questioning my character. Instead of pointing fingers you should help him get his story together cause that shit went down. And from the looks of it, the DA is coming for blood. What is it? Hmm? Have you lost faith in your loving son? The one you revere. Wow! This is Boston we're talking about. He will pull a rabbit out of his hat. He always does. It's been just a few months and already you want to blame everyone except him. He shot that boy and you know it. Why are you saying it was you? Why have you pushed that narrative? You changed the story to protect him?" Phoenix fumed, as he continued his rant.

"Where was all that protection when Denver got in that trouble. He had to fight his way out himself. And Dayton. Huh! Where were you when that white man wanted to kill Dayton for fucking his baby momma. Huh! Where were you pop. Memphis had to go see him. Scared him so bad the muthafucka left town. Memph handled that, not you! But as soon as Boston gets a hand slap, here you come. Ready to bury everyone in order to keep precious Boston protected. I know it was him. And for the record…No! I did not call the cops. Now if you'll kindly leave so I can get ready," Phoenix demanded.

Orlando stood with his hands in his pockets. It took him a minute to absorb the bevy of verbal assaults his son has just hurled at him. Orlando took a deep breath and exhaled slowly.

"Are you done?" he said.

Phoenix didn't respond. He had already regretted some of the anger filled words that had left his mouth. Orlando walked over to the kitchen island and sat at the chrome and white cushioned stool. He rubbed his hands together as he sought the words that would calm an already heated situation. Phoenix stood, still defiant. Orlando gave him a dose of reality.

"So, I see we're still not past this. The past is still a problem for us. Well…I'm going to help you process some of that. Dayton *went* to Memphis first and he responded before I had a chance to. If you think for one second, I would let some privileged white man say or do anything to any of my sons, then it is you who do not know me! I know you. I see the man you are. But you do not see me. You will. Hopefully you do before I am dead and gone. Because the one thing I don't want is for you to have to live with that guilt. The regret and wishing you had more time. As I have told you, my love for you is the same. I love all my children equally. Maybe you will when you have sons of your own," Orlando said, as he looked away before continuing.

"Secondly, let's go ahead and clear up the Freemont incident. Because I see you have confusion. So let's talk facts. I didn't want you to know but you're a grown man now. You can handle truth. And I trust you more than you believe I do. Boston shot at him and missed. I shot and hit. It happened fast. Boston believed it was his bullet that hit that boy but it wasn't. He didn't flinch until I hit him. It was dark but I saw everything. Boston always believed the boy was shot twice. He was young. He ran up and shot before I could stop him. The boy reached for something and I laid him out. He would have retaliated. I moved us after that. I took you out of that environment. You understand now! Boston was protecting me. The shit couldn't be avoided. That boy was hunting Memphis. He had shot at him once before. I looked for him. It was either him or Memphis. It wasn't *going* to be mine! There was no way I would have let someone take any of my children's lives if I could do something about it. None of my children. That included you. We stick together. No matter what. Do you understand. And I know how you feel about Rose. So yes, it crossed my mind that maybe you had it out for him. So I had to ask. You said no and I believe you.

We won't have this conversation again," Orlando said, as he stood.

Phoenix was racked with emotion. Orlando walked around the kitchen island and gave his son a long hug, patting him his back.

"I love you son. I don't know why you question that," he said. Phoenix fought back the urge to shed a tear.

"Love you too pop," he replied.

He did. His need for validation from Orlando was still a weakness he wanted to overcome. Phoenix knew he needed healing. The story of what happened helped. He always thought Orlando was covering for Boston. A thought that frightened him. Especially now that the past was coming to take revenge for a life stolen. Phoenix would rather it be Boston than his father. But now that he knew the story. it seemed Boston was protecting their father. Phoenix was ready to take a seat and let his wounds heal. He was being ridiculous and it stemmed from his feelings for Rose. He was still getting over their affair. It was something he had to do on his own. Boston was not his enemy. He was his own enemy.

*B*ronx awakened to a knock on the door. He sat up then moved to the side of his bed and strained to focus on the time displayed on the clock. "What the fuck," he mumbled. It was 8:45 am. Too early for a visitor. Bronx stood up and walked his long hall. He felt sorry for the person on the other side of the door. Any pamphlet carriers, delivery driver, nosy neighbors or concerned family would hear harsh words. He was mourning fine. He didn't need constant check ups and definitely not at eight in the morning.

"Pop!" Bronx said as Orlando walked past him. He closed the door and followed his father into the living room.

"Sorry to wake you. How have you been son?" he asked.

"Good! Better...I guess. Is everything alright?" Bronx asked. Orlando was acting like a man with the weight of the world on his shoulders. He and Cicely were the only ones who were allowed unlimited access to him. He loved his parents. And if Orlando was there so early it meant something had happened.

"How's Boston?" Bronx asked. Orlando glanced back at him as he made his way to the couch and sat down. He was glad Bronx's first question was about Boston. A part of him hoped that Bronx wasn't the mystery caller with all the pertinent information regarding Freemont. It didn't seem likely. Bronx wasn't the type. But Bronx also wasn't the type to screw his brother's wives and he'd lost his children. So Orlando wasn't sure what to make of his possibly mentally unstable son. He was there to find out. To ask all the right questions and gage for himself whether or not Bronx was the witness. There were lingering worries he wanted answers to. Was Bronx in love with Rose and seeking paternity for her child. And was he upset enough to want his brother out of the way.

"He's been better. He needs support. I can tell he's breaking down. Every day another piece of him is missing," he said, as he looked around at Bronx's fabulous home. He hoped he was coming across as relaxed and unfazed. It was quite the contrary. His mind was burning with questions. But Bronx would need to be taken along slowly. He was in a fragile state. Orlando smiled and got comfortable on his son's couch. It felt good to be there. Bronx let him in which meant he was feeling better. There were days the knocks went unanswered.

Orlando loved visiting his children. They lived such grand lifestyles and seemed to thrive effortlessly. It was a pity that they were still struggling with respecting boundaries. They had thrived in all other areas of their lives and he couldn't be prouder. No one consulted him any longer. They were all off into their own worlds. It was a good feeling. He had done his job. He had raised a tribe of well-established adults. No one was on drugs. No one was insane or mentally troubled. They all excelled in some way.

What Cicely had said about their children held a small amount of truth. They were jealous of one another on different levels and he knew it stemmed from him. But Bronx was one of the beneficiaries of Orlando's constant attention and praise. Yet still he too found himself at odds with one of his brothers. He had slept with Rose. Or at least that's what Heather's mother said. If that were true, it would be the biggest upset in their family. Bronx was the most stable. The smartest. The one everyone trusted. Orlando was there to do damage control. But first he needed to pick Bronx's brain. He was there to see how he was fairing since the funeral.

Whether life had normalized somewhat for him. But more than that he needed to see if Bronx's affair now had him an enemy of his own brother.

"You haven't been to see your brother. Everything okay?" Orlando asked. Bronx nodded.

"Why wouldn't it be?" he asked.

"Because you haven't been to see him. That's not like you. You are one of the first to show up and support. I know you're just getting your bearings. But still…You would never let him suffer something like that alone. Not you," Orlando noted. Bronx rubbed his goatee and walked to an adjacent sofa and sat down.

"I am not in a good way pop. I have lost everything. My world has crumbled. You have no idea. All of your children are alive and well. Not mines! My boys died before they had a chance to grow. A chance to thrive. Learn about life. Get married and have children of their own. They were robbed in the worst way imaginable. And I can't get them back. Can't hold them. I wasn't there! I should have been. Their mother was not responsible and I let her take them. This is on me. I let them down. And so, excuse me for not being concerned about Boston or anyone else for that matter.

He has my support. I am here. But I cannot be physically involved when I am so mentally devastated. Do you understand. Besides…What can I do? He needs lawyers not brothers," Bronx said.

Orlando took a moment. The words were hard to take. He could see the pain in his son's eyes and was not prepared for a rebuttal on the heels of such reflection. But he didn't agree. Bronx didn't sound like he was mourning in a healthy way. Saying he should have been there was saying he should have died alongside them. And that crushed Orlando.

"I don't know what you are feeling. You're right. But I have suffered through a horrible loss. When my father died, I fell into a bad way. I went down a destructive path. I fell into a deep depression. Then I fell further into despair when my brother, your uncle Dennis, died. I felt I was being punished. I get it son! Loss is terrible. And I couldn't imagine losing one of you. I love you. I'm here. You have a long way before the healing begins. But if you let depression take over, you'll sink into the abyss and heaven help you if that happens. You think your brother doesn't need you. That none of us need you. We lost them too. Part of your healing should include your family. And your brother needs the love and support of his family just as much as he needs good counsel," Orlando said, bracing himself for the hard question. The one that would reveal his true motive for the visit.

"I know pop. I want to. I just can't," Bronx said, looking down at the floor.

Orlando needed to say what he came there to say. It was a risk. Bronx could react in a way that pushed them far apart. It would be the first time. He'd never turned from his family. Orlando believed in their bond. And so, he decided to just say it.

"Does your absence have anything to do with Rose?" he asked.

Bronx raised a brow. His heartbeat began to elevate. He stared at his father realizing that the longer he took to answer, the more likely he would be unable to explain.

"No! Why would she keep me from my brother?" he said hoping his father backed away from that particular line of questioning.

Orlando smiled to hide his true feelings. He was disappointed. He could read the depths to which his son was involved with her. It was in his eyes. But his unwillingness to talk about it had backed Orlando in a corner and he wasn't prepared to challenge him. Bronx was too frail. He was still dealing with the worst loss a person could face. The death of a child. And he had lost two.

"There was mention of Heather feeling some sort of way about Rose and I just wondered if that came from something that hasn't been mentioned," Orlando said. Bronx shook his head.

"No! Heather didn't care for anyone but Heather. What was said?" Bronx asked.

"Her mother believes there was an affair between you two," Orlando revealed. Bronx's heart sank. He had told Chicago and Dayton had overheard. That was two people who knew. It wouldn't be long before Boston would hear about it. But Bronx wasn't ready to expose the affair. And he was beginning to regret mentioning it to Chicago.

"No! That's not true. I don't know where she got that from," Bronx said, his body tense from the awkward and premature conversation that he was not ready to have.

"I figured she was wrong. Marianne is just looking to blame. I asked because I know she is definitely capable. And I wondered if there was something more, that's all. But I will say this…Boston is not doing well. He is not as strong as you, contrary to popular belief. If something happened, no matter how innocent, tell him. Before someone else does and before she does. If it appears that he will be losing this case, I will confess. I will do that time. It would make me feel a lot better knowing that my family is intact. Strong. Close. And above all else, loyal. You all have to find a way to keep the temptations of this world from breaking your bond. When your mother and I are gone, you'll have your families. And you'll have each other," he said. Bronx teared up.

"What do you mean pop. You not doing no time. Don't say that. That's not going to happen," Bronx said, as he looked intensely at his father. Orlando smiled to keep him from worrying any further. But he couldn't take back what he said. He meant it.

"I will if it comes down to it. Sorry son! I'd do it for you to. I can't have my boys in jail. I've lived my life. I'm getting old. Better me than any of you," Orlando said, as he stood up.

"Well... If you want to talk, I'm here. I should get going. I don't want to add to your worries. I have to go see Max. It seems someone is talking to the prosecutor. Soon he will have enough to put your brother under the jail. They have a gun. The one that shot a bullet that lodged in the wall. But not the gun that killed him. The caller claims to have it.

They are supposed to be delivering it. I don't know what will happen if that happens. Your mother will be no good after that. She knows I am stepping in if I have to. No one wins in this scenario. None of us will get past that. Behind losing our grandbabies we can't really take much more," Orlando said. He hoped to appeal to his son. Make him think. If it was him who was willing to destroy, he wanted him to think about all the people he would hurt in the process.

"I'll talk to you later. Love you son," Orlando said, as he walked towards the foyer. A letter with a huge green triangle logo caught his eye. He glanced at it. The letters D-N-A displayed prominently on the sealed envelope. A sinking feeling went through him.

Bronx hugged his father. "Love you pop. I'll come by and visit with mom. She tried to call me earlier. Tell her I was busy. I'll call her later," he said. Orlando pat his son on the back and walked out. Bronx watched him walk to his car. He shut the door slowly, shaking his head in disbelief. There was no one who knew the details. He wondered how the police had anything. The only ones with detail were Memphis, Denver, himself, Boston and Orlando. Memphis was too private to tell anyone and even though he was married now to Kendra, he doubted Memphis would reveal such negative information to his wife. There would be no need.

Denver told his women nothing about his past. It was part of their issue with him. He was known to keep secrets. So Bronx was sure Denver hadn't said anything.

Orlando wouldn't have spoken to anyone about such a dark part of his past. Not even Cicely had all the details. And Boston had just one person who ever got close enough to know anything. And he didn't see Rose backstabbing him in such a way.

Bronx thought hard. He realized that he *did* tell someone. Two people. Dayton and Heather. He remembered when Dayton came to him complaining, and the emotionally charged conversation turned to the past. Bronx ended up telling his curious younger brother some of the details of that night. Then there was the pillow talk with Heather.

She was his new wife and his attempt at being open with her led to him telling her about the night he was involved with a shooting on Freemont. He was puzzled. If someone was talking it was from a small circle. Bronx looked off. Something he remembered. A conversation he'd eaves dropped on, as Heather complained during one of her rants. Bronx could remember the night vividly. He and Heather had a heated exchange. She appeared fed up with not being able to do as she pleased. Bronx spoke his mind and exerted his tough love, keeping her home and away from the drugs she so desperately wanted that evening. Heather responded by giving him the cold shoulder all day.

Later that night while they slept, he awoke at two in the morning and found her gone. Bronx remembered walking through their home looking for her. Heather loved to lock herself in bathrooms. He walked to each one until he finally found her in the bathroom on their lower level. There he stood listening as she complained to someone about feeling watched and how he scared her. It seemed the person on the other end wanted to know what she meant to which Heather replied;

He is not the man he pretends to be. He was a gang banger in his past. He's done something terrible. Him and his brothers. He is capable of great bodily harm. I have proof and I'm not risking my life or the lives of my children.

Bronx remembered the way her words made him feel. But he also remembered being concerned about the freedom and open dialog she had with the other person at the end of that phone. It was someone she trusted. Bronx initially thought it was her mother. But now he wasn't so sure. Whoever she was talking to could have the whole story. Heather was a blabbermouth. Especially when she was high. Bronx wondered who she confided in. He shook his head no. He hoped it wasn't who he thought. Faison.

"Chi. Where are you?" Bronx asked.

"Me and Jan getting ready for family night. We got the popcorn popped and we going to rent a movie with the kids. What's up?" Chicago asked.

"I need to swing by and get that bag of Heather's personal belongings," he said. Chicago paused.

"Sure B. It's still in my car in the glove compartment. You on your way?" he asked.

"Yep!" Bronx replied.

Bronx removed the phone slowly from the thick plastic bag marked with a large symbol and the word *Biohazard* on it. He could see dried blood on the phone. It brought back the pain of that night. Bronx sat the phone on the sofa and took a few breaths, dropping his head and trying to suppress the need to cry. If one tear emerged, it would be the beginning of an unstoppable force.

"Okay. Okay," he whispered, as he picked the phone up plugged it in. Soon the beginning of a charge allowed him to turn it on. Bronx flipped through the calls then the texts briefly, looking for something that stuck out. Heather's whole life was there. Bronx looked at her apps. She had tons of them. All things she found interest in, or used, were there. Her banking apps. Music apps. Dozens of downloaded games and other fun things. Bronx flipped through her pics. There were thousands. Too many to look at but he would still try.

"Blake," he said in a low voice as he looked at his youngest son's face. A pic of him holding a large water gun played at Bronx's heartstrings. Bronx remembered the day. He and Heather had taken the kids to a water park. He flipped through the pics stopping on one of Devon eating a cupcake compliments of a bakery they frequented. Bronx remembered the owner giving his sons free cupcakes after Bronx bought a box of them to take to Raleigh's house. He was dropping the kids off so he and Heather could go to counseling. It was another fond memory.

Bronx looked at dozens of photos then exited her gallery and went into her phone log. It wasn't long before his anger returned. Dozens of calls to Faison littered the phone list. Bronx exited the list and went to her messages. He scrolled her texts but was unable to find one with Faison's name. Bronx furled his brow. As much as she called him it was unlikely that they never exchanged text. Bronx began to read different texts. Soon he tapped on one that was extensive. The name was unfamiliar. A woman named Fallon. Bronx was sure he'd never heard the name before. He began to read the messages. It soon became apparent that it was a second phone for Faison. Bronx went back to the phone log. He could see that same name was tied to some of the later calls. It seemed Faison and Heather were hiding their calls.

Bronx went back into the messages and tapped on the name *Fallon*. He scrolled to the top and started to read. Bronx was in shock at what they had been talking about. He paused and sat the phone down. He needed a drink. He would be there for a minute and in order to get through it, he needed something to calm his nerves. Bronx went to his bar, poured a glass of cognac and returned to his bedroom. He sat back on a stack of pillows and got comfortable. He read a few of the more intimate messages then stared off. He took a sip then gulped down the drink in one swallow. "Alright," he said, as he sat the phone on the nightstand. He didn't have the stomach for it.

"Uhhh," Bronx jolted wake. Tiny beads of sweat covered the better top half of his body. He glanced at the clock. It was becoming impossible to sleep through the night. Nightmares and morbid thoughts that controlled his mental sanity plagued him. Bronx sat on the side of the bed. "It was just a nightmare," he said. His eyes dropped to Heather's phone. Something in him was ready to go through it.

Bronx opened up the list of messages Heather had with the person saved in her phone as *Fallon*. He scrolled to the top, bypassing dozens of texts. He began to read the dates, times and words of each text. He expected it would take a while. The texts dated back over six months. It was a daunting task. But he felt something was there. He just didn't know what;

Need to bump into you. I need something to get me through the night. I'm stressed. Can I come now.

Yep. Come now. Don't have me waiting like last time.

Ok. But I can't stop at the bank. He monitors the money I take out. He's always looking for proof.

I got you. Hope he don't follow you. He roll up on me this time, gon get his shit blew out.

Shut up. He's asleep.

You must of put that pussy on him. Jealous. Sad emoji.

OMG. No I didn't. He came home late and crashed. Besides…We not fucking right now. I got him on punishment. So I need some dick. I'm horny as fuck.

I got that too. Come on.

OMW.

Bronx scrolled past the texts as anger took hold. He always believed she was fucking and he was reading the proof of it and wishing he could resurrect her from the grave. Bronx scrolled until something caught his eye. He stopped. His eyes widened as he read the exchange;

This muthafucka has filed for me not to see my kids. Actually taking me to court to get custody. What man does that.

Damn sexy. It's always nigga's like him that do the most. Pretty boy ass nigga. What the fuck is his problem. Can he do that. You been busted using again.

No stupid. Of course not. He's doing it cause his punk ass brother's keep telling him to leave me and take my kids. As if they cut from the holy grail. Them muthafucka's is dirty. They may have money now but they weren't always businessmen.

What you mean?

They dressed up dope boys. And they did something that could get them locked up for life. I'll tell you about it when I see you. He lucky I don't just tell the cops. I'm not going to just give him my boys. I will play dirty.

Really. So that good boy, suit wearing bullshit is just for show. Knew it! I hate that muthafucka. You should tell what you know. Get his ass locked the fuck up. He won't be takin shit then.

Yea. And their father was covering it up. Now they friends with governors and mayors. How ironic. I could ruin them.

Do what you have to. If he plays dirty, then hit him where it hurts. If you know something, say something.

Otherwise you gonna fuck yourself. Fuck em. If you can't, I will. I ain't scared of that bitch.

Yeah. IDK. I'll see you in a minute.

Yep.

Bronx sat her phone down. He swallowed hard. It was worse than he suspected. He never imagined she would talk about things so detrimental to his family's way of life. Things he told her between the sheets in private. "Damn. Ok," he said, with a seriousness, as his guilty conscience began to resolve. In a split second he came to a conclusion that would now be between him, and that part of him that dwelled in the low waters. It was his fault. The axe had been swung by his own hand. And only he could undo it.

Chapter Eleven – Ride or Die

*R*ose drove down 18th Street on her way to meet Kendra at Little Rascals. She was anxious to get there and see what she was so desperate to tell her. Kendra was with her girls and unable to go into details. The women agreed to meet. Kendra was already in the area and so she just needed to get there.

Rose was nervous. Kendra wouldn't say anything more. The presence of her two daughters prevented her from talking. "Come on," she shouted, as a car jumped in front of her then slowed. Rose jumped lanes and went around the car turning onto Clark Street. She had a short drive to go before she would be there. Each minute was intense. The way her life was going she wouldn't be surprised by any new revelations. Nothing could be worse than Ashley possibly being Boston's baby's mom. And with the fallout after the sale of Rockwater, she had to brace herself for endless possibilities when it came to the St. Rocks and Boston.

He was fuming over her new money and appointed position within his company. Rose was locked in. If she wanted the five hundred million she had to take a role within Fritch's new company. She had yet to step foot in Rockwater. The agreed start date was still a few months away. But Rose was ready. She had already received some of the money. She was rich beyond her wildest dreams yet her world was crumbling beneath her. And she missed Boston. She was waiting on the ball to drop. Her last affair that would be his unraveling. Boston's calls had suddenly came to a halt. And she feared him. He was a plotter. Clever and bold. He would strike out.

Rose drove past Kendra and waved then drove around the back and parked in her usual spot. She had a new employee working. Tina was under the weather and April hadn't returned since the hospital stay, so she had to hire someone. A young woman named Miracle who seemed to thrive in sales. Eboni had taken on more of a nanny role and was only working at the boutiques occasionally.

"Miracle…How are things today?" Rose asked, as she walked into the main part of her boutique. Miracle could see Rose was distracted. She looked outside then sat her purse down and waited near the entrance.

"Everything is great! We're all sold out of the *BabeeTrac* Jogging Suits. I wanted to check with you before I placed another order. The price went up," Miracle stated.

"Oh no worries. Order them right away," Rose said, as she watched Kendra and her girls get out of the car.

Miracle glanced outside to see what had Rose's attention. She could see the woman and two young girls walking towards the store. Miracle was still getting to know everyone. It was overwhelming to be working for the wife of such a prominent man. She admired Rose. The astute businesswoman who was also kind and generous. Miracle felt lucky to have gotten the position at the store that was growing in popularity. Her cold call to the store and subsequent conversation with Tina ended with her being hired the next day.

"Hey," Kendra said, as her girls ran straight to the cotton candy machine near the lounge.

"Miracle...Can you do me a favor and get the girls some cotton candy. Kendra and I are going to step over here and talk for a minute," Rose asked.

"Sure," Miracle said, as she walked towards the lounge. Rose waited until she was no longer within ear shy of what would be revealed. It was a tense moment.

"Please don't tell me any bad news. I can't. Not now. Boston has stopped all calls. He's pissed because I struck a deal for myself when he is the one giving up on life. I don't recognize the man he is right now. He wants to plea bargain with the prosecutor. Actually plea! Can you believe that! Which means he'll have to do time. Even from jail he wants to control me. Give me what he wants me to have. And Orlando and Cicely have lost it. The family doesn't want me with him. They want me gone. I'm doing everyone a favor here. It's for the best, you know. It's just a matter of time before he finds out I've betrayed him," Rose said, as she tried to appear strong in front of her friend. The truth was she was heartbroken.

"You've apologized for all that. You made your peace. Any more secrets, then tell him Rose. You have to. And you must demand that he come clean. That's they only way you will heal. Don't turn from him now. The money is irrelevant. But of course he won't see it that way because he doesn't want to lose you," Kendra said then sighed before continuing with her reason for being there.

"Okay so don't flip out. I have no idea what all this means. I didn't see it. But um… Viv told me she saw Dayton put a stick in Brooklyn's mouth," Kendra said, her eyes peering into Rose's. She waited for Rose to accept the words. But the furled brows meant she needed more time.

"Rose. Did you understand what I said?" she asked. Rose's lips trembled. Her efforts to speak were in vain as her mind danced around the topic. She was sure Kendra did not mean a tree branch. Soon an image appeared. Rose covered her mouth and gasped. It couldn't be. Her worst nightmare was not coming true.

"What the fuck Kendra. Stuck what in her mouth? No! No!" Rose panicked. "Let's calm down and think about this. The only thing I could come up with is one of those testing swabs. Like DNA," Kendra replied. Rose took a step away.

"What the hell! When?" she asked.

"It had to happen that last time he came over. Remember that day he came to my house and spent some time with us? He stayed for a while. Remember?" Kendra asked. Rose nodded slowly.

"Oh my god. No! What has he done? I gotta go," Rose said, as she rushed off.

"Rose wait! Wait! You have to be careful. You know he can be violent. Wait!" Kendra shouted, as she ran behind her friend. All she could think of was April and the time she had to be hospitalized behind Dayton's fury. Rose's reaction now answered the question of which brother she'd had an affair with. Kendra misread the reaction. She had no idea it was Bronx. Her conversation that day with Rose left more questions than answers. She now stood bewildered at her friend and her reasons behind such a low-down move. She had done enough for a lifetime yet there was yet another notch on her tree of shame. She had obviously slept with Dayton. But Kendra had no time to blame. Her first reaction was to try to help Rose come up with a plan. But Rose was not having it.

Rose bolted towards the back door. Her greatest fear was being realized prematurely. It would devastate an already broken man and it would catapult her back into a spotlight she worked hard to dim. It was inevitable, but she needed to appeal to the person responsible. He had no right. It was Noor all over again. Boston deserved better.

Rose burst through the door. She could hear Kendra calling her name. She was aware of what it looked like. She wasn't going to confront Dayton. He had no dog in the fight. The DNA was taken for Bronx. She was sure. And she was going to confront him.

*T*acoma walked the yard with her two English Bulldogs, taking in the breeze. The sound of her lover's car was idling in the background. Marti still had not pulled off and Tacoma wasn't willing to run behind her this time. She was incensed and had not come down from the emotional high after their heated debate. Marti's strong opinion over something she was not privy to was not appreciated and Tacoma didn't mince words about her disapproval.

"Damn!" Tacoma mumbled as she watched Marti walk purposeful in her direction. She stopped, refusing to meet her half way. The yard was massive. She would need to come the entire way if she had something more to say. Tacoma hoped she picked her embellished words a little more carefully this time. The insults were hard to take.

"I am not leaving yet. I wasn't finished," Marti huffed. Tacoma looked away.

"Say whatever else you have to say and leave. I'm not going to debate with you about my family. What I do. You knew what it was when we first hooked up. I can't be ran. I run this shit. Mind your business when it comes to me and mine. I didn't ask your opinion on anything and the fact that you even know what happened pisses me the fuck off. Stay out my gotdamn phone Marti or we going to keep having problems," Tacoma shouted.

Marti felt like an outsider. She was always *minding her business*. Trying to keep such tight reins on her self-expression was proving difficult. The need to walk on egg shells in order to get along was waning. She was done filtering her thoughts and words in order to remain in the life of the only woman she ever loved.

They were supposed to be partners. Open to each other. Committed to a healthy relationship. Marti felt Tacoma was lucky to have her. She was loyal, honest and in love. Which was a stark contrast to her last love. Rumors of infidelity plagued Tacoma's previous relationship, and Marti waited in the background for the opportunity to tell her how she felt. She was ready to pick up the pieces and one day she got her chance. There was something about the consummate bad girl who was as tough as men, with enough charm and sex appeal to rival her sexy male counterparts. It didn't take long. Tacoma's old lover was still very much attracted to men and the two finally ended their tumultuous affair. Marti was glad it ended but always lived in fear of her ex returning. They were opposites and Marti wondered if Tacoma missed the drama and fire of the lover she affectionately called Sweetpea. Something else that hurt since Tacoma had no sweet nickname for her.

"Wow! I don't go through your phone Tae. You left it. Remember! Someone was texting you that day, like crazy, and I was just checking to make sure it wasn't an emergency. With all that's going on in your family I thought I should. But how can I ignore that text? Can I even trust you? I thought I could. But if you can do that to your own brother and sleep at night, then I wonder sometimes if maybe I made a mistake," Marti said. Tacoma leaned back, her eyes bulging wide.

"Can you trust me? Interesting! A few texts, and now you question us. Like I said Marti, I'm not going to keep going back and forth with you."

Marti shook her head slowly as she stared Tacoma down. She didn't get that her behavior was toxic. She didn't get to pick and choose who someone loved. It was on Boston who he loved. The move she made to get rid of Rose was not only dirty is what the type of behavior anyone would question. Paying Rose's ex friend to pretend her child was Boston's in order to inflict enough pain that she would leave, was a deplorable act and she wouldn't be sitting idly by while it continued.

"You don't get it do you. He knows who she is. He loves her still. He adores her. Too bad you don't know that kind of love. The kind that makes you willing to give a person a thousand chances, even after they deserves none. He sees her. Mark my word, that woman has scars the likes of which you couldn't begin to imagine. Yeah…I know things. I heard about her. She was in the system. So was I. I know what that means if you're not one of the lucky ones. You need to back off! He is no angel. In order for your little scheme to work it means he slept with that woman and that makes him just as bad," Marti said.

Tacoma stood speechless. She remembered Boston's excitement the next day after meeting Max's then girlfriend. She had never seen him so wound up. It was instant for him and he vowed that if he got her, he would never let her go. Even after the affair with Denver and the information he found out about his new wife, he still wanted to stay. He revealed then that he had "messed up" and refused to go into detail. She later learned that Ashley was his big mess up. But after the multiple affairs, she wanted Rose out. Even though Boston was having his as well. And Marti didn't like the interference. Tacoma was being what she hated in other people. Untrustworthy.

"I don't know you at all. I'm ashamed of this. Call me when the old Tacoma returns. The one who would never break her brother's heart by tearing him apart from his family," Marti said, as she turned and left. Tacoma watched her, as regret began to slowly take hold.

"What up," Tacoma said, as she entered Dayton's new condo. Bronx shelled out a million dollars to put his brother close to his favorite spot. Downtown Chicago. Dayton was still decorating and had just received the delivery of his new dining room set. Tacoma was anxious to see her brother's new pad. He had only been in it a week. Bronx was generous. And Dayton was happy. There were no conditions with the purchase. It was free and clear in his name and he owed his brother for showing him love. Orlando would have purchased him something fancy. But Dayton would rather it be Bronx. His easy to get along with brother who had no motive.

"What up. You bring me some food too? What you got in that bag?" Dayton asked. Tacoma walked in and looked around.

"Damn Dae! Who picked it out?" she asked.

"I did. I found it and Bronx just wrote a check. This muthafucka is a palace. Marble floors. Gold wallpaper. Bad ass chandeliers throughout. I love it here. I ain't left out in life three days. Been getting food delivered," he chuckled.

Tacoma walked to his new dining room set and placed the food on the table. "Get me something to drink," she said. Dayton went into his kitchen and returned with two coolers. "Boy! Not no damn cooler. Like a soda or something. Save that shit for one of yo bitches," Tacoma said. "You drink coolers. Don't front," he joked. "Yeah. But not with my food. I want a coke," Tacoma said, as she sat and got comfortable.

"You talked to pop?" Dayton said, as he entered with two cans of orange pop. Tacoma gave a look. "This all I had," he said in his defense, snapping the tab back and handing it to her.

"That good. Yeah…I went by to see ma. Pop was home. He was happy. Something about Boston and Max poking holes in the evidence. It looks like he might get out on bond. Max is meeting with the prosecutor. If they drop the charge to manslaughter, he'll get out. Max said after that, he will fight to get the charges thrown out altogether. He told pop it's easier if he can get the charges reduced first. It makes them look incompetent. Like they don't really have a case," Tacoma said. Dayton nodded as he dug into his meal of meatloaf, mashed potatoes and asparagus.

"I'm starting to have doubts about it. The shit aint right. And when Boston comes home…I'm worried," she said.

"Worried about what? We're good. He got other things to worry about. Like the fact that his wife took his money and split. He ain't checking for Ashley. That shit was nothing. He just gonna think she had it out for Rose and decided to make some shit up," Dayton said with a light chuckle. Tacoma didn't find it amusing.

Rose was never supposed to go and question Ashley. Tacoma could see the writing on the wall. Ashley was probably terrified of what Boston would do. Her fears could possibly blow their cover.

"No he won't overlook it. Ashley was long gone. We should have never did this shit. Ashley said she's seen Rose a few times. Now she running scared. She think Boston gonna show up next. I don't trust her. What if she tells Rose it was a set up. What if she calls Boston and tells him we paid her to lie. This is fucked up. This shit on you. Trying to get rid of Rose! Now look! This shit is going to backfire," Tacoma said, as she looked to Dayton for answers. It was his idea. It was her money. They were in over their head playing with the one brother who did not play games.

"Ashley not all that scary. More money will shut her up. I got this. And I ain't scared of him finding out. Not anymore. Everyone wants Rose gone. Nobody more than you. Admit it. You hate her," he said. Tacoma nodded.

"Yeah I do. But you don't. So what gives. Tell me why you want them to split up so bad," she asked. Dayton took a bite of his food.

"Same as you. She's trouble. Boston and Phoenix don't speak. Him and Denver stay into it. I mean...She is single handedly turning brothers against one another," he said. Tacoma glanced at him. There was emotion in his words. She wondered what was really eating at him. He never cared who his brothers fucked. And they stayed into some kind of disagreement. They were all high strung, sexually charged men with their pick of women. It didn't add up.

*T*he chime of the doorbell didn't wake Bronx from his afternoon slumber on his couch in front of the television. What was supposed to be a relaxing moment turned into him drifting off to sleep. "Mhmm," Bronx moaned, as he dreamed a sweet dream that was quickly changing.

He was at a park with his boys. The sound of their unmistakable laughter had him all smiles, as he ran toward their voice. The haze of the foggy afternoon began to thicken. Bronx ran through it. He called to them. The fog was too dense to see through and he could hear their voices fading. *Blake...Devon...*he called. Over here, Devon's fading voice said. Bronx became frantic. He wanted to see their eyes. Touch them. Take them out of the park and somewhere safe where he could protect them. Bronx moaned then turned on his side. The movement awakened him slightly. He bolted up. "Fuck!" he mumbled. Just then he heard the knock at his door.

"What!" he blurted, as he tried to get his bearing. Bronx stood up and looked at his watch. He walked to the door and looked out the peep hole. To his surprise Rose stood on his porch with her arms crossed looking around. It weighed heavy on him. A multitude of varied emotions flooded his already weakened heart. It was her. The woman he never expected to see. Not in a one on one situation. Maybe at parties. Or perhaps at cookouts. Never standing on his porch.

Bronx collected his thoughts and opened the door. Their eyes connected with an undeniable intensity. A lot had happened. With her. Especially with him. It was an intensity that neither one of them would foresaw or expected. Bronx opened his glass screen door and allowed her in. Rose walked in slowly. Her heart racing. He was the only brother she actually had feelings for. But she wasn't there to rekindle anything. She was there to stop him before her did something he would regret. Because no matter what the paper said, there was the reality of the situation.

Bronx watched the back of Rose still shocked that she was there. Part of him wanted to kiss her. Take her. But part of him feared the rejection. He took a moment to calm the vigorous beat of his heart. It would be worth the rejection.

Getting close enough to smell her. To feel her skin, if for a moment.

Rose walked towards his kitchen counter in silence. She took the time to lessen the anxiety that being in his presence was causing. A different woman stood before him. One who was slowly purging the inner broken part of herself. Being a mother had a surprising effect. One that was initially slow to take hold until Brooklyn's birth. The baby she had doubts about. The child who could change her life. Reality never sat so clearly in her path. There was never a threat to really lose Boston until now. She was desperate.

"I won't beat around the bush Bronx. I know you're probably wondering why I'm here," she said. Bronx took a few steps in her direction, stopping far enough away to read her body language, but close enough to charge her for a kiss if she so much as threw a small hint that he could. Bronx's hopes were dashed in an instant. She looked like a woman on official business. Gone was the sultry look. The seductive way of being. She stood like a teacher at the head of the class and he was the bad boy getting reprimanded.

"I know about the swabs. How could you? How! Think about what that will do. It will affect everyone. And Boston…He will lose himself. Not because of me so much as it is with you. I know losing the boys hurt. But this won't make you feel any better. I'm sorry that you can't get past that night we had. Neither could I. Not until I forgave him and fell in love with him all over again. When he came back home with Noor, I was the happiest girl in the world. I realized then that I could never live without him. Even now, with everything that he has done, I still can't. I deserve worse. I get it. I get him. I get you. I do. In another life it would be you. But I'm in this life, with him, until we say otherwise," she cried, realizing her last words should have remained unsaid. He was the only other person she loved. But it failed in comparison to Boston. And so, it needed to be said.

"She is mine. You know it and I know it. Her eyes…Grey! Her hair…sandy brown. Right?" he said. Rose stared at him. Bronx nodded.

"Yeah…I thought so. She belongs to me. He's in jail for murder and he's not coming home. I will wait. But you need to think about that. I want you with me. I know my family will disown me. I'll be good, as long as I have you. We can go away. You just have to say yes," he said.

Rose shook her head. She believed he had gone mad. The loss of the children had him speaking in a way she never thought possible. Not Bronx. The peacemaker. The tower of strength. The one who was fatherly with his siblings. And the one who found strength after their night of passion and refused to give her a second of his time. It was her who wanted more. She was angry at the way he treated her. Disregarded, as he pretended not to care. And now he was prepared to run off and turn from all that he loved for the sake of love. Rose wasn't going anywhere. And he needed to get back to reality. Her and Brooklyn could not save him from the current state he was in. Rose needed him to see it was sorrow guiding his words. Pain controlling his thoughts. What he wanted wasn't possible for the reasons she had already said. She loved Boston.

"Your family needs you. Boston needs you. This is not who you are. You pulled from me at a time when I was ready to continue betraying my husband because that is who you are. A man of honor. You tried to correct a wrong and you did. You stayed from me. Not one look. Not one call. All out of respect. You are someone with their morality intact. This is not you," Rose said, as she walked towards him. She stopped within a foot of him, and reached out to hold his hand.

"I'm sorry you lost your children but it's not fair to take Boston's in their place. Please don't," Rose said, as she kissed his cheek and walked to his door.

Rose opened the door and looked back. Bronx couldn't face her. She wiped her eyes. She understood. He had to get a hold of the wayward boat he had sailed on, and turn back to shore. It was taking him in the wrong direction.

"Brooklyn deserves her entire family. Not be the odd man out. I'm pregnant again. No one knows. I have left the home I share with him so I can be at peace. Your family is driving me crazy and I can't deal with the stress right now. Why would you put Dayton in the middle? He is determined for Boston to find out. You need to talk to him. You need to make things right. Even Brooklyn needs you. Think about how she would feel if she was the only one with such a checkered past. The daughter of one of the brothers. The shame it will cause her and it won't even be her fault. It could destroy things for her. I know a little something about being a destroyed little girl. Please don't do that to my child," Rose said, as she left.

Bronx was blown away by her words. He turned and walked to the doorway. He watched as she pulled off. He had a lot to consider. Reality was hitting hard. Bronx shut the door and leaned on it. His legs felt weak under him.

"What am I doing," he whispered. He wasn't sure. Was it love. Or was it lust he hoped would be love. The baby he hoped would replace a void left by the death of his children. Bronx rubbed his eyes trying to remove the sting of tears.

"My Devon. Blake. Ahhh…," he cried, as he fell to the floor. One minute turned into twenty. Bronx laid there curled in a fetal position while the images of his children took hold. The air was inadequate. His fast breaths and occasional bleats were like cracked windows allowing fresh air in. Bronx stayed there for over two hours. Again. It was another small step towards healing.

"Get the fuck out of here man!" the gentleman laughed as his noddle legs prepared to take him crashing to the ground. Bronx sat in his housekeeper's car watching as Faison and another young lady walked from an area of trees just beyond the apartment to the parking lot. They were heavily intoxicated or high or both. Bronx sat a pair of dark

Ray Bans covering his eyes. He looked like the feds staking out their prey. His well selected spot between the garbage area and a tree was perfect. And Lucy's inconspicuous car was the perfect blend.

The city light just above needed replacing. An annoying fact for the residents of Tuscany Garden and the answer to a problem for Bronx. Faison was being his same disgusting self, as he fondled the woman almost to a point of indecency, right out in the open. Bronx shook his head. It was the same way he handled Heather. A part of his character that nearly got his head blown off that fateful day.

Bronx was shocked at how cool he was. There was no bead of sweat. His hands did not shake. Only the rising of what once simmered beneath came from him. It was an anger that raged and he couldn't settle it down. The man, who by all accounts was the reason Heather was hooked on drugs, was now the man trying to take down his family. And Bronx was there to settle old scores. His problems were with him. Not his father and not his brother. The only thing saving him from the onslaught that would be his swift exit from this life was the fact that there was someone with him. Someone's daughter. Sister. Possibly someone's wife. He would get a pass this day.

Max walked out of the prosecutor's office smiling. It was a small victory for Boston. With no witness yet and without the gun that actually fired the shot that killed the victim, they didn't have much. The gun they had only proved Boston was there at some point and fired a round. He would be an accessory to murder at the least. Max asked that they reduce the charges and stop seeking *no bond* for his client.

The prosecutor was fired up and unapologetic of his belief that he had the right man. But the law was the law. He would have to get his witness in and on board for the stronger charge of murder or reduce it to a lesser charge. He was gunning for a win over the case that was now all in the papers. The new billionaire who sat in a jail cell awaiting trial on murder charges.

Max pushed the narrative that the prosecutor was going after a man simply because of the color of his skin. He threatened to help the papers push that story and the prosecutor was back-peddling. The St. Rocks were powerful. It was a threat that worked for the moment.

"Hey! Got some good news," Max said. Boston stared out with a spacey look that Max hadn't seen.

"What going on. Come on man. Don't lose it on me now. Not when I have good news. You're going home soon. Your case has to go before the judge again. The prosecutor is reducing the charges. They just don't have enough at the moment. You'll get a bond. This is just preliminaries. I am still fighting for all charges to be dropped. But it's a process like I told you. Reduced charges get dropped all day long. It's an uphill battle that I've fought and won many times. Trust me. They have zip. A bullet in the wall. A spit behind a building in a neighborhood you lived in. An area you trekked through, rode your bikes through. Circumstantial bullshit. I got this," Max said, smiling as he looked through his briefcase. He glanced up at his client. Boston stared at him. His spacey look was replaced with one of anger. Max slammed his briefcase closed and placed his arm on it and leaned in.

"Look! If you're mad, save it. This was the best I could do. Did you hear me. You're going home. What the fuck else matters at this point," he said.

"I heard you," he said, pausing. Max narrowed his gaze. "What?" he said, his client wasn't done. Boston looked like he'd been floored by the worst news ever. It didn't add up. "What Boss. What the fuck," Max said.

"I need you to take on another case," Boston said.

Max lifted a brow. He was in over his head in a murder case with a person who knew enough about that night, to successfully get a billionaire Fortune 500 company owner arrested. What else could Boston actually need.

He was in the fight for his life. Max couldn't see the need to pile more shit on top of the heap of shit he was in.

"What?" Max asked.

Boston looked fiercely at him and sat back. Max prepared himself. He could take on whatever Boston needed so long as it did not take away from his time on the case. They were not in the clear. There was a lot more work to be done.

"Spit it out. You push until you get your way. So let's have it. How bad could it possibly be," Max said. Boston smirked then look intensely at him. This was the man he robbed of his woman after she stole his heart. And he was now an embattled husband in an emotional war with her. His life needed to change. Starting with his home life.

"I need a divorce from my wife!"

Max stopped cold. He looked at Boston. His request was breaking one of Max's old rules. One he still was prepared to enforce. He was not going to go against his ex. Not then and not this day. Boston had nerve. He was not that indebted.

"Are you serious," he said, as he shut his briefcase and snatched it from the table. "You never cease to amaze me. You are asking me to help you divorce the woman you came to my home and took. My first love. The woman I planned to marry. Unfucking believable! Do I have to say it. Do I! Do you not know that the answer is a big fucking no! Absolutely not! Don't press your luck. I'm going to get your ass out of here. That is my only concern at the moment. Whatever the fuck you and her do is ya'll fucking business. I am staying out of it. Ask your father to help you with that.

I'm sure he'll get right on it. I know how your family feels about her," Max said. Boston furrowed.

"Was all that shit necessary. A *no* would have sufficed. And what the fuck you mean *how my family feels*. Somebody been feeding you bullshit," Boston said. Max stopped and stared.

"Listen…Don't shoot the messenger. She is on the outs with them. Enemy number one. Or did you not know that. They treat you like breakable glass. You are their precious Boston! They protect your ass from everything. So much so, that you're on the outside looking in. Maybe if you were less bullying and more open to allowing people to express themselves without fear, you would know what the fuck is going on in your own gotdamn family. Look…I have to go. You'll be home in a few days. The prosecutor will file the new charges and you will get a hearing on it. Be ready. Clear your mind. And don't get a divorce until this shit is over. You taking on too much. For real. That my best advice," Max said, as he left the counsel room.

Boston sat stunned. He wondered what was going on with his family and his wife. Max was harsh, but some of his words were spot on. Phoenix had embellished the details with Max, he was sure of it, but some things rang true. And if the family had in fact turned on Rose in his absence, no one was forthcoming with that bit. Maybe it was because they felt he had a bigger burden to carry than how they felt about his other half. But someone had been dirty. He was sure the information about his past with Carmen and the fling with Ashley had come from someone within his camp.

I have to get out of here. Get my life in order. This is all stemming from one person. It has to be, he thought, as he sorted through the details. Boston stood and walked to the doors. He was going home and he would deal with everyone then. He was in the fight of his life and was dealing with more than any one of them could handle. None of them had a right to be at war with his vulnerable wife. Only he had that particular privilege.

Boston stood up and walked to the adjacent door as the guard stood prepared to escort back to the gold section. That was the nickname of the area they placed high profile prisoners and anyone that needed extra protection from the general population. It wasn't special. Same cell. Same smell. Same shitty guards with shitty attitudes. He was over it.

Boston was heavy in thought. His life had been on public display. His faults and hers were continued public displays of two people not getting it right. Their love was supposed to transcend them into a bliss that few reached. They had been crazy about each other from day one. And now she wanted a divorce. Boston couldn't believe it. A divorce when he needed her most. And all because of one woman with all that she had put him through. Something else was wrong. He wondered if the pressure the family was placing on her was the reason. He couldn't pacify his family. He could only do what was in his heart and mind. With everything off the table; The money. The children. The sex. His brother's. The elephant in the room was them. Their relationship. Their bond. He had to be honest with himself and make the hard decision. Was it over.

Boston look at the other prisoners as he passed them. The glaring look of dismay in their eyes caused him to turn away. What pieces of them they'd left outside the iron wrought doors of Cook County Jail left vacancies in many of their spirits. He nodded at several men. His own strength was returning. He understood what a withered man looked like. Even the tough lost hope early on. The system wasn't designed for a black man to hold onto hope with a firm tight grip. But this walk felt different. His feet were lighter. His breaths were invigorating. Gone was the weight of the world. An energy noticed by his fellow house mates.

A man gave a thumbs up. Boston smiled at the elderly gentleman they called *Pops*. Soon he passed by Richie Rich. The man held his fist in the air. Another man named Spoons held his fist up to show his support. Not everyone took to the parade of sorts with its star prisoner at center stage. Some men were angry at the world and shouted obscenities hoping to garner some attention of their own. Anything to make them feel alive. But many showed their support. Men like him awaiting their fate as the world pressed on. Boston felt for any man who was innocent of the charges against him. It was no place for the guiltless. He had never felt so smothered. It was akin to being a caged animal. These men had families. People who were missing their contribution to the household. Some were fathers and husbands. So was he.

There was light at the end of the tunnel. He would be going home soon. The question was: Where was home? Was he going to his palatial estate on Cherry Hill Drive. Or was he going somewhere else. He had another home on Lakeview. He also owned a condominium in downtown Chicago. There were the new properties he purchased as investments in Colorado and Florida. Homes he'd never seen. He had been informed by his father that Rose hadn't been to their house on Cherry Hill in days. And that Eboni was back working for Chicago and had told everyone Rose moved but she wasn't sure where. It was the past being played out again only this time the infidelity was on him and Rose was gone.

Boston walked into his cell and stared at the small six by eight box he called home. A picture Noor painted with her fingers was taped to the wall. The painting comprised of just three colors and was better than any Picasso he could have hung in its place. Boston took a seat. It was time to explore his options. Dig deep into that part of him that was the essence of who he was. It wasn't easy coming to a conclusion about the only woman he'd ever loved. Thinking of her was torment. He'd always kept from it. His inability to see or touch her had almost driven him mad. Absence did not make the heart grow fonder.

Boston could picture her. As if she was right beside him. Her eyes appearing like an apparition. He could see the brown and green texture of their hazel color. He could see her mouth. Her smile. It wasn't long before he was wound up like a top. Boston shook his head. No matter how much love there was between them, they would be lost without trust. And if she no longer trusted him, she would soon resort to her old ways. He had to leave. He couldn't take much more. His strength was waning. There could be no more affairs.

And he wasn't so sure there wouldn't be affairs. At least on her part.

"Mr Hill," Max said, as he shook the prosecutor's hand.

"Sit," Allen said, as he sat at his desk. "How can I help you?" he asked.

Max had the winning hand for the moment. They were going before the judge but he was still perplexed. The prosecutor's case was weak. Unless there was more, he didn't understand why they were still pursuing murder charges of any kind.

"Well Allen, I was hoping you had something more on my client. Otherwise, this case will have to be dismissed. The judge will rule in our favor. Is it pride that stops you from doing the right thing," Max asked.

"No! It's the taxpayers. No one likes murderers. Even rich ones. Your client doesn't get a pass because of who he is. This office has no personal vendetta against Mr. St. Rock. Only that justice was carried out. You know I'm not in position to drop the charges. I still have a witness. He promises to come forward within the next few days. Especially after I told him the case could get dismissed by the judge. It piqued his interest. He's done hiding. Says he doesn't care what enemies he makes. That means I'll have the murder weapon soon. So you see…This isn't over yet. Boston St. Rock is a murderer. And this office puts all murderers, rich or poor, behind bars. He may be the toast of the town but that does not help him win sympathy. He can not evade the law," he said. Max's hopes were dashed. If there was a witness and there was a murder weapon that would point to Boston, it would be a terrible blow.

"You have built this entire case around circumstantial evidence and the promises of some caller you never laid eyes on. If he had something you would have it by now. The caller is using your office to burn my client, probably from some past wrongs. If you continue to pursue these trumped up charges I will express my concerns publicly. It's been over four months," Max said.

"This witness is the reason we have what we do so far. He is afraid of the St. Rock's. Talking to him and convincing him to come forwards was like trying to talk a turtle from its shell. It had to be on his time. We have one of the weapons so far," he said. Max snickered.

"All you have is a gun that matches the bullet in a wall. Nothing more. And spit out in the open. In an accessible area where anyone could have spit. Hell, if you go back there now with a forensics team, you'll find more. It's an open alleyway. It's weak Allen and you know it. I going for a dismissal. See you in court," Max said, as he stormed out of Allen's office. Allen gave a light chuckled as he twirled the pencil between his fingers. He was worried. The caller didn't give a date or time for his grand appearance and he had about a week before the hearing. If he walked into court without more than spit and a gun that wasn't the murder weapon, his case would dry up like the Sahara Desert. Allen sat straight and picked up his phone.

"What's the status on the origin of that call?" he asked.

"Still working on it. We're waiting on Pacific Telemanagement to give us the location," the investigator said. Allen slammed the pencil down on his desk. It seemed nothing was working in his favor against the rich entitled Boston St. Rock. He had no personal vendetta only the drive to make an example of the new money billionaire. It seemed the dashing self-made man was popular and many either loved him or hated him. He was described as egocentric and Allen didn't like what that represented. He disliked the man he'd only heard about. And now he sought to make him an example. Someone else didn't like him. Allen wasn't too sure it wasn't someone in his own family given the rumors of infidelity among the brothers.

"How long does it take. Geez! Do I need to go there and personally run the information myself. Pay phones are obsolete. Isn't there like two in the whole gotdamn city. How hard can it be," he voiced in opposition to the workings of the system.

An investigator identified that the number had the same first three numbers as old pay phones in the Chicago area. Allen was incensed. It seemed he was pulling teeth with every request. Nothing was easy and Allen Hill was used to winning. He believed he was working against a flawed system and the criminals were winning. It was tiring. But after years and some premature graying, he was looking forward to a nice clean exit from his current position and an entrance into politics. This was his ticket.

Allen hung up and leaned back in his reclining, ergonomic leather chair and spun around to view the city. His mind raced through the details. He was sure he was missing something. He had no doubts that the caller was either at the crime scene or privy to someone close to the case. He knew things that weren't released to the public. Not even the Knoll family knew some of what he had in the files. Max had ninety percent. He was leaving something to the last minute. Yet still he needed the witness. Otherwise it was still weak at best.

Allen turned back around and decided to go through the evidence once more. His phone rang. He hit the do not disturb button and continued reading. Suddenly his door opened. His new clerk Katherine entered. An attractive blonde in a purple dress and heels and who's bubbly personality was not welcomed in the serious environment of the prosecutor's office. She was a few months on the job. Allen liked the bright eyes law student with dreams of making it to the top of the food chain on the short list of who's who in the legal world. There were a lot of players but few stars. Only a handful were on a first name basis with the residents of the city and Max Stone was one of them. She'd seen him come in. Her smile and charming greet was meant to sway him for a more informal introduction. But Max wasn't swayed. And the irresistible blonde bombshell wasn't done.

"I pushed do not disturb for a reason. If you're going to work here you have to get something right off the top. The DND button is crucial. You can't be interrupting a thought. A call. A meeting. You get what I'm saying," he stressed.

"Yes," she replied.

"Good. Now since you're here...what was it?" Allen asked.

"I have an important call for you," she said.

"And we know it's important because why. Because they said so," he said, glancing over his glasses then quickly looking down at the papers before him. Katherine rolled her eyes. He was impossible at times but she still liked him. he was direct and sometimes brutal but he was rational and he could take her career places.

"Yes. They did. Won't give their name. Should I send the call through?" she shot back. Allen chuckled. Katherine was a handful but she was smart. He liked that she didn't take his crap. It would make her a good lawyer one day.

"Yes. Send it through," he said.

"This is Allen," he said, as he held the phone. "Hello," he said still waiting for the caller to speak. Allen's brows creased. The thought of his time being wasted on a useless call was aggravating.

"Hello," he said. Suddenly a shaky voice uttered something barely audible into the phone.

"Wait! There he is again. Hold on," the voice said nervously. Allen held the phone. The caller began mumbling indistinctly. Something had the person on edge and Allen had no time for pranks or wrong numbers.

"This is Allen Hill. Did you call to speak with me?" he said, as he struggled to hear the words clearly.

"Someone is following me! Your office promised my identity would be confidential. You fucking promised me. I told you what she told me. That those men were dangerous. Now look. I'm not safe. I want to be put in witness protection right now," the caller said. Allen stood up. His eye widened. This was his witness and he was in danger.

"Where are you? I can have you picked up right now," Allen said. The caller held the phone. The warm office he complained about for the last two years now felt like a blazing inferno. If his witness was being followed then his life was in immediate danger. Allen began to fear for his life. It was hard to say whether the man was being paranoid or in fact was being followed. It wasn't a risk he was willing to take. Allen realized he knew nothing. No face. No address. No name. No work address. Nothing. If the man disappeared, he would never be able to wrap up his case.

"What's your name? I can't help you if I don't know who you are. At least tell me your name," he said.

"No! Someone in your office knows my name. And now my life is in danger. You people.... I can't trust you! I have to go. I'll be there tomorrow. Get me what I need or you get nothing. I want to be relocated to Fort Worth, Texas. I want money to start with. And I want a new identity. If I can't get these things, I'm out," the caller said.

"I can't get that by tomorrow. I have to put in...," Allen said before being interrupted.

"Then I'm out," the man said.

"Wait! Wait! Okay. Just come in. I'll get started on it now. But you have to trust me," he said. The man chuckled.

"I don't have to trust nothing but the man upstairs and my momma. That's it. And I don't trust her ass. I don't trust shit. I gotta go," he said before the line went dead. Allen looked at the phone then slammed it on the receiver. His secretary came running back in.

"Are you alright?" she asked.

"I need Robin Christi on the line now! If you don't know who she is, get acquainted. I need a social security package with everything including tickets to Fort Worth, Texas and two thousand dollars for my witness. I needed them yesterday. Now go," he said. The secretary stood waiting for more direction.

"Sir!" Katherine said.

"I don't have time to explain. Go talk to Terry. Terry Childress in Operations. And I advise you not to go to her all bewildered and scatter-brained. She will have zero tolerance."

*B*ronx stood in the shadows of the small wooded area next to the apartment complex of Faison Wilson, hoping he would make an exit. He had been stalking him the better part of the last week and was ready to silence the man who was going after his brother for reasons completely unknown. Bronx figured that Faison believed the killer was him when he made the first call. Faison probably thought all he had to do was give the information and the case would go to trial. He probably never counted on having to get more involved.

His long distance shot at the heart of his rival worked. Bronx was feeling the heat. Rose's words about a child who would be at a disadvantage hurt him deeply. Brooklyn was his child. And he would do anything to prevent her from having anything but a normal childhood if he could help it. He also owed Boston for the betrayal. For the inability to say no to a woman difficult to pass up. That night she walked in his room in nothing but the smallest, thinnest lace gown made him fold. It was game over.

Bronx was ready to clear his conscience. He had to undo what Heather did. His come-clean discussion that poured from an open heart ready to give completely had hit like a raging bull. Stories of mayhem that he never thought would come back to bite him in the ass, was fuel for a fire. The stories were meant excite. Entice. Women liked bad boys. And Heather was the type to covet such dangerous behaviors. But now those words were the catalyst for a man with more than a hundred reasons to want him destroyed.

Bronx emasculated him the day he held the gun in his hand and threatened what he thought was his wife's lover. And now Heather was dead. An unfortunate tragedy he was sure the man was blaming him for as well. It seemed the man was looking to right a wrong. It was ironic. So was he. They were in the same boat. Only one of them wouldn't make it out.

Bronx tried to blend in with the locals. His rich boy swag and upper echelon flare was hard to flatten. He was effortlessly fluid in ways that were now a detriment to his plan. It was important to stay from prying eyes. He stood in black denim and a black button down shirt with a blunt in his mouth meant to give a reason for his presence among the trees. It was a spot for users. He could see dozens of cigarette butts, condoms and a hypodermic needle among the debris.

A man and woman walked in the distance. The man whistled and waited for someone to come to their balcony. Bronx stood behind the tree. A baseball cap concealed most of his features. Suddenly someone approached him from behind.

"Hey. Can I get a smoke?" a voice said. Bronx turned around. It was surprising to see someone was able to get so close to him so fast. The man moved like a cheetah. Swiftly and without detection. Bronx tried to appear relaxed, as his heart nearly pumped out of his chest. This was exactly what he hoped to avoid.

He shook his head no and leaned back on the tree. The man narrowed his gaze. "You got a dollar man?" the man asked, as he walked closer. "Naw," Bronx replied, looking the man over. *Get the fuck on*, Bronx thought. He had no time for the homeless man. Handing him a dollar would make him stand out. He had money. Plenty. But it was the wrong time to be generous. No one in that area freely gave away dollars. The man gave up and walked away. Bronx shook his head. He was now on edge. But he was still undeterred.

The wind picked up. Bronx looked around. The lighting in the area was faulty. It seemed pitch dark in certain spots where the street lamps were out. Soon it would be an area that was a lot less friendly. Crime was rampant at the Tuscany Gardens apartment complex. Chicago's Southside was a place one needed to show respect and pay attention. Bronx looked around. The homeless man's ability to get so close so fast only added to the fact that he was not safe. It was a moment where he should have felt rattled. Bronx was amazed at his ability to sharpen at a time he should have been more scattered. The unregistered 9mm that sat discreetly on his side was loaded and ready.

Bronx was irritated at the time it was taking to make his move. It was best to leave and return at a later time. His car was a block away in front of an abandoned home. He chose the block specifically for that reason. Residents in most low income areas minded their business. They also didn't have cameras on every house. Bronx exhaled sharply, as he walked away. It was risky to be seen. The locals were familiar with all the faces of the neighbors and he stood out regardless of his efforts not to.

Bronx walked slowly hoping to blend in with the community. Suddenly, movement from the corner of his eye caught his attention. Faison exited the building holding a large bag. He walked up to the couple and handed them something then walked away. Soon another man whistled and Faison turned and walked to the man. Another exchange, and Faison was soon on the move once more. Bronx waited. He leaned against the tree and pretended to be taking in the air. It was nerve wrecking trying to keep up with everything from all angles. But it was a necessity. It was time to make a move and get out of the area undetected.

Bronx emerged from the trees as Faison walked around the building. He looked back at the homeless man who had asked him for a cigarette. He was the only person who had been close enough to describe him. The man was too far and too drunk to be mindful. Bronx blew off the interaction as something that didn't matter.

He watched Faison's movements. A breeze brought along with it the stench from garbage piled up near the side of the building. Soon another man whistled and Faison turned and walked towards him. Another exchange, and Faison was again on the move. It was obvious Faison was cemented in the community. Bronx had to be careful. Someone so well known and pivotal to an environment would also have eyes on them. Many eyes for many different reasons. Bronx looked to see if there was anyone else in close proximity looking to get what they needed from the busy neighborhood supplier.

Faison looked uneasy as he walked on the side of the ten-story tall building. He glanced at his cell phone then stuck it in his pocket. His eyes darted around. A quick scratch of the inside of his arm gave a hint as to what he was feeling. It was all too familiar. The rubbing up and down against skin that felt like it was crawling. The uncomfortableness. The constant drag across the nose. All telltale signs of drug use.

Chirp Chirp.

Faison hit the remote of his old classic with dark tinted windows. He opened the car and grabbed something from the front seat then proceeded to walk towards the garbage area. Bronx sped up in an attempt to catch up to him.

The large garbage containers were concealed behind a six foot tall enclosure. Faison walked in quickly and tossed the bag over into the bin. He stood for a moment and counted the money handed to him then stuffed it in his pockets and turned to walk out.

"Where you going?" Bronx said, as he approached him. Gun in hand.

"What the fuck man," Faison said, as he held his hands up. Bronx could tell Faison wasn't quite sure who he was. But soon Faison's eyes opened with the intensity of a man whose mind made the connection.

"Man...Listen...I ain't did shit. I swear. It's not me," Faison said.

"Sure it's not. You been wreaking havoc on my family for a long muthafuckin time. Got my wife on drugs. Kept her on drugs. Even let her use in front of my boys. For what...so you could fuck her. Now you coming after me and my brothers. Yeah...What did you tell her...You would blow my shit out," Bronx said.

Faison pleaded. It was useless. Bronx had seen the text. He'd read what was left of a conversation between two people feeding off of one another and speaking on unmentionables. There was no telling what had been said during one of their ravenous drug seeking binges. It was the stuff people died over. Talks of murder and threats of bringing the information to light was a dangerous road to be on. Their beef went back years. And Faison had reached the end of his road.

"You're done," Bronx said, as he pulled the trigger, releasing two bullets into the middle of his chest and one in his head. Bronx turned and ran. There was no surviving three well placed bullets from a 9mm. The layout of the building worked in his favor. The garbage area was near an alley which made for a perfect getaway. Bronx headed east down the alley towards the street where he left his car. His heart pounded fiercely. He sweat profusely as the weight of what he'd done took over.

But the plot that began long before Heather was killed in the car crash warranted the harshest of penalties. Heather wanted Bronx to pay for trying to keep her children from her. It was supposed to be him rotting in that jail.

Bronx walked up to his car. He looked around and peeled away in the night. He hoped the spot under the broken street lamp on a blighted block helped cover him. He drove fast until he reached the main street. "Come on," he mumbled in a deep and frustrated tone, as he drove behind a driver keeping with the speed limit. Bronx jumped lanes and hopped on the Ryan Expressway. He leaned his chair back then exhaled sharply.

The breath released the built-up tension simmering beneath the surface. Bronx felt like a stranger in his own body. Murder was not something he thought he'd ever do even though he knew he was capable. He was the son of Orlando St. Rock. A man who walked silent but carried a big stick. Even though Orlando was now focused on being a great father and grandfather to his growing family, it still didn't erase the fact that he was a force to be reckoned with when they were coming up. His father once told him; *Enemies not dealt with could alter one's life.* Especially an enemy plotting on such a diabolical scale. But it was over. No witness meant no case.

Chapter Twelve – Blindsided

There were two pieces of evidence your honor. Two. And a witness that has yet to come forward. One is a gun discovered in the ground under a newly constructed building. The gun was tested and was inconclusive as to whether it fired the shot that resulted in the victim's death or the bullet found lodged between the bricks of the building. The other was semi dried spit found a few feet from the victim. According to the report, the spit had begun to dry. Which meant it could have been there for over an hour. The location was an area frequented by the residents of that neighborhood. Although the DNA ties it back to my client, he was young and was frequently riding his bike in and around that alley. He could have spit on the ground at any time that evening. That is not proof of his presence during the commission of the crime. Unless the state has more evidence, I move to dismiss the case on lack of evidence, your honor," Max said, as he stood next to a nervous Boston.

Boston smiled internally. Max was going hard out the gate. He initially said they would go with the reduced charged. But he changed gears after finding out that the prosecution still had no witness. Allen Hill stood defiant and not willing to give up. He interjected with theories and more accusations. The judge allowed him the floor.

"Your honor, we have a witness who is afraid to come forward because the defendant's family. Supposed businessmen. They are thugs and bullies your honor. My witness was followed on two occasions by what he described as Mr. St. Rocks people. The state always had the names of the St. Rocks as possible people to look at. But we never had enough to make a case. The gun, is in fact registered to Mr. Orlando St. Rock, the defendant's father. It was buried behind a building about a block away in an area that was sold as vacant land and built upon. He had access to the gun. The guns is his. The spit is his. What more do we need. He has a better chance of hitting the lottery your honor," Allen said. Max chuckled.

"He has hit the lotto. My client is a well-respected businessman with a newly acquired deal that has made him one of the wealthiest men in Chicago. If you ask me, this is more about name building than justice your honor," Max shot back.

"Okay. Enough! I have reviewed the evidence. And I am well aware of Mr. St. Rocks status and position within this community. But the laws are not meant to protect criminals, rich or poor. With that said, I must look at the evidence and make an informed decision based on evidence and evidence alone. I don't believe there is enough to pursue a charge of murder. The evidence doesn't place him there. Spit in a public area is not a smoking gun. Nor is a gun buried in the ground. It is not against the law to bury a gun. Only to conceal evidence of a crime committed with that gun and the state has not proven that. The state has also failed to produce the witness. The evidence on record is circumstantial. Therefore, this case is dismissed. Mr. St. Rock you are free to go. Take care sir," the judge said.

Max turned to Boston and smiled then grabbed his hand with both hands and gave him a firm hand shake. It was a powerful moment. "Thank you, your honor," Boston said, then looked over at Allen Hill. He glanced back at Orlando, his mother Cicely and his brothers Chicago, Memphis, Austin and Dallas. Raleigh walked in and sat down in the last row. She smiled at him and gave him the thumbs up.

Allen Hill stared through him. It was obvious it wasn't over. A dismissed case could be re-opened and Boston was sure Allen Hill would do everything in his power to re-arrest him. It wasn't over.

"Congratulations," Orlando said, as he hugged his relieved son.

"Let's get out of here," Memphis said.

"Congrats brother. I knew this was bullshit," Chicago chimed in. Boston hugged his brothers then walked to Cicely.

"My baby is coming home. You okay," she asked, as she held his face in her hands. His ordeal was almost the death of her. She had gone to see her physician because of the stress of it all. But he was coming home and she couldn't be happier.

"Yes ma. Don't cry," he said, kissing his mother on the cheek and rubbing a tear from her face. Raleigh stood close by him. As if he would blow away in the wind. Cicely gave a smile. He had no idea the torment she had gone through and still was. She believed one of her other son's had turned on him. She hoped it would come out so she could talk with whomever was responsible. No matter what, they did not do such hurtful things to one another.

The family walked out. Max walked alongside of Boston, taking a call and handing a woman a business card as she walked alongside him.

"I can help you. Call me," Max said, as he continued walking with the St. Rocks. The woman put his card in her purse and went in the opposite direction. Max was a busy man. People watched him in court. He was dynamic to see. Shrewd. Charismatic. And he knew the law. There was always someone waiting to get a card. Someone who wanted him to put out a fire. His fee was too high for most people but Max had other talented lawyers and he always helped them with their cases. His practice was thriving.

"You know he's not done," Boston said, looking intensely at Max.

"I know. If that witness ever comes forward were screwed. But he'll back off for now. I have a press conference lined up shortly. Gonna give him something to think about," Max said. Boston snickered. It was the reason he hired him. Max was a beast. A formidable adversary. They were very much alike. Boston had respect for him. He was indebted.

"Thanks. I still owe you," Boston said, as he and Max walked from his family to have a private conversation.

"No! Were good. Go celebrate. And stop the nonsense about a divorce. You went through a lot to get her might as well keep her," he said with a chuckle as he walked away. Boston chuckled at the thought. Max was right. His history with her felt like a decade and they weren't at five years yet.

"You ready," Chicago called out. Boston turned back.

"Yep," he said, walking quickly to catch up to them.

Boston jumped in the back seat of Orlando's silver Escalade. His brothers climbed in their own SUV's and followed Orlando back to the family estate. It was time to celebrate. Jan and Kendra were there with Aurora cooking a huge meal. The best liquor money could buy was being delivered and Orlando had the owner of *The Smoking Den* delivering a box of *Majesty Reserve* cigars. It was going to be a grand celebration. No expense sparred.

Orlando looked in his rear-view at his son. He could see Boston wasn't in a celebratory mood. He glanced over at Cicely, then out the rear view at Chicago as he trailed behind them.

"You okay son. I know you're worried. I couldn't locate her. Don't worry about that. We will get right on it in the morning," he said. Boston looked at the mirror. His eyes met his father's.

"Has anyone spoken to her. Kendra maybe? Aurora?" he asked.

"No. Not since about a week ago. She's just upset. She'll surface," he replied. Boston sighed.

"Take me home. I want to get one of my cars. I'll meet you at the house once I get myself together. I can't go straight there. I need a long bath. A drink. And I need to clear my head," he said.

"Of course," Orlando said.

Cicely turned around to look at him. She hoped to help soothe what she was sure would be his anger after he discovered the things their family had put Rose through. Cicely was aware of Tacoma's visit to Rose and although Tacoma never told her what all was said, Cicely was sure it was nothing nice. Tacoma could be rough and did not hold her tongue. There was Orlando's visit in which he too was tactless and said things he later regretted. Then there was her visit. They had all attacked Rose verbally and she wished they hadn't. Boston was the king of his world. It was up to him to move forward in life with her or chose to cut his ties. It was time for damage control and then at some point a conversation. She would need to tell her son she overstepped her bounds.

"Your aunt Freda is there. So are all your cousins. We have a big dinner for you. Make sure you come. Everyone wants to see you," she said, her voice filled with worry.

"I will. I just need a minute," Boston said.

Raleigh looked over at him as he stared out the window. She felt bad for him. It was rare that she got angry at her family but they had gone too far. It was obvious he was thinking about Rose and probably planned on trying to find her. It was his words to her years before. That he needed Rose more than he'd ever needed anything or anyone. He wouldn't be happy. He was coming home to nothing.

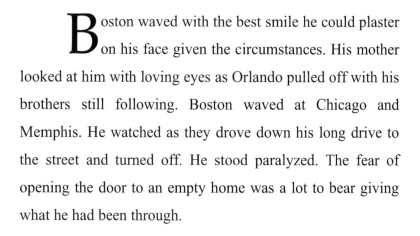

Boston waved with the best smile he could plaster on his face given the circumstances. His mother looked at him with loving eyes as Orlando pulled off with his brothers still following. Boston waved at Chicago and Memphis. He watched as they drove down his long drive to the street and turned off. He stood paralyzed. The fear of opening the door to an empty home was a lot to bear giving what he had been through.

His emotional purge of the word *divorce*, from his mental melting pot of feelings was premature. Boston walked slowly to the door and said a quick prayer. He wasn't mad about money. He wasn't angry that she hadn't been to see him. He wasn't even mad that she questioned his loyalty. He was ready to tell all and get back where they were. They were in a good place before the arrest. Nothing else mattered.

"Hello," Boston called out. He was hoping Orlando was wrong. Boston moved through the house quickly. First the living room and then on to the media room. Each disappointment pushed him to the next room with hopes of a reconciliation. He trotted up the stairs and walked swiftly to his little girls' room. The rooms were still filled with furniture. It was hard to say for certain. Boston was stressed. He walked quickly to his bedroom, looking in each bedroom as he passed. Rose mentioned moving the girls closer but he was against it because of how loudly their love making was. Rose laughed at his reasoning but agreed. There were times she was louder than him. Boston pictured her face. He needed sex like he needed air but at that moment just seeing her face would soothe the sexual beast in him.

"Rose!" he called out just as he hit the doorway of his room. Boston's hoped were destroyed in an instant. The bed was perfectly made. The entire house so perfect, it looked as though it were staged. Boston entered his room and sat on the bed.

"Damn," he mumbled, as he tried to come to terms with no wife. No babies. And no relief from his pinned-up desires to make love to her the way he'd dreamed about. Sex lately had been with himself as he pictured her face. Every detail. Her modelesque good looks that were exotic and unforgettable. Visions of her mouth on his penis as he jacked himself on the loneliest of nights. It was those moments that got him through the time. He never thought of himself as the type of man to jack off. There was never a need. He was a head turner himself. Women wanted him. All ages. All nationalities. It was nice to be desired by such a large pool of women. But there was only one who touched every part of him. Only one whose eyes, mouth, voice, body and feminine prowess had him whole heartedly. Rose.

"Let me speak to Kendra," Boston said to Memphis. Memphis held the phone then put his hand over it.

"Tell Kendra I said come here," he said, before removing his hand from the speaker.

"What's up? You on your way?" he asked.

"Yeah. I just need to ask Kendra something right quick," Boston said. Memphis looked towards the hall. He could see his wife coming. She moved hurriedly, as he waited.

"What's wrong," she said. Memphis held his hand over the receiver once more.

"He wants to talk to you. Have you been talking to Rose?" Memphis asked.

"No. She changed her number. I told you... I don't know where she is. I swear. I wouldn't lie about that Memphis. You know I wouldn't," she said. Memphis looked intensely at her then handed her the phone.

"Hello," Kendra said.

"Hey sis. It's Boston. I need Rose's new number?" he said.

"I really don't have any way of contacting her. Did you try Tina," Kendra said, as she looked for her husband to save her from the intense call of her brother-in-law.

"Yeah. I'm standing here with her now. She said you knew," Boston said in a matter of fact tone. Kendra turned from Memphis and rolled her eyes. She hated being in the middle. And her husband's lack of interest had just pissed her off.

"Listen Boston...I talked to her last week. She didn't tell me where she was going. She went to see Bronx. That's all I know. Maybe he knows where she is," she said, unaware she was saying much more than she should have. Boston held the phone.

"Bronx! Why the fuck would she go see him? Now of all times when pops said he wasn't taking visitors," he asked, as he walked away from Tina slowly. Tina put her hand over her mouth then walked away. She eyed Jerry as she left her living room. It was shocking that Kendra had said that. Tina couldn't believe it. Kendra was obviously nervous or intoxicated.

"Kendra!" Memphis shouted.

"What," she turned to him and said. He approached and took the phone from her.

"Boss. Boss…," he said, as the line went dead. Memphis hung up the phone and looked at his wife.

"What did you say? Bronx? She went to see him? And you telling Boston with all they been through. Why was she there Kendra?" he shouted.

"I don't know. All I know is she went there. Probably to check on him. I don't know. She never said why. Ok. All I know is she is going through something. She found out Boston has children. One by a friend of hers. But she said she did something too and she thinks they're toxic. That's all she said. I swear," Kendra cried.

The small amount of liquor she'd drank was wearing off under the stress of her husbands soured mood. Memphis peered at her once more then left the room.

"Memphis wait! Wait! Is he mad at me? What are you mad about?" she asked, as Cicely walked in. Kendra was stunned at her husband's abrupt departure. Cicely had been standing close enough to hear it all. It was enough to cause an alarm. Boston would take the visit as something inappropriate regardless of how unbelievable it sounded. That wasn't Bronx's style. But then this was Rose. Her curvaceous figure, twenty seven inch waist and ass for days would be Bronx's undoing. He was a strong man. But not pitted against someone like Rose. The femme fatale with the face of an angel.

"It's ok. Memphis will be fine. What did Boston say?" Cicely said, trying to gather his state of mind. He was bound to find out sooner than later. The timing was horrible. He hadn't been home a full day.

"He didn't say anything. I was thinking that maybe Bronx knew where she was since he was the last one to see her. What is the big deal? I've been to see him too. We all have. Why is that so wrong?" Kendra asked. Cicely touched her arm.

"Nothing really! But she's gone. So, of course, Boston doesn't want to think his wife would go visit anyone. You understand," Cicely said unwilling to say much more. It was all still speculation. No proof of an affair. But Heather's mother seemed sure of what she said.

"I didn't mean to make him think anything like that. We need to find her. And Bronx may know," she said. Cicely nodded.

"He might," Cicely said then turned to her husband. "You need to find Boston. Call him please!"

Kendra's eyes opened wide. It was apparent that something was up. The visit to Bronx was not innocent.

"Boston…I'm sorry. It's nothing. I'm telling you, it's not what you think," Tina said, as Boston stood with his hands on his hips.

"No! It is what I think. You're wrong. She tried to tell me. Something that she believed was unforgiveable. She said it to me that last time I spoke to her. The night she told me about my own shit. Look…I have to go," he said. Tina saw the life drain from his eyes. He looked as though he'd seen a ghost.

"Wait Boston. Come back. Let's talk about this. Wait," she yelled, as she ran behind him. Jerry exited the house and stood on his porch. Dusk was approaching. It would be dark soon. He watched as Tina stood on the side of Boston's black Escalade. He looked intensely at his mother in law. There were no words. No consoling. Nothing.

"Where's ma," Bronx said, as he entered the St. Rock Estate. He was met with surprised looking stares.

"Bronx," Aurora said, as she walked to him slowly and hugged him.

She hadn't seen him in weeks. He was back to not answering his door. She once walked around to the back of his house and watched as he lay on the couch and ignored her knocks on his window. It was good to see him out. She was elated he was in a mood to celebrate although whether there would be an actual celebration remained to be seen.

"What up?" Austin said, as he bumped fists with his grieving brother. Out of everyone, he was the one who hadn't seen him since the funeral. His knocks too went unanswered. One by one, the siblings hugged and greeted their brother. Bronx looked around. He hoped to lay eyes on Boston for the first time since that fateful day at the hospital.

"Where's Boss?" he asked, as he looked around. His eyes met Orlando's.

"He…um…well the truth is were not sure he wants to come yet. He seemed anxious to get home," Orlando replied.

"Oh!" Bronx replied, as he walked up to his father. "Pop," he said, as he hugged Orlando.

"Son," Orlando replied.

Cicely came out of the kitchen with their housekeeper and began to cry at the sight of her son standing in her home. "Bronx!" Cicely said, as she walked up to him. She wasn't expecting him to be there. Not with his absence at the other events the family held. He had missed the barbeque. The birthday celebration for Raleigh and the get together Aurora threw at her home.

"Hi sweetheart. It's so good to see you," Cicely said. She checked him over like he was glass that would break.

"You hungry. We have food. We have deserts. I have your favorite. Apple Pie," she said. Bronx smiled. He wondered why the room stood so still. It was unsettling. His family had him feeling strange. It was a first. He didn't expect them to be so off putting.

"Sure ma," he said, as he followed her into the kitchen. Orlando looked over the faces of his other children. Their silence was eerie even for him. Orlando turned and walked into the kitchen with his wife. He could hear Tacoma voicing her concerns. He couldn't find Boston. No one knew where Rose was. And Bronx was the new man in the middle.

Boston drove to Bronx's home and pulled up slowly. He peeked through the window then began to bang on it. He waited for movement. Anything that signaled he was inside. He grabbed his phone and call him then sucked his teeth when the automated voicemail was instantly activated.

"Fuck!" Boston said, as he got back in his car. "Naw," he said fuming as the thought of Bronx being at the estate crossed his mind. "Hell naw," he said, as he rubbed his neatly trimmed goatee that he found the time and strength to groom earlier in the evening.

Boston made another call. He was aware that calling any one of his brothers would not get him anywhere. They would be in protect mode. He wouldn't get to Bronx so easily.

"Hello," a tired Max said.

"Hey. It's Boston. You talked to Phoenix. I need him to call me right now," Boston said.

Max looked at his clock. It was late.

"Uh. I haven't talked to him in a few days. What's wrong?" he asked.

"Nothin man. Just call him for me. He's not going to pick up for me. You know that nigga moody as fuck. He probably back with a stick up his ass. Do it for me please," he said. Max looked at his resting wife.

"Sure. But then I'm going back to sleep and cutting the ringer off. I have to get up at five," he said.

"Yep. Thanks!"

Boston ran a red light in his frazzled state. He would take the chance and he hoped he was right. If he was wrong, his family would expect him to stay. They would slow his movements. And if they were aware he was now in full rage, they would cover Bronx like a veil.

Boston checked to see if his ringer was on. He wasn't sure what Phoenix knew. He needed to talk to the only other person who kept up with Rose even if he did so in private. He was the furthest away but the closest to all things regarding his wife. Boston hated it but it was what it was. Phoenix still believed he was Rose's first love. Boston didn't doubt there was some validity to it. But a decade was a long time. Things change. Boston couldn't control his brother's heart. He didn't plan to. He only wanted information. He was sure Phoenix and Rose were over. Phoenix would have never come to the jail if it wasn't. He would have never contacted Max by request. It wasn't his style.

Boston drove around to all of Bronx's old spots. Bronx wasn't doing family events. He hated to be coddled and Boston was sure he was avoiding all the St. Rocks like the plague. His phone rang. Boston was shocked. He didn't really expect Phoenix to actually call.

"Hello," he answered.

"Yeah. What's up," Phoenix said.

"Every fucking thing. Is Bronx fucking my wife," Boston fumed. Phoenix paused. He wasn't sure he heard him right.

"What the fuck did you say. What do you mean. Bronx? Like Bronx. Come on man. You out and you paranoid. What the fuck Boss," Phoenix said as he realized that Boston being out and talking like that meant he was on a rampage.

"Where are you?" he asked.

"Looking for him," Boston replied.

"Don't do that. That man lost his kids. You fuckin trippin," Phoenix replied.

"You still in Florida?" Boston asked.

"Yeah. But now I need to come home. You hunting my brother. You need to get control of your life. Your shit man. Nobody touched her. Everybody is on with their life. You living in the past. I'm down here with my lady. I don't think about her. Neither does Denver. And now you need to find someone else to blame for her lack of interest in you," Phoenix said. Boston blew up at his brother's harsh words. Phoenix had gone too far.

"Oh you want her muthafucka. And you're wrong. She has been with somebody. She pretty much confessed when my ass was locked up. When I find out who, I'm going right back to jail. I'm sick of ya'll fucking with her. She's sick," he said. Phoenix held the phone.

"Sick! Sick how," Phoenix asked.

"Nothing! Fuck you! Saying that stupid ass shit to me muthafucka," Boston ranted. He was being unreasonable.

"You trippin and I ain't got time for this shit. You need to relax. Go home. Sleep that fucking anger off. Rose will be back. She always comes back. She's terrified of yo ass just like everybody else. But I'm not. And neither is Bronx. Don't go fucking with that man, please," Phoenix warned.

Phoenix's had old wounds that were still fresh. Talks of Rose opened them once again. He was on the mend. But he worried about his brother. Boston sounded unreasonable. He was now capable of anything. Bronx wasn't safe. He was too fragile to think logically. No one knew the tables had turned. Bronx had crossed into dark waters. It was Boston who wasn't safe. Bronx was capable of much more.

Boston pulled up at his parent's home. "Say that shit to my face. You touch her and you won't live to talk about it. Try me muthafucka," Boston said. Phoenix chuckled.

"Look...I'm not your problem. Ge the fuck off my phone," Phoenix replied. Boston sat in his mother's driveway. Phoenix hadn't hung up yet. He was sure it was out of fear of what he was going to do.

"I have to go. You should watch what you say when it comes to her and I," Boston said.

"Yeah. I know. Where are you?" Phoenix asked. Boston took the phone from his ear and pressed *end call*. He was right behind Bronx's car at his mother's home. He couldn't answer that question although he was sure Phoenix's next call would be to Austin, Memphis or directly to Bronx. He was going in. And he had no questions. Brooklyn looked a lot like Bronx's children. The light eyes and hair. Her complexion. She was lighter than Rose. Boston found it strange since he was dark skinned and Rose was more of a caramel color.

Boston's mind raced. He remembered how angry Bronx was at the hospital. His absence during the entire time he was locked up which was something totally out of character for him. Then there was the fact that he wasn't at the hospital for the birth. He was the only one missing in action. At some point, everyone showed up. Even Phoenix. Boston was sure he wasn't wrong as he exited his car and walked up to the house.

The front door opened and Tacoma and Dallas stepped out on the sprawling porch to greet him. They were also there to check his temperature and he knew it. He decided to play it cool. He needed to get past them without doing damage. He was getting to Bronx one way or another and they would get hurt trying to stop him.

"Boss," Dallas greeted.

"Hey," he said as he hugged him. He could see Tacoma and Marti staring at him out the corner of his eyes.

"Hey Tae," he said, hugging his sister. Her intense glare seemed to penetrate his soul.

"Hey. I am so glad you home. Come eat. I got your Louis XIII ready. Pop got Majesty's to smoke. The whole family is here," she said. He was sure she was telling him that to prevent him from clowning. But it wouldn't suffice.

"Boston!" his aunt Freda said, as she embraced him. Boston hugged her as he stood in the doorway looking around. He got in just a few more feet, before being grabbed by his aunt Carol on his father's side.

"Oh Boston. So glad your home. And congratulations. I saw an article about you in the magazine," she said kissing his cheek.

"Thanks auntie," Boston replied, as he scanned the faces. There were more than thirty people standing or sitting. His other aunts. Cousins. Nieces and nephews. The house was packed and more were expected to come.

Boston kept his eyes scanning the room. Soon Bronx emerged with a smile. Boston glared at him. Bronx furled his brow. He had never seen the look. Boston continued to allow his family to hug him and touch his arm. They seemed to need a piece of him. As if there needed to be proof it wasn't a mirage. Boston walked slowly past them. He glanced at Bronx as rage fueled inside of him like a roaring fire. Bronx looked at Orlando. Their father could sense the danger of Boston. He knew him. He could sense the rage. Smile and all, it wasn't good.

"Hey son," Orlando said. "Can I borrow for a minute?" Orlando said to his sister, as he tried to intervene on what looked to be a planned attack. Just then, Boston pulled from his father and rushed Bronx.

"Ah! Oh no. Stop!" the voices said as Boston tackled his brother. He picked him up and flipped him on his back and began beating him in the face. Bronx managed to kick him and stand up.

"Muthafucka," Bronx said, as he tried flipping his stronger and professionally trained brother to no avail. Boston locked his arms around Bronx's neck as Orlando tried to pull him off.

"Boston! Stop this now!" Orlando demanded. Boston was unreachable through words. His red rage filled eyes and non-existent senses had taken over. Bronx hit him in the side and Boston punched him in the center on his eye knocking him back.

Cicely ran from the kitchen and over to her son's. Memphis ran from the back to help. Orlando had somehow been knocked back and was still trying to get his bearings as Austin helped him to his feet.

"I'll kill you muthafucka," Boston raged, as he flipped Bronx once more.

"Stop it. Stop this," Cicely said, as she held her mouth. Memphis grabbed Boston and pulled him back. Boston snatched from him.

"Touch me again! I dare you. Touch me one more fucking time," he said. Memphis got in his face. He was stronger than Boston and wasn't worried about Boston flipping him. Chicago grabbed Bronx as he tried to charge at Boston.

"Stop that. What is happening here," Cicely said, as she suddenly doubled over.

"Ma!" Dallas said, as he ran to her aid.

"Something's wrong with ma," Aurora said, as they helped her to the couch.

"Ma! Say something," Dallas said, as the family began to panic.

"Call 911," Freda shouted.

"Call 911 now!" she repeated. Orlando pushed his family out the way and held Cicely's face.

"Honey…Baby…Say something. Oh god. CeCe talk. What hurts. Say something," he said, as his eyes filled with tears.

"I'm not waiting for no ambulance. Get her in the car, I'm taking her myself," Orlando stated.

"That's not a good idea pop. They'll be here in a minute. They have stuff on the ambulance that they can give. Just wait," Dallas said. Orlando touched Cicely's face again. She held her eyes closed as she winced in pain.

"Get her an aspirin. Who has an aspirin," Boston shouted. Kendra ran to her purse.

"I have aspirin," she said.

"Give it to me," Boston said. He crumbled the pill up and put it in his mothers mouth.

"Swallow ma. Please. Swallow. Can you swallow," he asked. Cicely's mouth moved slightly.

"What about some water," Marti blurted.

"No! She could choke. It'll go down," Boston said, as he looked at his father. Orlando gave a stern reprimand of disapproval that Boston hadn't seen in years. Fears set in. If Cicely died because of him he would die inside.

"I'm sorry ma," Boston said, as he covered his mouth. His eyes were wide with fear. He stood over Orlando staring down at the face of his first love. His mother. It was because of what she went through that Rose was still able to hold onto him so firmly. Rose was Cicely. There was something he knew that no other St. Rock knew. Her strength was endearing. She had been through enough trauma to break one's spirit yet her spirit was intact. She married and raised 13 kids. She was the epitome of a woman.

Boston got down on his knees and put his head on her head. "Come on ma," he cried then kissed her cheek. Aurora ran from the room. It was too much.

"My momma," she cried. Chicago ran behind her to comfort her with his wife Jan close behind. It was a devastating blow to them all.

"She'll be alright Ro. She will," Chicago assured. Jan rubbed her husband's back. She was sure he was two seconds from a nervous breakdown. Jan looked off. The sound of sirens in the distance became louder.

"I think they're here," Orlando said, as he held Cicely's hand. Boston didn't move. Orlando rubbed the back of her hand as Boston kept his eyes closed and his arms over her.

"Open the door for them," Orlando instructed.

"Okay Boston. They're here. Move out the way," Orlando said. Boston held his mother.

"Okay son. Move out the way," he repeated, as he pulled on Boston's arm. Boston stood quickly and walked away with Dallas and Raleigh right behind him. They followed Boston to the bathroom but he shut the door before they could enter. Orlando pushed the coffee table back as the EMT entered.

"What happened?" the man asked.

"We don't know. She grabbed her chest then bent over. We had to help her to the couch. She hasn't said a word since," Raleigh cried.

"Please help her. Please," Aurora said.

"Okay. We're going to move her to this stretcher," the EMT said. "Check her vitals," the man said to his partner. They placed a pulse oximeter on Cicely and attempted to move her on to the stretcher.

"Don't! I got her," Memphis said, as he stepped in and picked his mother up and put her on the stretcher. Cicely's 5'6, 160 pounds was like a rag doll in his arms. The EMT stood back. The house was full of men giving them glares. It was understandable that the family would be freaking out.

"Let's get her to the hospital," the man said.

"I'm riding with her," Orlando interjected. Soon his sons voiced their desire to be with her.

"Me too," Memphis chimed in.

"I'm going," Dayton said.

"We have room for just one person. Sorry," the EMT noted. Orlando stood next to his wife.

"You all meet me there. Which Hospital is she going to?" Orlando asked.

"We're taking her to Northshore," the EMT said.

Orlando nodded. He looked around at his children. There wasn't a dry eye in the room. Freda grabbed her purse and left out with her children in tow. She never looked back. Her only interest was beating them to the hospital so she could be there when her sister arrived. Chicago and Jan followed her.

"Let's go," Ralph said to his wife Aurora.

"What's taking so long. Get her out of here," Bronx commanded. "We are sir. We're just making sure she's secure," the nervous EMT said, as he raised the gurney and rolled Cicely towards the door.

Raleigh walked up to him. Her big brother looked to be in the most fragile state. He had lost his family six months prior. It had been a long road for him. He was still in mourning. Raleigh stood next to him and took his hand. She held it firmly. It was traumatic to watch Cicely being rolled out of her house. She was in good health. They couldn't imagine what had happened. They only knew one thing, the fight brought it on.

"No!" Raleigh shouted. Dayton walked over and hugged her as she cried in his arms. What was supposed to be good times had turned into a tragic event. Cicely still hadn't said anything. Her tight eyes were now open and she looked terrified. Her eyes were fixed on the ceiling above. Orlando touched her face hoping she would look at him. It broke his heart when she didn't.

"Pop...We'll see you there. Alright," Austin said.

"Yeah," Orlando said, as he looked back.

The EMT rolled Cicely to the ambulance and placed her inside. Orlando climbed in as Memphis and Austin stood directly behind him. "Watch your step," Austin said. Orlando reached for a handle and stepped inside the truck with blaring lights. It was an eye piercing reminder that his wife was in a medical emergency.

Chapter Thirteen – Filtered Through

*T*he family of forty plus men, women and children filled the room that was designated for them. The adults sat around quietly. The younger St. Rock children were rambunctious and required constant monitoring. Freda tried to keep up with her great nieces and nephews with the help of Aurora, Jan and Austin's wife Janice. Kendra sat quietly next to Memphis overwhelmed with feelings of guilt for having naïvely told Boston about Rose's visit to Bronx.

Orlando paced the floor until Chicago approached him. "Come on pop. Sit down. You're gonna wear yourself out," he said. Orlando sat down for a moment. Chicago looked at Bronx. Their intense and readable facial gestures suggested it wouldn't help. Their father would be up again in a matter of minutes to start pacing again.

Chicago felt his phone vibrating. He took it out and saw it was Boston calling and immediately stepped away from Bronx. Bronx had a feeling who it was and tried to listen in on the conversation but Chicago continued walking until he was near the windows. His family had enough drama for one evening and Bronx had enough for a lifetime. He had hoped for a better outcome. Bronx was supposed to tell Boston. A conversation over the phone first to give him time to absorb the blow. From what Bronx told him, it was Rose who was the aggressor. It didn't make it better but it would take more of the heat off. Boston told Memphis that she was being taken advantage of. A conversation that Memphis told Chicago. The brothers weren't sure what Boston meant by the remark. She was not a child. She was seducing men. In Bronx case, it seemed she went after him. That was not someone being taken advantage of. That was a person very much in control.

"Hello," Chicago said in a low voice.

"How is she," the solemn voice said. If Chicago had not looked at the caller id and saw it was Boston, he would not have recognized the voice.

"We're waiting for the doctor to come out and update us," he replied.

"They haven't said anything at all," Boston asked.

"No. Only that they suspect a heart attack but they wouldn't confirm it," Chicago said, as he glanced behind him, mistakenly making contact with Bronx's eyes. He turned back around and held the phone listening to his brother's breaths.

"You alright?" Chicago asked.

"Yes. I won't be if anything happens to her," he said. Chicago nodded.

"None of us will. Just pray for her. You coming?" he asked.

"Yeah. Soon. I'm still at the house. Should I bring anything for her?" Boston asked. Chicago thought for a moment. He remembered when his wife gave birth to their children how much she wanted her own gown and house shoes.

"Yeah. Bring her a gown and slippers," he said.

An hour went by with no update and no Boston. A nurse entered to tell the family that the doctor would be in to speak with them. Her short but brief words had them on pins and needles. There was despair in her initial demeanor that she tried to cover up with a plastered on smile. The family was used to being at hospital's for more joyous occasions. Orlando walked to the window and looked out at the night sky. It was filled with stars that seemed to have an extra sparkle in their gleam.

"You alright pop. She's gonna be ok. Mom is strong," Memphis said.

"Yeah I know. I guess I never imagined her leaving here before me. That just can't happen. She knows that. We discussed that. So she will fight," he said. Memphis pat his father on the back and went to speak with Austin. He could tell his father needed a moment.

"You good," Memphis asked Austin.

"Yeah. This is crazy. I'm pissed. I could kill Boston. I swear, she better make it through," he warned. Memphis stared at his emotional brother.

"She will. That woman is strong as an ox. She'll pull through. Watch! You still leaving Friday for DC?" Memphis asked.

"Hell no! Not now. That shit on pause. I can't. I'm supposed to start a new job. I'll be running the National Organization for Social Justice. It's a new branch of a much larger organization. It's always some shit. Now look! This family of ours. I swear man...That's why I'm leaving. Because I can't do this any longer. I can't. The dysfunction is insane," Austin said. Memphis shook his head no. He didn't agree.

"We not that bad man. It could be worse. We rich. We have families. We have each other," Memphis noted. Austin shot him a look.

"Really! With all the drama and dirtiness between us. Now Bronx fucked her. And I was mad at Boston for the longest over the way he treated Phoenix. But now I'm on his side. Why they keep fucking his wife. And what the fuck is up with her allowing it. They don't have to worry about me. That bitch could stand in front of me butt ass naked," he said.

Memphis had no rebuttal for words that had a lot of truth. He felt Austin's pain. They had some healing to do. A lot of the issues stemmed from behaviors as young boys and their teenage years that were never corrected. Now as men, they crossed boundaries still. And at the center was jealousy that still seemed to be growing among them.

"We can get better though. If everybody talks. Get to the root. Show love. It can happen. We need family counseling man. Not a new city with a bunch of muthafucka's you don't know," Memphis said.

"Maybe! But I have to go. For now at least. I'll be back and forth for a minute until ma is good. She gonna pull through. And I'm going to be there for her when she does," Austin said, as he watched two nurses walk by.

The women were on lunch break and took a moment to see what all the fuss was about. Word had spread of the family full of dashing young men waiting on news of a loved one. It warranted a peek. Austin smiled at one of the women. She smiled back at the caramel complexioned charismatic gentleman with almond eyes and dark facial hair trimmed to perfection. His low-cut beard that covered his lower jawline and around his mouth was one of his best features. His tall muscular frame and bowed legs were another.

Memphis noticed them but tried not to pay too much attention. His wife was standing less than three feet away. So was Austin's wife Janice. But Austin was a flirt. The things he complained about, he was just as guilty of. The St. Rock men loved women. Women ruled them although they begged to differ. They were rough enough not to be taken lightly by their counterparts but soft when it came to women. They had great lives. Awesome women. If only they could get to the root of their past

Bronx walked up to Orlando. He had something to say and he wanted a moment alone. The timing was perfect. Orlando stood by himself near the window. Bronx looked around at his family. No one seemed to be gunning for a chance to have a word with his father and so he walked over slowly.

"This is my fault," Bronx said in a melancholy tone. Orlando's eyes quickly met his.

"There's something I didn't tell you. I should have answered honestly when you came to my house and asked me. We..um...did have something. A long time ago. Once. And I have regretted it. I'm ashamed. And now ma...," he said, as he dropped his head. Orlando reached out and placed his hand on his shoulder.

"It's not your fault. I blame Boston more. But you bear some responsibility in this. You know their history. Of everyone, I expected better from you. You have to make this right and talk to him. Your mother can't take any more of this. The stress this has caused. These issues between you all. You and your brothers should have each other's back. This is a cruel world. You'll always be faced with envy. Jealousy. I raised strong self-assured black men. It's to be expected. But you all should stand as one not be each other's worst enemy," Orlando said.

Bronx had planned on talking to him he just needed more time. He needed to heal and he needed to stop lusting after Rose. There was a deep rooted jealousy that grew once he discovered Rose was pregnant. Things had only escalated after she had the baby. The DNA letter that arrived answered his question and he tossed the letter in his fireplace. No one needed to know the results. Because he agreed with Rose. Brooklyn would have a harder life given the circumstances. He didn't want that. She needed to be stable. Raised with the parents she expected to care and watch over her. Rose was now doing her part. She had changed her whole life around. He needed to do his part.

Rose's visit stuck with him. Her words burned a hole through his heart. Burning the letter was the only way to allow the baby a real chance at normalcy. She was his. And he believed Rose knew it. Out of all the words she said that day, she never said Brooklyn *wasn't* his. He was sure she would never want the results. Her words were final. Brooklyn was Boston's. And so, she would be.

Orlando perked up when he saw a physician entering the lounge. The family parted like the red sea as he nervously walked up to the man in the light blue scrubs and a skull cap. His facial expression was hard to read. Everyone looked him over. Would he smile to suggest she was going to be fine. Or was it more a worried look he bore, signifying she was not. Orlando took his time. He would be next if the man said she was gone. He could take just about anything but those words. As long as she was still fighting, there was a chance.

"I'm Doctor Solomon. Are you the patient's spouse?" he asked.

"Yes. How is she?" Orlando asked, as everyone stood around.

"I'm one of the resident Heart Specialists here at NorthShore. We have her stable for now. But she is not out of the woods yet. She's in what we call the Cath Lab right now. There, they will check blood flow and check the heart and valves. After that we will get an MRI of all her internal organs plus there are blood test we need to run. Right now, that's all I have. As long as she doesn't have any major blockage, we expect that she will recover. But it's too soon to say," he said. Orlando was speechless. He wanted to hear him say she would be fine. An uneasy feeling overcame him.

"How long before we know something more?" Orlando asked. "An hour. Maybe a little longer. Afterwards she'll go to the ICU and rest. It's late and only one person will be allowed back to see her," the doctor said.

"Thanks Doc," Orlando said. Other family members chimed in with a *thank you.* They hoped he was a skilled physician who could save their loved one. He gave off much better vibes than the nurse who had been in. Dr. Solomon was aware that his patient was the mother of a newly famous Chicagoan who had just became a billionaire. Boston was in all the papers. This was a family who would pay for the best of the best and he was one of the best. There was no need for them to call another physician. He was Harvard educated and had done his residency at Cedars Sinai in Los Angeles. The hospital had already called him in. He was Cicely's best option.

"Alright! Hang in there. I'll be back with another update soon," the doctor said as he walked away. Orlando looked at his children.

"You should all go home. I'll call you. I know you're tired," he said, as he scanned their faces and the faces of their significant others. Some of their spouse's he'd known for years.

Jan was close to Cicely. They went shopping and talked on the phone. So did Austin's wife Janice. Kendra was new to the family but her outgoing personality made it easy for Cicely to bond with her. Missing was Dayton's girlfriend April and Columbus' wife, who never seemed to be available for any event, good or bad. Denver stood alone as usual, since he and his last wife split. Even Aurora and Raleigh's husbands were well cemented into the family. Tacoma's girlfriend Marti was the newest partner to come along and they were still getting to know her. She was still well-liked and respected. She brought a sense of normalcy to Tacoma who could be a bit wild and unpredictable. He could see no one was anxious to leave. "Alright then," he said, as he went and sat on the thick cushioned two-seater. He was tired.

"Oh my god. Raleigh. I just heard," April said, as she rushed in. She quickly looked around until her eyes met his.

Dayton sat off in a corner alone, not being very sociable, as he tried to settle the fear of losing his mother. He was further from reconciling now. Boston was responsible and he vowed to never lay eyes on him again if Cicely didn't pull through. April could see the empty shell of a man as she had expected.

She ran over to him. Dayton stood up then released a tear as she stared him down. She hoped he wouldn't break down. He didn't have her to talk to. She had purposely tried to break him as she stayed from him even though her heart begged her not to.

"Dayton…Baby…I'm so sorry. She will be fine. Watch! She will," she said as he grabbed her in a tight embrace. Aurora smiled. It was a relief. He was the next St. Rock to come unglued over a lost love.

"I missed you. I'm sorry. I won't ever touch you again. I need you Cola," he said. April chuckled. She had told him to stop calling her that. Now it wore beautifully. She called him Thor. He asked her why once and she told him he had a big heavy hammer. Dayton laughed and embraced the cute moniker. He was proud. She would know. She brought out the beast in him.

"Nothing happened. You know that right? You should know that I would never…," April said.

"Yeah! I know. It still hurt that I couldn't see you. You can't go back there. I got you. You don't need his help," Dayton said. April never saw him so serious. He was a man's man overnight. He looked different. He talked different. She needed to see if they would be better together this time. They weren't over.

"Good! Cause I'm going home with you. So whoever she is, she has to go now," April said, with a light snicker.

"Stop playin! Don't nobody stay with me. That's your crib," he replied. Dayton paused. He hesitated to say the next words. He had never said them. He wasn't quite sure he felt it until now. "I love you Cola," he said. April swallowed hard. It was a long time coming.

"Me too. I love you."

Orlando nodded off occasionally. Chicago didn't doubt his father was starting to wonder where Boston was. He checked his phone then dialed Boston once more. Bronx walked over to check on him.

"How you holding up," he asked.

"Alright. I'm trying to get Boston. He at the house still. He was supposed to grab her slippers and gown then head here. Knowing him, he out looking for Rose," he said.

"I'll run and get her stuff," Bronx said. Chicago became tense. If Boston was still there that wouldn't be the best idea.

"I'll ride with you," Chicago said, knowing it would be better if he was there. Boston's state of mind couldn't be good and Chicago wouldn't be able to live with himself if either one hurt the other badly.

"Alright. Let's go now," Bronx said, as he headed over to Orlando to tell him they would be returning with Cicely's thing.

"I'm going to take the children home honey. You call me. I'll put them to bed and come back if you need me," Austin's wife Janice said. Austin kissed her then touched the head of his eight year old son. "Everything will be fine. She'll be fine. Go get some rest," Austin said, trying to keep a strong front for himself. Janice worried about her husband whose strained relationship with Boston was now further damaged. Coupled with the issues he had with his father's tunnel vision, it was enough to drive him out of Chicago.

Janice didn't want to go. She didn't want any life but the one she presently had. It was filed with good living and a family she had bonded with. It was his dream to pursue a political career and the move to DC was the stepping stone. Janice would support any dream of his. But now that Cicely was ill, she hoped it would light a spark in her husband to reevaluate his decision and stay home.

Janice didn't see herself as the wife of a politician. She was a bad girl turned good girl with a past her husband didn't know about. His political career could open the doors to things she hoped to keep hidden. His rise could expose her. She was the daughter of a preacher. A reputation she hoped would clean up the fact that she used to dance topless among other things. Janice smiled at her husband and kissed him before gathering her children to go home. "I'll see you later hun," she said.

Raleigh also decided to leave and get her kids home and comfortable. She demanded that someone call her as soon as they knew something. Tacoma had already left. She was too tired and too emotionally drained, and promised to be back by morning. Aurora and all the men decided to stay a little longer. She sent her children home with her husband Ralph. Cicely was more than her mother. She was also her best friend. She wasn't leaving without knowing.

"Where's Chicago and Bronx?" Austin asked Dallas.

"I think they went back to the house to get ma some stuff," Dallas said, as he flipped through his phone.

He leaned back in the small but cushiony chair and got comfortable. Austin joined him and laid back on the chair and closed his eyes. He was not a night owl. He needed some type of rest. But first, he checked his phone to see if Boston responded to the text he shot him. It read;

Hey where you at? Don't be like that man. That shit over with. You need to be here. What was that about anyway?

The text had gone unanswered. "Damn! What is this nigga issue," Austin said, as he stood up to go outside of the lounge and call Boston. He was determined to talk sense into him. "Be back. I'm going to see where Boston is," he said to Dallas as he turned to leave out. He looked through his phone as he walked out into the hall and nearly knocked Rose over.

"Oh," Rose said, as she jumped. "Rose!" Austin said, looking at her and her family. Tina stood holding a sleeping Brooklyn as Jerry stood behind her holding a sleeping Noor.

"Austin! How is she?" Rose asked, as her eyes darted between his.

"We think she'll be ok. It's been over an hour since we talked to the doctor. He seemed hopeful," he said. Rose looked down. Phoenix had given Tina an earful in search of Rose after he'd heard about the fight. He was upset and was already booking a flight back to home. If it wasn't for the call from Phoenix they wouldn't have known about Cicely's emergency. Rose hadn't talked to Kendra out of fear that Kendra would disclose her location. She was fully aware Boston was expected to be released and was terrified of what he would do if he found out Bronx asked Dayton to get a swab of Brooklyn's mouth. Her fears of his reaction were now realized. The attack was just what she thought would happen. And she still wondered what was in store for her. There was a time her betrayal led to him sodomizing her in his new house. He always seemed remorseful but in light of what had occurred, she wasn't sure he wouldn't resort to something extreme.

"How's Cicely?" she asked.

"We don't really know yet. We're waiting for some test. It will be a while. They running all kinds of test of her. But so far, she stable," he replied. Rose sighed then smiled. "She will be ok. I know she will," Rose said. She looked through the glass and scanned the faces looking for her husband. She looked at Austin with curious eyes. He was not in attendance. That wasn't like him.

"Is Boston here?" she asked. Austin looked intensely at her and shook his head no. Rose sighed. It wasn't a total surprise. He was somewhere cooling off. The report she got from Phoenix was shocking to everyone except her. She knew that once he found out about Bronx it would be tragic.

"I was just getting ready to call him. He said he would be here. He was at the house the last time I checked. He supposed to bring her robe and slippers but he never showed," Austin said. Rose instantly worried.

"Ma I have to go! I need to check on him. Can you take the girl's to your house. I can come get them in the morning," Rose said.

"Of course baby. You call me," Tina said. Orlando exited the lounge followed by Dayton and Memphis.

"Rose!" Orlando greeted.

"Orlando," Rose said in a soft and unassuming voice. The last time she'd spoken to him he ripped her heart in two chastising her for something Boston asked her to do. But she wasn't keeping score. She was past it all. The only thing that mattered was Cicely and Boston.

"Hey," Dayton greeted.

"Hi," Rose replied with a smile. The moment was awkward but Rose was happy she was at least greeted. They probably blamed her indirectly. And she was trying to shake the guilt of it all.

"Well…I'm going to go find him. I'll be back," Rose said, as she turned and walked to the elevator. Orlando followed her and approached as she waited. Tina hoped he was careful. She was aware of his vicious verbal assault on her daughter and she wasn't having it.

"Rose…I just want to apologize for the way I talked to you. I was out of line. It's not my business what you and my son decide. It's also not my business what you decide to do as his wife. Only god can be invited in to a marriage. All others must stay out. I apologize for the bad blood my words brought on. I'm aware that Tacoma also said some not so nice things all fueled by my anger," he said. Rose gave a warm smile.

"Thanks Orlando. That means a lot. It's not about me right now. I'm praying she gets better?"

"We're supposed to hear something soon. It's been a while so that's a good thing. She's still alive. She'll be fine. You need to find your husband. He feels guilty. I know he's blaming himself. He's at our house," Orlando noted.

"I'll find him. He'll be fine," Rose said.

"We all will. Tell him this is not his fault. Tell him I love him," Orlando said. Rose smiled.

"Okay! We'll be back," she said.

Chicago and Bronx pulled up to their parent's estate. "He's inside," Chicago noted.

"Yeah. Hope he cooled down," Bronx said.

"He did. But he sounded depressed when I talked to him. He knows this shit his fault. He ain't going to make it worse. Besides...I'm here. He can't fuck with me. I'll flip his ass like a rag doll," Chicago said. Bronx chuckled even though it wasn't a joke. He was right. Chicago and Memphis were the strongest brothers. There would be no win attempting a brawl with either of them.

The men walked to the door and rang the bell. Chicago walked to the closest window and peered inside. "I don't see any lights on. I know he ain't in here sleep," he said. Bronx banged on the door then flicked the bell repeatedly.

"He's not gonna answer. You got a key?" Chicago asked.

"Pop keeps it in the bushes. Don't ask me which one. Under one of them rocks," Bronx replied.

"Aw naw man! We got to look under a bunch of rocks," Chicago griped.

"All I know is it's one of the lighter colored rocks. Come on! We'll find it," Bronx said.

The men searched through the rocks. Chicago stood up and looked around. "Damn finally," Bronx said, as he pulled the key. "Make sure we put it back. He'll get mad if it ain't there," Bronx said.

Bronx turned the lock on the thick glass custom door and opened it slowly. Chicago entered past him. "Boss!" he shouted as he looked around in the dimly lit entryway. He immediately walked to the grand room. "Maybe he upstairs," Chicago said.

"I'll check the library. That's where all the liquor is. His ass might be passed out in there," Bronx said.

Chicago headed up the stairs while Bronx made his way towards the back of the house. Bronx looked in the kitchen first before heading to his father's favorite room. Chicago made it to the top of the stairs and walked slowly past the bedrooms and the bathrooms, looking inside each one for his brother. He hoped to be the one to find Boston.

He still didn't trust Boston and Bronx to be in each other's presence. Tempers were still not evened out. Bronx was playing the good brother which was hard to read. Chicago figured he had to be mad. Getting jumped on like that was humiliating and not to mention emasculating. He was older. But Boston was faster. He was trained. It wasn't fair. But it was what it was.

Bronx was not a loser and that's where the complications came in at. Chicago was aware of Bronx's dangerous side. They were the oldest of the siblings. They ran in circles together and did things that no one spoke of. He was quite aware of who was really the most dangerous.

"Boston!" Chicago said, turning on the lights as his brother sat with a drink in his hand looking down at the floor. "Why you sitting here like that? What the fuck. I thought you were on your way. Everybody's worried," he said. Boston glanced up at him.

"Are they?" he said sarcastically. Chicago sighed.

"Yeah man! What the fuck. They are. Especially pop," he said.

"Umph," Boston replied.

"You trippin still. You haven't calmed down. Come on Boss. Let's go to the hospital. We should be able to see ma soon. Don't you want to see her. Does she matter in all this?" he said. Boston stood up.

"Say it again," he said. Chicago snickered.

"Ok. Now you really trippin. Let's just go. Bronx here. We both came to get you," he said. Boston jerked his head back.

"Her things right there on the bed. I'll be there. I ain't riddin with him," Boston said, as he walked to the window and took a sip of his cognac. Bronx walked in and looked at Chicago.

"Let's go. He said he gonna get there on his own," Chicago said.

"Alright. Just wait in the car for me," Bronx said. Boston kept his back to them. His crinkled brows and tight jawline was out of their view. He wasn't ready for any talks. Especially from a brother he trusted who had ultimately betrayed him. It was enough to cause a volcanic eruption. His low simmering boil was increasing with each minute.

"Uhh...Ok," Chicago said, his raised brow signaling his thoughts on the matter. Bronx nodded in assurance. Chicago nodded back. He had to trust him. He didn't think Boston was mad enough to charge at him. It seemed that would have happened the minute Bronx walked into the room.

"I'll be in the car," Chicago said, hesitating then turning and leaving out. Bronx watched then turned to his heartbroken brother.

"I uh, don't really know what to say. I just know I'm sorry. I can't tell you how that happened. Something innocent that ended up being something I was ashamed of," he said. Boston sighed loudly but kept silent as he continued his gaze out at the back of the property. Bronx shook his head. It was a hard conversation to try and have. He wasn't sure if he'd say something to trigger another attack. He had no plans to thwart it with a bullet. His mother would surely pass if any one of her children died before she did. Part of him believed that Boston would have every right. The words needed to be said. He had many sleepless nights thinking about it. It was risky. Boston could flip out hearing the details. But if he lost another fight to him, it would be the karma he deserved.

"It happened once," Bronx said. Boston exhaled loudly and dropped his head. He wasn't sure he wanted to hear it. But he still loved his brother. They were close before this. He had no desire to hurt him. He just wished Bronx hadn't stuck the knife in on an already delicate situation. It was still unbelievable that he was the one who Rose tried to warn him about. Bronx continued.

"You were out of town on business in Michigan. She sounded stressed and was complaining that Noor was driving her crazy. I told her to bring the baby to me. I was weak. I missed Heather. And she was hard to resist. I just...I can't take it back but I would," Bronx said, his deep powerful voice low and solemn. Boston didn't say anything as his feelings took hold. Then remembered the night vividly. He had only ever been to Michigan once. He was well aware of the day it happened. And now he believed he understood why she did it.

"She came that night because I was out of town with Jodi. That's what she does. Gets mad when I do something then strike back. We were working on things. You had no right to touch her. You don't know the half of her issues. Or even our mother's past issues. She was sexually tortured. Abused most her life. Just like ma was," Boston said. Bronx's stared wide eyed at his brother. It took a minute for the words to filter. The shock consumed him whole.

"What! Abused! What you mean? And ma? Where you hear that at?" he asked.

"I heard her," Boston said, as turned his head slightly then looked back out the window.

"She was abused by our grandfather. I heard her when I was a kid. Kept it to myself all those years. Rose reminds me of her. Sweet. Delicate. Rose needs support and understanding not for everyone to try and fuck her. Whether she came to your house or not, you shouldn't have touched her. You should have called me. She's sexually aggressive. It's her way of dealing with shit. I didn't tell anyone but I shouldn't have too. She is off limits. That's not my piece of ass that's my wife," Boston said, turning around to face his brother.

"I'm telling you because so much has happened and I can't hold this shit in no more! My wife has problems and I understand them. I'm waiting her out because one day she will heal and this shit will be behind us. That's the mother of my children. My wife. I did my dirt. My whole life. It's almost like this is my karma for the shit I've done. The women I've hurt. The shit back on Freemont. The universe makes you pay it back in the worst way. Usually with something you really love. And these are the dues I must pay to be happy I guess," Boston said. Bronx gave his undivided attention. He felt even worse. It weas a lot to absorb. But he had a better understanding. And there was a new cross to bear. It hurt to hear his mother had been molested. The anger in him wouldn't stay silent easy.

"It's hard to believe. I know. Hopefully one day ma will talk about it. I want her to know what I heard. And I need to tell her about Rose. It's a long overdue talk. Right now, she thinks Rose is a whore. I know she does. She's not. She's broken. You understand," he said. Bronx nodded slowly, still in shock by the discovery that his mother was sexually abused.

"If I ever see our grandfather…," Bronx said.

"Yeah. I know. Me too. But he already paying for that shit as we speak. He knows we're living like kings. Karma paid him back. He wants to be in our lives and he can't. His children want nothing to do with him. He lives in Maryland on the streets. He will die on them muthafucka's too. I won't give a nickel to his cause and I better not find out he's gotten help using my money. Freda talks to that muthafucka. Mom won't though," Boston said, as he took a moment then asked the most important question.

"Is my baby yours?" he asked. Bronx was shocked at his candor.

"No," Bronx replied. Boston felt an instant relief.

Bronx gave a half smile. It wasn't exactly the truth but it was what would be moving forward. Anything else would be a disturbance of the worst kind. He trusted Boston with his child. He would be the best daddy. And he would get to see Brooklyn whenever she came around. His life would also get better. It started with fixing his torn relationship with Boston. Everything else would fall into place. He believed they made a few steps closer to getting back their brotherly bond. Enough had been said for now.

"I better go. Chicago probably nervous as fuck sitting out there. And just so you know…she came to see me about a week ago. She was worried about me thinking Brooklyn was mines. She cut into me. She wanted to make sure I didn't think it. Don't be mad about that visit. She was definitely there for you. You can't get rough with her. She said she's pregnant," he said to a stunned Boston.

"Act surprised! Because I'm probably not supposed to tell you," Bronx said. Boston was floored. He knew exactly when it happened. Their moment at the jail. It was a gratifying feeling. They had another child on the way.

Bronx smiled then turned to leave. He stopped abruptly and turned back to his brother. Boston looked intensely at him.

"One other thing…That little problem of yours. The witness. Taken care of. Ain't no witness," he said, as he left out the room. Boston stood stunned. He walked quickly into the hall and watched as his brother headed to the staircase. Bronx stopped and looked back. Their eyes locked in an understanding gaze of what that meant. Boston nodded once. Bronx grinned then hit the staircase. Boston looked off. He couldn't say he wasn't thankful even though it was hard to celebrate given what that meant. Boston walked back in the room and picked up his cognac and took another sip. No witness meant he could stop looking behind his back for the cuffs that were not coming. He would find out who it was later. It was apparent that the enemy was not a brother of his. He could relax. He was wrong.

*R*ose pulled up to the St. Rock estate with her stomach in knots. Boston had no way of contacting her so she had no idea of his current state of mind. She thought of calling him but didn't think he would be in the mood to talk to her. She wondered if he hated her for the affair with Bronx. His affairs failed in comparison. Ashley was a friend. Bronx was a brother. The latest brother. The third time. Her undoing.

Before all this they had come to terms with the past and loved each other enough to stay together. She forgave him for what she classified as his attempt at doing her as she had done him. It was the best she could come up with. She had no proof of any affair before she started with her affair with Denver. She believed he was faithful. She had checked under every rock. Put someone on him. And nothing. She no longer blamed him.

Rose sat for a moment and thought about her role. Her brokenness that was causing confusion and pain for a man who loved her from the moment he laid eyes on her. His relentless and undeterred pursuit captured her heart. It was the same for her. She would never be the same after that day he waltz up to the condo she shared with Max and stole her heart after she opened the door to him. She remembered locking eyes with him. She remembered how nervous she was as he walked behind her. A stranger. A man who she did not know. Anything could have happened. But she knew it wouldn't. She could feel him. She understood he would be a gentleman and after just an hour talking with him over dinner, she knew she could never stay with Max.

He left that evening. Only to return and whisk her away when his tormented soul could take no more. Rose shook her head. No matter what he did, it didn't warrant her response. She was there to lay it all out. Come clean. Tell him whatever he wanted to know. Even if it exposed things not yet said, she was willing. It was the only way to move forward. And after the talk they would move forward or decide to part. Rose hoped he would stay. She wanted him still. More than ever.

The grand home seemed lifeless. Rose was glad to see that it was lit brightly enough to make finding the spare key easy. Orlando kept it hid in the bushes. She had watched as

Boston retrieved it on several occasions when his parents wouldn't answer the door. Orlando teased that he would put Boston and Dayton's name on it since they used it so often.

Please be inside, Rose thought, as she stared at his Escalade. The house was dark. He was newly released and like most prisoner's, she was sure he needed to release himself. The thought made her jealous. She wondered if Jodi flew in for a special night with him. Something was keeping him from Cicely. Besides shame, there was nothing better to help soothe a stressed and sex starved man than a sexual tryst. She couldn't blame him. She told him she was leaving him. Then changed her number so he wouldn't be able to contact her. She was again, in no position to be angrier than he.

Rose approached looking around at the massive windows for the silhouette of her distraught husband. She reached under the bushes to feel for the brick with the key underneath. She pulled the light colored one and then grabbed the key and let herself in. Rose sat her phone down as she walked carefully into the grand room looking around.

"Boston," she called out as she continued. She made it to the kitchen then continued on into the grand room. "Boston," she called out again, as she walked toward the back and into the library. Rose peeked in and decided to scale the staircase to the second level. As she passed the foyer, she noticed a glass of liquor sitting on the table. The house was immaculate except the one tumbler that was out of place. She couldn't believe a party had happened just hours before.

She ascended the stairs then stopped half way and sat down. Her tough exterior was cracking beneath the surface. The brave face she had plastered on for the world to see the last few months was a facade. "He's not here," she said. It was dark throughout the home except for the lights from outside that shined through the windows. Rose stood up like an old lady with back pains. She was tired. Her strap shoes that wrapped around her legs and up to her knees were wearing her feet out. They were beautiful but challenging. Rose felt for the knot and begun to try to loosen them when she heard a sound.

"Boston," she said, as she stood up and went up the stairs. There were seven bedrooms on the second level. She hoped to hear something that would narrow her search. Her feet were begging to be released from their beautiful prison. But Rose was determined to find him first.

Rose walked into the third bedroom. It was the room he'd slept in the few times he was too intoxicated to drive home. Rose imagined it would be where she would find him as she walked inside. She stopped at the door. There he sat in the dark, twisting the Baccarat tumbler before taking another sip. His eyes danced across the etching of a horse as he picked up the bottle of Louis XIII and poured more.

"Boston. Why are you sitting in the dark? Why aren't you at the hospital?" Rose asked. Boston gave her the silent treatment. Rose trembled slightly when she noticed a Gurkha Black Dragon cigar next to him in the ash tray. It brought back memories of when he picked her up smoking one just before his rant the night he took her to Denver's condo to confront them both. She also remembered the time he smoked one as they drove to the home where he sexually brutalized her. If he was back to being that man, she would exit his life because she was no longer that woman.

"Answer me Boston. Say something," she said. Boston turned up the glass emptying the contents into his mouth then picked up his cigar and lit it.

"Cicely is better. You ready to go see her?" she asked.

"No. Not yet," he replied.

Rose walked to him slowly and stood over him. He kept his head down. He was defeated. He had fought the good fight and lost. What he thought were ripples early on were giant waves still ingrained in their relationship. She reached down and touched the top of his head then slowly rubbed it. Boston tried to light his cigar but Rose reached down and removed it from his hand. He wasn't that man any longer. They were in their third year of marriage. The newness had not worn off yet. She had a long time to be with him. There was no one else and there never would be. They had more children to make. Brooklyn was his. She had to be. Because only his sperm would find its way to her eggs. Only he could possess her so fully. And she had no intention of proving otherwise. She was pregnant with their third child and they were not going to regress. Not if she could help it.

Rose kneeled before him. She was shocked to see his eyes red and swollen. She looked down in shame. He needed something she never gave him before. The truth. Her truth. From her mouth. Not Tina's version of a child exposed to sex. Or Ashley's recollection from cleaned up stories and half-truths. But her past as only she could tell. He knew some of it. He knew the *easier to deal with* version and the *not so bad given the circumstances* version. It was time to mend her husband and clear up his confusion and anger. It was all she had left.

"Can I talk and you listen?" she asked. Boston nodded slowly, still too upset to talk. Deep down he feared saying something that would hurt her. He understood her better than she thought. He was curious as to what she would say. How much of her life she was willing to share. He wiped his face and then stared into her eyes. Even under the cover of darkness, he peered into her soul. Rose could see him. She could see his desperation in trying to make sense of her. She started slowly. It was a hard conversation to be had. One she never spoke on until now.

"I didn't have a normal childhood. Not at all. Tina exposed me to men early. She was a kid with a kid. She used to take me with her when she turned her tricks because there was no one to watch me. I was a little child sitting in the back seat while she smoked and climbed on top of men. Or she would drop down on their laps. It took me a long time to realize what she was doing. I could hear the sounds but I didn't understand. One time, a man reached his arm in the back and was rubbing on me while she was doing what she did. He had the most disgusting look on his face. After that, things got worse. It would have been better for me to continue watching her have sex then what I endured in the foster system," she said, as she fidgeted with her hands. She couldn't look him in the eyes. Not when she felt so dirty. Speaking it was reliving it. But she continued. He needed to know.

"I ...um...there's was this one family. Six brothers and two sisters. Just to get a check, that family took on two foster kids. Myself and this other girl. We were both ten years old. We were treated so badly. We always ate last if we ate at all. And when the family went on vacations, they left us home locked in separate rooms with nothing but a jug of water and crackers. Sometimes they would give us spam and maybe some other cheap food like cheese or sardines. It was... really terrible," she said, glancing at him before looking away. Boston's inflamed eyes couldn't take much more. He had already cried himself into a headache over his mother, now Rose was speaking her truth. He couldn't imagine what was coming next.

Rose could get through it if she kept her eyes off of him. The details were smothering. She could only breathe if the pressure of seeing his shock was removed. Rose continued.

"Things got really bad," Rose said, taking in a deep breath as images of her painful past appeared. She wiped her nose then sniffled as she continued. She didn't try to wipe the tears. The flow was heavy and it would have been useless.

"They started to keep food from us. I used to let the father touch me just so I could get enough food to feel full. Soon that wasn't enough. He wanted sex. He stuck his penis in my mouth. At first it was horrifying. I hated when he came up those stairs because I knew what I had to do to eat. I hated it. I hated him. Then his sons started. The father told me if I didn't keep them away, he would starve me. I stayed with that family for five long years. I was having a lot of sex. For me sex meant I would be okay. All my life. If I had sex with someone, they would be there. I would be protected somehow. And I used sex as a weapon. As a way to get a person back. I know it sound weird. It was all I knew. I got better. But I didn't really change until now. Having them changed me! Having you changed me!" Rose said.

She shook her head vigorously as if she was shaking off the filth of the images that played like a movie in her head. Boston wiped her tears. Rose looked up at him. The pain in his eyes at what she had gone through helped her continue with a story that was ripping at her soul. She had worked hard to forget the details. But he was worth it. She would relive them if it meant him understanding she was damaged beyond belief. That it started with her mother and she never caught a break until she was old enough to fend for herself.

"I didn't tell you the whole story because I was ashamed of it. You would have looked at me differently. You would have pitied me. I guess I feared not being good enough. Who wants to be married and have kids by a woman with that kind of past. But then you started with Jodi and... Then I just...," she said then abruptly stopped and dropped her head in her hand. Boston pulled her to him and held her face. He kissed her repeatedly on her lips. She didn't have to say anything more. He knew what ailed her. And he loved her still.

"I loved you too much to leave. I wanted kids with you regardless. Only you. I want more. We were not done. And I didn't pity you. Your mother told me some of this. I'll admit I didn't know the half of it. I knew you were abused. You just needed time. I figured we'd be ok one day. My mother went through the same thing," he revealed. The words tore through Rose.

"Cicely!" Rose asked, the words shooting through her fragile core. Boston nodded. The admission causing his eyes to water. Rose wiped his eyes then placed her face on his.

Boston tried to find the strength to talk about it. He hadn't seen his ill mother yet. To bring up such a devastating part of her life was opening yet another wound. Her abuse came from her father. He was estranged from Cicely, her sisters and their children. The grandfather he wanted to strangle for old times' sake. He hated the man and he never laid eyes on him. All the family had was a single picture. Boston continued.

"She doesn't know I know. She thought she was alone in the house that day. No one knows. I'm not sure if she ever told my father. I overheard her talking to aunt Freda and aunt Carol one day. My father wasn't home. She was just ballin. I'd never heard her cry like that. Even when she got mad at pops sometimes, she never got that upset. I was in shock. I was pissed. I never knew why we couldn't meet him. Then there it was. The reason hit me like a fucking brick. He had reached out to my aunt asking to come to Chicago. Freda told him no then called my mother. She said my pops would kill him if he knew. And that she would kill him if she ever found out he touched one of her kids. So he never came here.

It was safer for him. He'd be fucked up by now. I never told anyone. I just went to the park and sat on a swing and just cried. I wanted to kill him," he said. Rose wiped his eyes.

"It was hard knowing that happened to her. She stayed strong. She's a stand-up woman. And the best mother a man could ask for. If I lose her... I won't be any good. Not even for you," he said.

"Don't say that. She's gonna pull through. She will," Rose said, touching his face and hoping she was right. She didn't doubt Cicely's death would be the end of him.

"I wanted to protect you. I couldn't leave you. You're just like her. A good person who was just hurt. You just needed love and support. Not me leaving you. Plus, I loved you too much so...," Boston said with a smile. Rose perked up. His smile lit a fire in her. He was her guardian angel. Her rock. Her support. Her husband. He was forgiven for his past. It seemed he had forgiven hers.

"You deserve better! You deserve everything" she cried.

"Then give it to me because I don't want *everything* from anybody else!" he replied.

Boston pulled Rose onto the bed and kissed her passionately, as they rolled on the bed.

"Careful, I'm pregnant," she said. Boston pulled away.

"I know. Bronx told me," he replied with a smile.

Rose's lip trembled. Her love for him had never been more profound. She rubbed her thumbs across his thick eye brows. Then traced down his face and pulled him back to her lips. Their deep love for one another wiped away what had scarred them. She felt safe with him once again. The way she felt after she'd met him for the first time. He understood her. He would protect her. No longer did she need to use sex as a weapon. Or as a shield. They were recommitting again with the promise to be true because they had no interest in anything other than each other and their growing family.

"I love you," Rose whispered. Boston kissed her neck.

"I love you. I will always love you," he said, as he looked intensely into her eyes.

Rose kissed his hand as he held her face. She had been through hell and back. But he had her now. She would never be mistreated by him or any other man. She needed him and he was there because he needed her. This was day one of their new journey. His grandmother's words were etched firmly in him. He remembered what she said about his future wife. About love and loyalty. And the art of forgiving.

You must always love and be forgiving. You have to cleave to your wife and she will cleave to you. If she says she is sorry she deserves your forgiveness for whatever she has done. Because sometimes women are in a place of pain and a lot of women need to heal from whatever they have gone through. Help her if you love her. And if you do wrong, apologize to her. It starts with saying you're sorry. A genuine apology should wipe the slate of a god-fearing man and woman.

They were words that humbled him. Words that would haunt him when he was faced with what his grandmother meant by women go through a lot of things. His mother had also been sexually abused. A past she healed from and was able to overcome it enough to marry raise her own children. Boston carried her pain in him and his discovery of Rose's past had only made him cleave to her more. Because he had faith in their love. It was love that helped Cicely forge ahead. And it would be love that would help his wife do the same.

"No one else matters Rose. They don't. If you want us to start over, we will. I forgive you. But it stops now! I expect more from you. Yes, I had affairs. I'm not proud of them. But I am not seeing anyone. That was in the past. And I realized that it wasn't fixing my problems. You're the only person I ever loved. Ever! And I promise to be true from this day forward. Like we promised when we married. I will handle my responsibilities, but you are my wife so we will deal with them together. I have not seen anyone. We were starting over. You have to believe me," he said. His feelings on the matter had been filtered through. He was never more sure about anything.

"I know. I know baby. I do. Me either. I wasn't doing anything. After the girl's something in me just felt different. I can't let them down. We're good. No more! No one else gets to come into our world and wreck our happiness. I love you and I promise you from this moment on, you never have to worry about me. It's only you forever!" Rose said, with passion as she fell in love with him all over again.

Boston kissed her passionately. His tongue dove into her mouth searching for the essence of her. Rose was prepared for him. The short skirt and no underwear were in preparation for a husband home from prison who she was sure needed her. Boston wasted no time mounting her and entering her slowly. She was again with child. He would make love the way he always did when she was carrying their child. Slowly and methodically. Rose pulled him in. His rock hard entry filled her completely.

"Mhmm," she moaned. Boston thrusted inside her slowly at first picking up the pace, as he stuck his finger inside her lips and watched as her mouth wrapped around it. "Damn," he whispered. Rose chuckled. It was his weakness. Her mouth. Her lips. Her pussy. Her ass. Everything about her had him under her spell. An enchantment he was not ever going to give up.

The power of his thrust gained momentum. He could take no more. She gripped him with the powerful grasp of her well-honed kegel muscles. Boston cupped his hands under her ass and picked up the pace.

"Uhhh!" Rose shouted. His thick, ten-inch cock had her in her first orgasm as she dug her nails into his back. Boston pounded her fiercely. He couldn't slow down. He couldn't take it easy. He stayed out just enough to protect his baby but was inside of her warmness just enough to explode.

"Rose...Rose...," he called to her, as he gripped her ass firmer. Soon his jerks signaled the release of his man juice. Rose could feel it running out of her as his slowed pumps allowed some to release. "Mhmm," she moaned, as she kissed the side of his head. Then waited for him to notice she needed his mouth. Boston kissed her intensely then laid his head inside the tuft of her neck. He was drained. Soon he was asleep. Rose eased from under him and closed her eyes. She soon joined him rest.

Boston awoke to a sleeping Rose laying on his chest. Soon the vibration of his phone sounded again. He grabbed it and slowly eased from under his wife and took the call once he exited the room.

"Hello," he answered.

"Boss," Phoenix said.

"Yeah. What's up. You here yet?" he asked.

"No. Can't get a flight. Not for another two hours," Phoenix replied.

"You should of told me earlier. I would have sent my plane. By the time he gets there now, you'll have a flight out," he said.

"Yeah. I know. Why you not at the hospital. Pop worried about you. He said ma gonna be alright. They've been letting them back one at a time. He said you won't answer the phone," Phoenix said. Boston sighed. He was exhausted yet relieved. His mother would be okay.

"I'm going. Rose and I fell asleep. We leaving out now," Boston said.

"Alright. Well…I'll see ya'll soon," Phoenix said.

"Yep," Boston replied.

He hung up then looked at his watch. It was after midnight. He felt ready. He wasn't sure what held him back. Part of him wanted to go but he couldn't be there if she wasn't coming home. The guilt would have been tremendous. Rose helped. There was relief in talking to her and getting back on good terms with her. A relief in finally telling someone about his mother. Someone who understood. His wife and mother had a lot in common. Something that made him decide to never give up on her.

He believed if Cicely could overcome it, then so could Rose. He would be there to ensure she got better. He loved her. There was nothing more to say. He owed no one any explanation about why he took her back over and over. One day Cicely would need to tell her story to her other children and maybe then they would understand. For now, it was her and him against the world. Now all he needed was his babies and to go see his mother. The women of his life.

"Rose," Boston said, shaking her woke.

"Umm. What time is it?" she asked.

"Twelve-thirty. Let's go. Where's my girls?" he asked.

"Tina has them. They're sleep Boston. We can go get them in the morning. You're going to see Cicely?" Rose asked.

"I want us to go together," he said.

"Of course," Rose replied, as she sprung up ready to go.

"Hey…Look at me. She is going to be alright now. She will," Rose said, pulling him to her for a hug.

He was still not right. Rose needed them to get there. Boston was a man who needed to see, hear and touch. He needed to see Cicely's face. Until then, he would be incomplete no matter what the report on her condition was.

Part Two available now on Amazon!

The story that gets more toxic!

More intense!

More shocking!

Get ready!

Thank you!

More Books By

Smokey Moment

Standalones

The Twin

Her Sister's Husband

Wife on Paper

From Nothing to Wifey

The Need to Have Him

I'm Not His Cousin

Keeping Him Quiet

That's Still My Wife

Gifted

Beauty is Sleeping

Baby Girl

The Bird in the Bayou

Hood Wife

Love Among Shadows

♛

Two-part Sagas, Series or Trilogies:

Ways of Kings I

Ways of Kings II

Of Flesh & Water I & II

Stray I

Stray II New Life

Stray III Covenant

A Savage Love (Series: Books 1-9)

Don't Judge Us: We Gotta Eat (Books 1-3)

Sins of the Father (1 & 2)

Note from the Author

I had a great time creating and developing this nine book series. A story filled with juicy, jaw dropping drama. Each book getting more powerful. A lot of time and effort went into building the characters. The feedback I get is surprising. I had several fans ask if these men were based off of real characters. It warmed my heart that they were so engrossed in the characters, that they wanted them to be real. Me too. I wish they were real. Someone please point them out (Lol).

Follow me and sign up to my email list so you see when I release new books. As with all my work, I promise to deliver the best that I can create. I've seen your reviews and messages and I know what many of you want in a series. Thank you for being my roadies on this journey. That is why I do this. For you the reader. I love to entertain. And there is more to come

Please leave a Review for the book on
Amazon

Thank you for your support!

Smokey Moment

For information on use of this material please contact WordRoc Publishing at the email provided. If you are an author looking for publishing services, feel free to contact us for consideration of your publishing needs. If you are a producer, promoter or screenwriter, send request to WordRoc directly.

Email us: wordroc@gmail.com

Thank you!

Made in United States
Orlando, FL
06 December 2024